STORM
WARNING

Kathryn Brocato

A KISMET™ Romance

METEOR PUBLISHING CORPORATION
Bensalem, Pennsylvania

This book is respectfully dedicated
to
Dr. Albert J. Love
and
Dorothy Love

KATHRYN BROCATO

Kathryn Brocato is a scientist and business owner who has been a life-long reader and writer of romance. A true believer in the happy ending, she is married to her own romantic hero, Charles Brocato. When she isn't writing, Kathryn enjoys bird-watching, the martial arts and computer studies.

ONE

"Mama, the last person on earth I care to see is Devon Rayburn. That's why I'm wearing my Sunday dress and putting on makeup."

With that, Valerie Dallas, slim and elegant in a cool navy dress and high-heeled pumps, picked up her purse and her grocery list. Her silver-blond hair was swept into a perfect chignon at the base of her neck, and thanks to the miracle of modern optical science, her light-green myopic eyes were not hidden behind thick glasses.

Meg Dallas, a plump blonde in a jogging suit, looked up from her computer screen and scanned her daughter. She returned immediately to the computer screen and pecked out a word.

"Whatever you say, dear. It'll be a shame if you don't call him while you're in town, after what he did for you during that mess with Jonathan Wade."

Valerie cringed. "Mama, I'd appreciate it if you never mention that unmentionable incident again. It was the most embarrassing thing that ever happened to me in my entire life, and if I never have to think of it again, I'll be grateful."

"Anyone can make a mistake, dear," Meg said absently. "Although I have to admit, Jonathan Wade was a doozie. Did I tell you he's disappeared?"

"Yes, Mama," Valerie said patiently. "You told me last night when I got in. Is there anything you want from the store?"

Meg stared at her computer screen. "I can't think what's gone wrong with this book. I got to the eighth chapter and I suddenly realized the book isn't working. You can't imagine how frustrating it is." She backspaced over the word she'd just typed. "Get whatever you want for supper. It looks like I'm in for another long night."

"Okay, Mama. I'll be back in an hour."

Valerie walked out onto the front porch and stared at the overgrown front lawn. It was June in the small Southeast Texas town of Winnie, and the grass was growing wildly. Meg had been busy on another book, and probably hadn't even looked at the lawn.

Valerie grinned and crossed the thick grass, conscious of the tall fronds of pigweed, among other grasses, swiping her calves. Five years ago, Meg had succeeded in selling her first book, a romance novel. Since then, she'd received rejection after rejection, but she showed no signs of either giving up or of selling another. Her proposals and completed manuscripts arrived back in the mail with the regularity of utility bills.

In the meantime, she'd ignored all housework and yardwork, and had generally ignored the pots and pans in her kitchen as well.

Valerie admitted Meg had a right to live as she pleased now that she'd succeeded in raising her two fatherless daughters. She just hoped Meg didn't die of malnutrition or grow some strange new species of killer-mold in her refrigerator.

Valerie's preparation paid off. Although she met several people she knew at the grocery store, she met no one she really cared to exchange more than a casual greeting with.

As for Devon Rayburn, it was the busiest time of day for him. Despite what Meg had said about seeing him often in Winnie, most of his business activity was confined to the nearby suburbs of Houston to the west and Beaumont to the east.

"I'm back, Mama," she said, shoving open the front door.

As she pushed two sacks of groceries inside, Meg barely glanced up from her screen. There were three more sacks in the car, and Valerie trekked back and forth through the tall grass with them, grumbling with every step.

"Mama, this grass is terrible. Have you had it mowed at all this year?"

"The grass? What about it, honey?"

"It needs mowing. I've got these little black things all over my hose. If it were raining, my legs would be wet. Have you even looked outside this spring?"

"Why should I look outside?" Meg asked reasonably. "I go out in the morning to get the newspaper. I'll take a look around the house after I've finished this book. For better or worse," she added darkly.

Valerie hauled a sack to the kitchen table. "By then the county's liable to be after you. Maybe you should get a goat."

"What do I want with a goat?" Meg asked, totally at sea. "Nasty critters. I hate goat's milk."

"Not for the milk, for the grass-eating capabilities," Valerie said, hauling another sack.

Meg glared at the screen. "That's an idea. Maybe a cute goat named Billy could bring Blake and Pamela back together again. Pamela's refusing to marry Blake, and I haven't got the faintest idea how to make her."

"Have Billy butt her from behind," Valerie recommended.

Meg brightened. "Maybe that's it. Of course I'll have to go back to the very beginning and explain why Pamela would have a goat in the first place."

"She's allergic to cow's milk," Valerie supplied, passing through with a third sack.

Meg thought about it. "That would mean I'd have to change the third chapter, where they have a wonderful picnic and make homemade ice cream. Goat's milk ice cream just doesn't sound romantic."

Valerie passed by with the fourth sack. "You're right.

It sounds hideous. Why not have them eat goat's-milk cheese and wine?''

"I don't know," Meg said slowly. "I'll have to think about it. Goat's-milk cheese. I'll have to go buy some and see what it tastes like."

Valerie carried the fifth sack through the room. "I can answer that. It's an acquired taste, like beer. You have to cultivate it."

Meg shook her head. "Forget Billy. Maybe a big dog." She hit the page-up key repeatedly. "I'll just have to read it through from the beginning and see what suggests itself."

Valerie chuckled and went to her bedroom to change clothes. In a writing-fit, Meg couldn't be forced to participate in everyday life; she could only be enjoyed. Valerie had been enjoying her mother ever since Meg plunked her first typewriter down on the kitchen table and announced she was going to become a writer.

It was nice to be home again after two years on tour with a group of gospel singers. Valerie had never become accustomed to living out of vans, buses, or motel rooms. Home had always been important to her, in terms of her own plot of ground to cultivate as she pleased.

She glanced out her bedroom window at the tall grass disfiguring the large backyard. Perhaps she'd have time to dig and plant a small garden. Perhaps she could even bully Meg into looking after it.

She hung up her dress, recalling that two years ago she'd been glad to get away. The infamous incident of Jonathan Wade was winding up, and she had just graduated from Lamar University in Beaumont with her degree in music. She went to Fort Worth to apply for a vacant music teacher's job, and at church one Sunday, a vacationing musician heard her sing.

A few days later, she was on the road with the Shelby Winthrop Quartet. The pay was more than she'd have made teaching music, and the experience was invaluable.

She'd learned a lot of other things, also. If Devon Rayburn saw her now, he wouldn't know her.

Valerie grinned at herself in the mirror as she pulled an old blue T-shirt over her head. Thanks to the wonders of hair stylists, her formerly lank, mousy-blond locks were thick, lustrous, and lightened to a spectacular silver-blond.

Her green eyes were framed with gently darkened brows and lashes, all of which showed, thanks to contact lenses.

She owed it all to Shelby Winthrop, who hadn't an ounce of jealousy in her. Shelby had been like a big sister to Valerie, more helpful than Valerie's own big sister had been.

Valerie glanced at the photograph of Barbara Dallas that sat on the dresser. Barbara looked like Miss America, and everyone spoke of the sweetness of her character, but she'd never had much time for Valerie.

And why should she? Valerie reflected. Barbara had been one of those girls born to make other girls envious, and having a tall, lanky, mousy sister who wore thick glasses must have been a terrible burden to her.

Valerie was by no means tall, but her five-foot-seven frame had towered over Barbara's curvy, five-foot-two. Barbara resembled Meg, whereas Valerie took after their father, Charles Dallas.

Charles had been tall, blond, and full of life and laughter. He'd been a daredevil private pilot, and had moved his family to Winnie because crop-dusting had answered his need for both flying and excitement, until the day his plane had refused to gain enough altitude to clear utility wires lining the rice field he was seeding.

Meg claimed Valerie had inherited Charles's unusual light-green eyes. Where Barbara's eyes were pure green, Valerie's were a shade Barbara had called split-pea green. Valerie had been ready to cry at the description. Then Devon had studied them and said the proper description was peridot-green. Once Valerie had discovered peridot was a jewel, she'd taken pride in her eyes. If Barbara's eyes were like emeralds, her own were like peridots. It had made all the difference in the world.

It was too bad Barbara and Devon hadn't gotten married the way everyone had supposed they would. Something had happened between the couple soon after Valerie left for Fort Worth. Barbara married Harry Kilgore soon afterward, and was moving up rapidly in the investment-banking world.

Valerie took out her contacts carefully and stowed them in her case, first placing her glasses where she could lay her hands on them. Without the glasses, she'd barely be able to see five feet in front of her nose. Then she took the pins out of her hair and brushed it back into a ponytail before pulling on an old pair of shorts. She had a day of housework ahead of her, and it helped to be cool and comfortable.

In the kitchen, Valerie spent time unpacking the grocery sacks and restocking the kitchen shelves and the refrigerator. When Meg was alone and writing, she usually ran out to Dairy Queen whenever she felt the pangs of hunger. Valerie had spent several hours last night cleaning the remains of various Dairy Queen feasts from the cabinets and the refrigerator.

Meg wandered into the kitchen and opened the refrigerator. She stood looking blankly at the shelves a moment, then asked, "What happened to my steak fingers? I was sure I left a basket in here."

"You did, Mama. It had mold an inch thick on the fingers. Have some turkey wieners."

Meg closed the refrigerator. "I don't feel like cooking, dear. I can't think if I have to cook. Would you like something from Dairy Queen? I'd better run over there before the lunch crowd hits."

"Not today, Mama. You go back and work some more. I'll cook lunch and call you when it's ready."

"I could sure use some coffee," Meg said plaintively.

"Coming right up, Mama."

Valerie put on a pot of coffee and began broiling a pair of chicken breasts. She'd taken a month off to visit her mother, and it was a good thing she had. Meg's diet was a nutritionist's nightmare.

Meg received the high-protein, low-calorie lunch with

indifference. Probably, she didn't realize what she was eating.

"I just can't figure out what's wrong with this story," she said, as she downed broccoli spears. "I've got a beautiful, red-headed heroine and a hero who looks like a surfer. What else could an editor want?"

"A good plot?" Valerie tried, dredging up what she could remember about novel-writing from the one seminar Meg had dragged her to.

"That goes without saying. I mean, how many ways can a boy meet a girl and not get her until the two-hundredth page?"

"Mama, all the editors want something new and different. Something fresh. Isn't that the word?"

"Fresh!" Meg said. She stabbed her chicken breast with a fork. "If I hear that word one more time, Valerie Dallas."

"Sorry, Mama. I was just trying to help."

"Sit still and listen. There are only a few basic romance plots. Boy meets girl, they split up, and meet again two or more years later, whereupon the hero discovers a baby resulted from their encounter. Or, boy meets girl and it's instant hate, until the two-hundredth page, wherein they realize they were falling in love all that time."

"Oh, come on, Mama."

"Well, I don't think much of that one, either. Maybe I should. Maybe that's my trouble."

Meg brooded over the dilemma, and Valerie replenished the vegetables on Meg's plate.

"Actually," Meg confided, "I'd be lousy at that plot. I like people who like each other, don't you? I mean, if I meet a man I quarrel with every time I meet him, I'm going to make damn sure I don't meet him very often."

"True, Mama."

"Of course you're supposed to throw them together, like in a cabin in the wilderness, where they can't avoid each other."

Valerie poured more coffee. "That sounds more like the way to begin a murder mystery."

"My feelings exactly," Meg said.

Meg lapsed into silence once more, still brooding over the basic romance plots, Valerie presumed.

"Did you think to check the mail while you were out, dear?" Meg asked suddenly.

"No, Mama. I forgot. I guess I've gotten used to having it delivered. Are you expecting something?"

"I'm always expecting something," Meg said gloomily. "One of these days I'll get a phone call instead of a self-addressed package."

Valerie bit back a smile, recalling the packages and letters addressed to Meg in her own handwriting that had arrived with great regularity. It looked as though the contents of Meg's daily mail hadn't changed.

"Don't worry. I'll run out this afternoon and check the post office for you."

"That would be nice, dear. Leave a big pot of coffee, will you? I need all the stimulation I can get."

"Sure, Mama. Have you been getting any exercise while I've been gone?"

"Exercise?" Meg asked vaguely as she rose from the table.

"Yes." Valerie pantomimed jumping jacks. "Bodily motion. Walking. Jogging. Calisthenics."

Meg turned toward the living room impatiently. "I don't have time for that. Once I've sold another book, I'll invest in one of those bicycles you can ride while you read or watch TV."

"Exercise may be what you need," Valerie suggested. "Once you get your circulation moving and more oxygen going to your brain, you'll be able to come up with an original plot idea."

Meg was not impressed. "I haven't got time for exercise. I've got to get back to my computer."

"You can go walking with me later this afternoon," Valerie said.

Meg didn't reply. She'd already turned on her computer and inserted her program disk.

Valerie shook her head and carried the dishes to the

sink. It looked as though she had come home just in time. If something wasn't done, Meg would wind up in the cardiac wing of the hospital. If she didn't wind up a candidate for the local nut house first, Valerie thought, grinning.

A glance in the living room revealed Meg with her stack of romance-writing publications opened all about her, searching diligently for a suggestion as to what had gone wrong in her own writing.

The house had been largely ignored since Valerie had been gone. Even though Barbara lived barely thirty miles away in Houston, she'd obviously made no effort to help Meg in any way. Consequently, Valerie spent an hour after lunch cleaning the stove and scrubbing the kitchen floor. The refrigerator needed a good cleaning also.

"This is terrible!" Valerie muttered, staring at the dishes full of bites of molded food.

She'd cleared out the Dairy Queen sacks the night before, but her nerve had failed upon confronting the remaining items.

A strange odor permeated the room every time the refrigerator door was opened. Worse, there wasn't an ounce of baking soda in the house.

"Damn it all!" Valerie grumbled.

She threw a head of what she presumed had been either cabbage or lettuce into the plastic garbage bag she'd placed at the ready. A carton of solidified milk, from which emanated a horrifying smell, followed.

"What on earth is that dreadful smell?" Meg asked from the doorway. She came into the room and refilled her coffee cup. "I can hardly work for the odor."

"I'm cleaning out the refrigerator," Valerie said, adding the contents of three bowls to the sack. "How old is this carton of milk? It's gone totally solid."

Meg looked vague. "Maybe a week or so, dear. I really don't recall. Why don't you just put it back in the refrigerator? Then maybe it won't smell so awful."

"Mama, it needs to go out in the garbage."

"Exactly my point, dear. If you leave it in the open air, I can't get a bit of work done for the smell."

Valerie snatched up the plastic bag and hauled it out back to the garbage can. Meg was right. It was difficult to work with that odor in the house.

Removal of the chief offenders helped, but the plastic refrigerator liner had absorbed enough of the odor to perfume the air every time the refrigerator door was opened.

Valerie resignedly went to her room and picked up her purse. Until she had scrubbed down the inside of the refrigerator with baking soda and water and left several dishes of baking soda sitting on the shelves, the odor would remain.

"Going out, dear?" Meg asked. "Don't forget the mail."

Valerie groaned inwardly. How had Meg gotten along without a maid so far?

"Mama, we're going to have to do something about this yard. That grass is almost a criminal offense."

Meg never looked up. "Call Devon. He loves to mow grass."

"Mama . . .!"

Valerie shut up and closed the door behind her a bit more loudly than was respectful. She marched across the tall grass and glared at it belligerently.

She stopped first at the post office, thankful she still had her key. Meg's box was crammed full, indicating that she hadn't checked it for over a week, and Valerie had to spend a few minutes standing at the window while the postmistress fetched the inevitable self-addressed package.

Valerie took one look at it and wondered if she could just hide it under her car seat until she was ready to go back to Fort Worth. Its arrival meant that Meg's already disjointed existence would become even more chaotic.

She leafed through the stack. Other than the usual sales circulars, there were several envelopes from editors—Meg wrote wonderful query letters—and two large manila envelopes. Meg had recently branched into confession writing to offset the romance-novel rejections.

Valerie drove to the grocery store once more, conscious of her long, bare legs and unbound breasts beneath the ancient T-shirt. She'd just be here a minute.

She nipped inside and gathered up four boxes of baking soda, miserably conscious that just down the aisle her former classmate, Jennifer Devilier, was filling a basket. Jennifer had been like Barbara, outgoing and exquisite.

She scuttled around to the cleaning aisle, where she picked up another bottle of floor cleaner. She'd used the entire bottle she'd bought that morning on the kitchen floor.

"Val?"

The voice came from a man who had just rounded the corner. Valerie felt that even the marrow of her bones was reacting to it, and kept her head down. Perhaps if she ignored him, he'd assume he had the wrong person.

She grabbed blindly for a second bottle of floor cleaner.

"Valerie?"

She turned slightly, keeping her back to him, but it wasn't working. He came closer. She could feel his presence at her back.

He touched her shoulder. "Valerie Dallas? I knew that was you."

Valerie turned reluctantly, conscious of a roaring in her ears and a dizzy spinning of the environment before her eyes.

She shoved her glasses higher on her nose and pretended to peer at him through them.

"Dev? I'm sorry. I was thinking so hard, I didn't hear you come up."

Her voice sounded weak and quivering, even to her own ears. Brazen it out! she told herself.

She drew herself straighter, then wished she hadn't. Devon Rayburn's smiling gray eyes immediately zeroed in on her chest.

"Were you thinking so hard about which wax to buy?" he asked, grinning.

"Right. You know Mama. She hasn't scrubbed the kitchen floor once since I've been gone."

Devon laughed. "Has she ever sold another book?"

"No, and it's about to kill her. See you later, Dev. I've left her alone with the computer and the coffeepot."

"Wait a minute, Valerie. She isn't going to do anything drastic in the next five minutes, is she?"

No, but I will, Valerie thought, gripping the baking-soda boxes.

She gripped so hard, three boxes shot out of her hands and struck Devon on the center of his chest.

He bent to pick them up for her, and Valerie watched helplessly as a bottle of floor cleaner left her grip and bounced off his head.

"I should have gotten a basket," she said when he looked up at her and laughed.

"This is the first time a woman has ever attacked me in a supermarket with handfuls of groceries," Devon said.

Valerie stared at him. Devon Rayburn was six feet tall and tanned and muscular from all the work he did out-doors. His hair was light brown and had been bleached by the sun to an unusual shade of streaked golden brown that contrasted with his deeply tanned skin and sparkling gray eyes.

Devon still had the ability to send her heart into what her mother's book described as a "spasm," and she could only hope he didn't realize that . . . especially considering the embarrassment Valerie had suffered when Barbara had pointed it out two years ago.

Devon stood, holding her groceries in his arms. "Here, I'll walk out with you," he said. "I only came in for a cold drink when I thought I saw a body I remembered."

Valerie felt like a red-alcohol thermometer with a flame applied to its bulb and wondered if she could disappear down an aisle if Devon's attention were diverted.

Devon showed no indication of diverting his attention.

He glanced at her. "For God's sake, Val. What on earth have I said?"

Valerie tried to look unaware of her glowing complexion. "Not a thing, Dev." She searched desperately for something to say and could come up with only one idea. "Are you still into mowing lawns?"

"Of course I am. Is this an invitation to exercise my professional skill on your mother's lawn, by any chance?"

"Please. I can hardly get across the yard to my car. You know how she is when she's writing."

"Lord, yes!"

Valerie shot him a surreptitious glance but was unable to look away. His tanned face was alight with laughter, and deep grooves on either side of his mouth appeared.

"Hi, Dev. Is that you, Val? My word, you still look about sixteen," Jennifer Devilier appeared at the corner. "I didn't know you were coming home. I saw Barbara last weekend and she didn't say a thing about it."

Valerie shrugged, and wished she hadn't. Devon's eyes had dropped once more to her chest.

She clutched the two boxes of baking soda that remained in her hands before her unconfined breasts. "I didn't know myself until a couple of days ago. How have you been, Jennifer?"

"Oh, so-so. I'm divorced now, you know. Say, why don't the two of you come to a little party at my house tonight? I'd love to have you."

Valerie began, "Thanks, Jennifer, but I—"

"She'd love it," Devon said. "And so would I. What time?"

Valerie noted that Devon didn't ask where Jennifer lived. He'd probably already dated her once or twice.

"Barb said you're singing with a gospel group," Jennifer continued, looking Valerie over closely. "Somehow I just can't picture you singing gospel."

"I know," Valerie said. "I have that natural punk-rocker look."

"You? No way." Jennifer giggled. "I'd have thought you would sing stuff like 'The Good Ship Lollipop.' You look so much like a little girl."

Valerie sighed and wondered if she'd ever outgrow being Barbara Dallas's little sister.

"I don't think she looks like a little girl," Devon said, eyeing Valerie.

Valerie's color once more approached the hue of a radish.

"Oh, my God. Look at that. She can still blush. God, Val, I'm so jealous. We're the same age, but I don't think anything could ever make me blush. Isn't that sickening? Jaded, at the age of twenty-four."

Jennifer had never been malicious, Valerie recalled. She'd just been honest.

"It's all that wholesomeness," Valerie said, and edged back slightly. "Well, it's been nice seeing you, Jen. I've got to get home. Dev, it's been nice—"

"I'm coming out with you, Val. See you tonight, Jen. We'll be there."

Valerie reflected on the truth of the maxim about running into everyone you know when you're only entering the supermarket for five minutes in your worst state of personal grooming.

"I want to talk to you some more, Valerie," Devon said. "You didn't mind my accepting Jen's party invitation for you, I hope? You're sure to meet some of your friends there."

"No, Dev. I probably need to get out," Valerie said, resigned.

"Good. I'll pick you up at seven."

"What?"

"I said, I'll pick you up at seven tonight. I'm taking you, remember?"

Valerie wondered how much of the conversation she'd missed. Fortunately, she'd always operated by the rule that stated if you acted as if you knew what was going on, you'd soon find out.

"Oh, Yes, Sure, Dev. I was thinking about the yard. You're really going to have to do something about that yard. Either that, or I'm going to have to buy a lawn mower."

"Buy a lawn mower when you've got Rayburn Lawn Maintenance on your side? Be reasonable, Val. How can

I stay in business if everyone goes around buying lawn mowers. I'll be by this afternoon. Is that too soon?"

"Five minutes from now wouldn't be too soon," Valerie said, pleased she'd found a subject to cling to. "The yard is in terrible condition. You'd better send someone with hedge-trimmers also. Give it the works."

"I'll take care of it," Devon promised. He took the boxes of baking soda from her, placed them on the counter, and watched as she paid for them. "Does someone at your house have a bad case of heartburn?"

"Mama soon will . . ." Valerie began, and laughed. "I picked up her mail, and it looks like she's got a manuscript back and heaven knows what-all else. She must send out five query letters a week."

Devon chuckled. "I remember all the fuss when she sold her first book. Lord, it was wonderful. Why can't she sell another one?" He took the sack and followed her out to the parking lot.

"I'm afraid to read anything of hers and find out," Valerie replied. "Maybe I'll suggest she try a professional critique."

Valerie began to feel more cheerful. Talking to Devon was easier than she'd ever thought it would be. Two years ago, she'd been certain she could never look him in the face again.

Devon smiled. Once more, the grooves on either side of his long, mobile mouth captivated Valerie.

His eyes caught hers, and she turned scarlet once more.

"Valerie . . ." he began.

She rushed into speech. "Well, Dev, it was awfully nice running into you. For the yard, I mean."

That made a lot of sense, she berated herself, and reached for the sack.

Devon held on to the sack. "Valerie, if you're going to turn red every time I look at you, I'm going to request a mirror. Have I got some kind of strange dirt on my face?"

"No," Valerie said in strangled tones. "Excuse me,

Dev. I really do have to get home. Mama is waiting for the mail.''

Devon set the sack on his hip and balanced it with one hand. He used the other to tilt her chin up and scan her face.

Valerie wondered if it was possible to die of a heart palpitation while a man touched your chin. Her only defense was to pretend a great interest in a woman coming out of the store.

Devon smiled. He leaned forward suddenly and kissed her lightly on the lips. ''Welcome home, Valerie.''

Valerie felt the kiss almost as if he'd given her what she used to call the ''full-tongue'' treatment when, as a teenager, she'd spied on Devon and Barbara.

''I'll see you in a few minutes,'' he added. ''Your yard is the type I like to take care of myself.''

Valerie stared at him, feeling as though the concrete parking lot had dropped out from beneath her. Overhead, the afternoon sun was beating down, and the Gulf Coast humidity was pressing in on her.

''Sure, Dev,'' she managed, and got herself into her compact car.

He grinned and added, ''Maybe you'd like to have dinner with me one night. For old times' sake.''

''Sure,'' she said, and choked before she could add, ''Dev.''

''Are you all right, Val?''

No one could be all right while her entire life was passing before her eyes.

''Sure, Dev.''

''You're beginning to sound like a broken record, Val. I'll be at your house in a few minutes. I'll have to stop by the equipment barn first.''

She clamped her mouth shut and looked up at him from the safety of her car. No man had a right to look that trim and tanned, she grumbled inwardly. No wonder Jen Devilier was willing to invite Valerie along in order to make sure he attended her party.

STORM WARNING / 23

Devon leaned in and looked at the pile of mail on the front seat beside her. "Is that all from editors?"

"Most of it."

"Lord." He laughed and backed off. "See you in a few minutes, Val . . . By the way, you look great."

Valerie started the motor by grinding the starter, then had to take her attention off Devon's well-shaped backside long enough to start the car properly.

She watched him climb into a pickup truck several cars down, then glanced at herself in the car mirror. Her glasses obscured her eyes, and her hair looked like a bat had tried to make a nest in it.

But Devon had always been polite. It was part of the reason she'd been secretly in love with him two years ago.

At least she'd been stupid enough to think it was secretly. Barbara had taken great pleasure in humiliating her with the truth.

Valerie backed out carefully, recalling Devon's kindness on the most mortifying day in Valerie's young life. He'd always been soft-hearted, and had treated Valerie tenderly . . .

She heard a crash, followed by a sickening crunch, and felt her car jerk slightly. She twisted around and saw nothing. Hoping she hadn't run over a child, Valerie flung open her car door and got out.

Devon pulled his truck up beside her and leaped down. "You've totaled a grocery buggy," he said, grinning.

TWO

Valerie arrived home and walked into the house minus her grocery sack. She stalked back outside to fetch it, grumbling at fate.

Fate had it in for her. Even though the store hadn't charged her for the buggy, the embarrassment of reporting it to the manager had been another humiliating incident in Valerie's life.

As she entered, Meg said triumphantly, "I think I've spotted the problem. The story is over! It ended with Chapter Seven. No wonder I couldn't get going in Chapter Eight. There wasn't anything else to say."

"So now you can go back and add a few more chapters in the middle, right?" Valerie paused at the sofa and deposited Meg's mail. "Maybe I should take all this and hide it in my room until you've fixed the problem."

Meg whirled to glare at the pile. "Oh, no! My manuscript!"

"I ran into Devon at the grocery store," Valerie said. "I've hired him to do the yard."

"The yard's fine," Meg said absently, approaching the sofa. "Would you mind making me a cup of fresh coffee, dear? Add a drop or two of the crème de cacao. I'm going to need it."

Valerie carried her sack of baking soda into the kitchen

and washed out the coffeepot. As soon as it began perking, she fled to her room, where she put on a bra and took down her hair. She settled for putting her hair back in its ponytail and taking off her glasses in favor of her contacts. It wouldn't do to let Devon know she was changing her appearance drastically for his benefit.

She had just carried Meg a cup of steaming coffee doctored with the chocolate liqueur when she heard a truck pull up out front. She stepped out onto the front porch and watched as Devon unloaded a powerful-looking lawn mower from the small trailer attached to his truck.

He saw her and waved. "This is the worst yard I've seen all summer," he called.

He came toward her, and Valerie saw his eyes drop briefly to her breasts, then rise to her face once more.

"The summer isn't over yet," she said. "Look out, Dev, or I'll start talking to Mama about the backyard wildlife sanctuary movement. I read an article once about natural lawns and their value to local wildlife."

"This lawn is a natural disaster. Unless, of course, Meg has taken up raising pigweed as a project."

"They never explained how you got the good stuff like wildflowers and millet to grow in your yard. I think you're supposed to let the animals seed the yard."

Devon grinned. "So plant some pecan trees and call it a grove. Every squirrel in Chambers County would love to call it home."

"I'll mention it to Mama. Well, I can see you're itching to reduce this natural wilderness to a state of manmade neatness. When you're ready, cold drinks await."

"I'll take one now. I saw you and forgot what I'd gone into the store for."

Valerie groaned inwardly. She'd hoped to have some of the smell in the kitchen dissipated by the time he was ready for a cold drink.

He followed her inside, and Valerie remembered Devon had once been treated as a member of the family. No doubt old habits died hard.

"Hello, Meg," he said. "I've come to do your yard."

Meg was sitting on the sofa with a thick sheaf of paper on her knees, a letter in one hand, and the cup of doctored coffee in the other.

"The yard's fine," she said. She waved the letter. "I can't believe this. This editor says my dialogue sounds wooden, and that I should read it aloud to get the feel."

Valerie said diplomatically, "Try it, Mama. It might be good advice."

"But I do read my dialogue aloud!" Meg wailed. "It sounded so good when I read it."

Devon sat down beside her and took the stack of paper. He turned over the cover page and read, *Loving Livvy*.

"The girl's name is Olivia," Meg said.

"Oh." Devon leafed through the stack. "Sure looks like a lot of work."

"It *was* a lot of work," Meg said glumly. "Oh, well. Another one bites the dust. I'll have to put it in the closet with the others and think about it. Maybe it can be revised."

"Why can't you send it to another editor?" Valerie asked.

"I would if I didn't have the uncomfortable feeling this editor was telling me the truth." Meg sipped coffee and brooded.

"Well, put it up and get back to the one you're working on," Valerie said. "Stay here, Dev. I'll bring you a cold drink."

It was a relief to have an excuse to keep Devon out of the kitchen. She hastily opened one box of baking soda, sprinkled the white powder on a plate, and stuck it in the refrigerator.

Valerie reentered the room with a cold drink and caught her breath when he looked up and smiled at her. She actually felt her heart perform a strange new maneuver and had to pretend she'd forgotten something in the kitchen. Snatching up Meg's coffee cup, she fled.

By the time she'd recovered her composure and returned with a freshly doctored cup, Devon was studying the letter from the editor while Meg instructed him about the terminology.

" 'Livvy is too virginal,' " he read. "I don't suppose you'd care to explain that one for me."

"It means Livvy doesn't come across as a liberated woman of the nineties," Meg said, still brooding. "She behaves like a nice girl who grew up during the early sixties—such as myself. In those days you didn't go to bed with a man on the first date."

Devon and Valerie both choked back laughter.

"Our biggest worry was deciding whether or not to kiss a man on the first date," Meg added.

"Perhaps Val can fill you in on the biggest worry of a woman in the nineties," Devon said with a perfectly straight face.

"Cast your mind back, Dev," Valerie said. "On your first date with Barbara, did you keep your hands to yourself?"

Devon laughed. "That was the eighties. Meg is concerned with the nineties. Things change, you know."

"They haven't changed that much," Meg said suddenly. "It's a mind-set. When I was young, you were supposed to get married and stay home. Now you're supposed to build a career while you raise a family. Maybe I should do research by getting a job."

"Why don't you just interview Barbara?" Valerie asked.

"I have, dear." Meg fell silent.

Valerie eyed her, but something about Meg's silence warned her not to pursue the matter until Devon was busy with his mower.

She glanced at Devon, discovered him watching her, and promptly felt the heat rising in her face once more.

Devon grinned. "What are you thinking, Val?"

"I was wondering whether or not to apologize for bringing up Barbara. I forgot that the subject is bound to be painful for you."

"It isn't painful for me," Devon said instantly. "Barb and I made a mutual decision."

Valerie doubted that, but didn't argue. "It isn't any of my business," she said, examining her toes carefully.

Devon smiled and turned his attention back to Meg, who had grabbed the editor's letter from his fingers.

Meg stared at the letter once more. "Well, I suppose I'd better put this story in the closet for a while," she said forlornly. "If I change Livvy's character, I'll have to change the whole story."

"You're in the middle of another story right now," Valerie reminded her. "Come back to Livvy when you've gotten the problem ironed out of it."

"I hope it's problem and not *problems*," Meg muttered.

"You're improving with every book, Mama."

"I can't be," Meg said reasonably. "I sold my first one, remember. Since then, I've been going backward."

Valerie couldn't think of a reply. She rose and took Meg's empty cup.

Devon stood also. "I'd better get busy on the yard."

"The yard's fine," Meg said. "It's too hot to mow. Why don't you take Valerie to the beach? She looks awfully pale."

Valerie choked. "Mama, Dev has to work for a living. If he isn't mowing our yard, he'll be mowing someone else's. Besides, if I don't finish cleaning out this refrigerator, one of these days you're going to open it and something's going to reach out and grab you."

"It isn't that bad, dear." Meg returned to her manuscript and her letter.

Valerie shook her head and went to the kitchen. She didn't realize Devon was behind her until he spoke.

"What on earth is that awful smell?" he asked.

Valerie whirled. "It's Mama's refrigerator. Be thankful I've already gotten rid of most of the cause."

"Lord! No wonder you bought up all the baking soda."

He smiled at her, and Valerie felt her heart respond by speeding up its rhythm. How many times in the past had she stood like this in the kitchen talking with Devon and wishing she were Barbara?

"While you're mowing, I'm going to be scrubbing out the fridge. Want another cold drink?"

"Thanks, but I'd better get started. I'll keep a better eye on your mother's property, Val. If I'd known she was letting it grow, I'd have done something sooner."

"If *I'd* known she was letting it grow, I'd have called you," Valerie said, grinning. "What's bad is that the yard isn't the only thing she's letting grow. You should have seen what I harvested from the refrigerator."

Devon tossed his soft-drink can into the garbage and studied the old hurricane-tracking chart Valerie had taped on the refrigerator door. It had the paths of all the storms of the season two years ago carefully tracked in different colors of ink.

"Barb lives only half an hour's drive away, and she visits regularly," Devon observed. "Doesn't she ever open the refrigerator?"

Valerie shrugged. "I doubt it. You know Barb. Housework isn't her forte. Investment banking and succeeding in the business world are the only things she thinks about."

"Yeah," Devon said dryly. "I know."

Valerie cast him a sidelong glance as she pried open another carton of baking soda.

Barbara had complained about Devon's lack of ambition in the business world. The fact that he had built Rayburn Lawn Maintenance into a business employing thirty men and women somehow escaped Barbara's definition of "business."

Barbara had succeeded in pushing Devon into entering and graduating from law school, but nothing could force him into practice. Hence, Barbara had dumped Devon as soon as Harry Kilgore, a junior officer in the bank Barbara went to work for, showed an interest in her.

"I'd better get your little pocket of wilderness into compliance with the code," Devon said. At the kitchen door, he turned and looked back at her. "Go take your bra off. You'll be a lot more comfortable."

He exited, laughing, and Valerie had to restrain herself from heaving the baking-soda box at his muscular back.

She ripped the old tracking chart off the refrigerator and got busy with the hot water and baking soda, grumbling aloud at her stupidity. It wouldn't have taken her five minutes to put on a skirt and blouse for that trip to the grocery store.

When she'd finished the inside of the refrigerator, and had set two more plates of baking soda on its shelves, she went to the living room, where Meg was still poring over her rejected manuscript.

"I've been reading over my dialogue," Meg announced.

Valerie picked up the empty coffee cup. "Have you reached any conclusions?"

"I think the editor is right, much as I hate to admit it. I'll have to test the dialogue another way."

Valerie pulled aside the curtain to peek out the window. Devon had finished the backyard and was mowing the front, using his own pattern of mowing. He had taken off his shirt, and his tanned skin gleamed with sweat as he moved rapidly across the overgrown grass.

"That's wise, Mama," she said absently. "This one will sell, I know it will."

She wondered how Devon's smooth, tanned skin would feel beneath her fingers if she were to stroke them over the rippling muscles of his back.

Meg glanced up. "I hope so. If it does, I'll dedicate it to you, dear. And to Devon. He was very helpful just now." She was silent a moment, then added, "I never did see why Barb threw him over like that. Harry Kilgore is a stuffed shirt."

Valerie thought so, too, even though she'd never met the man. She'd received one letter from Barbara in the two years she'd been gone. The number of lines devoted to describing Harry, as opposed to the number of lines it took to adequately express Barb's enthusiasm for investment banking, had been remarkable.

Valerie took one more good look at Devon. Who would want a junior bank officer when she had a magnificent specimen like Devon right there in her embrace?

She studied the hollow of his throat as he approached

the window and fantasized about tasting it with the tip of her tongue. He'd taste salty . . .

Devon looked up and she hastily dropped the curtain.

Not for the first time, Valerie wondered if Barbara's intelligence had been adversely affected by the Houston water.

She went to the kitchen and began on the cabinets, forcing herself to stay busy so as not to spend the entire afternoon admiring the play of muscles across Devon's back. She'd peeked out the curtains once more when she delivered another cup of coffee to Meg. Devon was bending over a weed trimmer, preparing to edge the sidewalk.

It was too much to resist. Valerie made a fresh pot of coffee so she'd have an excuse to return to the living room with fresh cups of the crème de cacao-treated coffee. Each time, she spent a moment feasting her eyes on Devon's bare torso.

When he moved to the back, she stayed busy at the kitchen sink where she could admire the way the sunlight played over the muscles of his chest.

Devon had always liked yardwork. If she stayed in town a month, she could have him back again in a week.

Valerie grinned at her thoughts. She was willing to pay good money so she could enjoy watching Devon while he mowed the yard.

When he'd finished, he reloaded his equipment and appeared at the front door with his shirt back on.

Conscious of disappointment, Valerie led him back to the kitchen.

He sniffed appreciatively. "Smells better. Did you add perfume to the baking soda?"

"I bought some super-duper air fresheners this morning. Have a seat."

She poured a cola over ice and plunked it down before him, then poured herself one and sat down opposite him.

Devon gulped the drink. "I saw you at the window, keeping an eye on the job."

Valerie knew better than to deny she'd been watching him.

"You have to keep an eye on the yardman, you know," she said. "Otherwise he'll sit down under the oak tree and charge you by the hour."

"How'd you like my new technique?"

"It was great. You should patent it."

She had no idea what he was talking about. In truth, she hadn't paid a bit of attention to his methods.

"So how long are you going to be in town?" he asked. "Your mother needs a keeper, you know."

"I've noticed," Valerie said. "I may have to hire someone to come in and clean once a week. I'll definitely have to put her on your list for the works every two weeks. I'm surprised you were able to get it done so fast."

Devon laughed. "Honey, when you make your living doing yards, you develop methods for working faster." He looked at her with his intense gray stare. "I'm an equal-opportunity employer, you know."

"Yes, I know. You're a great man, Dev. If the government ever gets after you, call me for a reference."

"I'd rather offer you some temporary employment," Devon said.

"What?" She wondered if she'd heard correctly.

"You used to be good at riding mowers, as I recall."

Valerie remembered riding behind Devon on his first tractor, then following his instructions and mowing her own yard and her next-door neighbor's with it. Of course, she'd done it to be near Devon, but she'd pretended enormous enthusiasm for the machine.

"I can't believe there's a dearth of willing employees out there," she said cautiously.

"This is an unadvertised position."

"And?"

"I need a personal helper. During the busy season, namely right now, I trouble-shoot and do small jobs like this one."

"You call this a small job? It was a jungle out there," Valerie said, grinning.

"We're used to apartment complexes and estates," Devon reminded her. "Individual homes are small jobs.

A guy with a pickup truck can take care of them. *If* he has the right helper."

Valerie stared at him.

"I suppose you think it's easy, doing a yard like this alone."

He drew in a breath to continue, and Valerie nipped in with, "Sure, Dev. You reduced this jungle to order in less than an hour. You barely worked up a sweat. I can tell you need help."

Devon paused, eyed her, and said, "I could get through in half the time, and do twice as many jobs. Lucky for you, I remember your youthful enthusiasm."

Valerie flushed uncomfortably. She'd wanted to be near Devon so badly, she'd almost been guilty of following him around. She'd pretended an even greater enthusiasm for yardwork than he'd had, and he'd let her push his mowers, edge a lawn or two, and operate the weed trimmer. She'd even learned the proper way to trim a hedge to impress him.

Devon laughed. "Think about it. Does Meg really go back and forth to her car without noticing that she needs a scythe to cut a path?"

Meg appeared in the doorway, manuscript and cup in hand. "May I have some more coffee?" she asked plaintively. "Oh, Dev. I'm so glad you're still here. Would you mind doing me a big favor, dear?"

Devon rose politely and pulled out a chair for her. "Of course not, Meg. What is it?"

Meg settled at the table and set several sheets of paper before him. Devon eyed them suspiciously.

"I want to listen while you and Valerie read my dialogue,' she said. "Maybe it'll help if I hear someone else read it aloud."

Valerie doctored another cup of coffee. "What's wrong with the tape recorder?"

Meg eyed her reproachfully. "I need fresh voices."

Valerie shut up and sat down as Meg passed her some duplicate pages.

"You're Livvy, and Dev is Rex."

Valerie stared at her sheets. "Who's Peggy?"

"What?" Meg fumbled through her copy. "Oh. I'll do Peggy."

Her words slurred a bit, and Valerie glanced up in concern.

"Okay, Dev," Meg said.

Devon rattled his papers. "Who reads the narrative?"

"The what?" Meg fumbled with her copy once more. "Oh. I will." Several sheets floated to the floor. She retrieved them, shuffled them, and read: " 'Livvy and Rex stared at each other across the large sofa. Livvy longed for the comfort of Rex's arms, but she had to maintain her distance.' "

Devon passed a hand across his mouth and read: " 'Livvy, why are you sitting over there? Come here.' "

Meg read: " 'Olivia quivered. Would she be able to resist Rex if she did as he asked?' "

Valerie took a deep breath. " 'Rex, please don't ask me to. You know I can't.' "

Devon bit his lip and managed to read: " 'Why can't you? You have the most kissable lips I've ever seen, Livvy. If you don't come here, I'll come to you.' "

Meg, who had tilted her head down and cocked her left ear forward, jumped after a moment of silence and grabbed for her pages. She read: " 'Rex moved closer and let his hand play in Olivia's long black hair.' "

Devon read: " 'Livvy, you aren't afraid of me, are you?' "

And Valerie replied, " 'Yes, Rex, I am. You make me feel . . . unlike myself. I'm afraid of the way you make me feel.' "

"Oh, God!" Meg said suddenly. "That's awful."

Valerie scanned her script. "You've leaped ahead, Mama."

Devon burst into laughter. "She was making a comment on the dialogue, Val. That little line isn't in the script."

Meg waved her empty coffee cup. "Pour in a dot of coffee and a lot of cacao, darling. That's a good girl."

Valerie blinked but accepted the cup without comment. She poured in coffee and added a drop of liqueur.

Meg went on. "I think I'm beginning to see what the problem is. I never realized it before, but Livvy does sound like a Victorian nitwit. How embarrassing. Read on, please. Let me hear the worst."

Valerie started to say it wasn't that bad, but bit back the comment. Meg was extremely serious about her writing and had a right to make her own judgments.

Obligingly, Devon read: " 'Livvy, you know how I feel about you. I'm coming closer, darling.' "

Meg sipped coffee, scowled at the cup, and read: " 'Rex moved until he was sitting beside Olivia, his muscular thigh resting against hers. He let his arm rest along the back of the sofa, touching her shoulder with his fingers. Olivia felt her body pressing against the arm of the sofa and quivered.' "

Valerie was so busy watching Meg rise and grab the bottle of crème de cacao, that she failed to respond until Meg waved the bottle at her.

She heard the splash as Meg added a generous dollop of liqueur to her coffee. " 'Rex, you're frightening me.' "

" 'I never want to frighten you, Livvy. I adore you. Put your hand right here, dearest. Feel the way my heart beats when I'm near you.' "

"Your line, Mama," Valerie said, watching with concern as Meg gulped doctored coffee.

"Read it for me, dear. I want to get the feel."

Devon grinned at Valerie, and Valerie aimed a kick at him beneath the table.

With considerable feeling, Valerie read: " 'Rex took Livvy's small palm and placed it on his chest just over his heart.' " She paused for effect. " 'Rex, please!' "

The corners of Devon's long mouth had tucked in. He read: " 'Feel my heart, Livvy. It beats for you.' "

"Oh, God!" Meg said. She poured straight crème de cacao into the cup and swallowed a generous amount.

"I'm surprised the editor didn't drop it on the roof via jet airplane."

"Mama, you've had enough crème de cacao. For that matter, you've had enough coffee. Put that bottle back."

"I have to fortify myself, dear. Read on."

Valerie went back to the manuscript reluctantly. " 'Olivia's pulses fluttered as Rex's big palm flattened over hers, holding her hand over his rapidly beating heart. She looked up, and promptly drowned in his hot gaze.' "

Meg let out a long howl.

Startled, Valerie dropped her sheets and half rose. "Mama?"

Meg's howl trailed off into deep laughter. She clutched her sides and bent over.

"Oh, Lord!" Valerie said. "She's hysterical."

"No, she isn't. She's high." Devon smiled reassuringly.

Meg slid down the cabinet and sat on the floor, still clutching her sides and howling with laughter. Tears had begun to pour down her cheeks.

"Oh!" she groaned. "Oh! That has to be the worst thing I've ever written in my life. The closet's too good for it. Throw it in the garbage, Val."

Valerie began to feel alarmed. "Mama, you'll change your mind—"

"Not if I have any sense," Meg said, wiping her eyes. She got to her feet with assistance from Devon and came to the table. Getting a fix on the manuscript, she read: " 'Rex drew Olivia into his embrace and covered her quivering lips with his hard, hot mouth.' " She paused and said, "Lord, it sounded so good when I wrote it a year ago."

Meg laid the manuscript aside and looked around for her coffee cup.

Valerie rose at once and poured her another cup, minus the crème de cacao.

Meg said, with dignity, "Sometimes a little booze helps give the needed detachment. That was the first love scene in the novel. I'd thought it too terribly tender for words."

"And now?" Devon asked.

"It's too terrible for words. Dev, you're a true friend. It isn't everyone who'd be willing to participate in a novelist's creative process. Val, dear, fix him something to eat. Shall I run out to Dairy Queen?"

"Mama, I want you staying away from Dairy Queen. I'd hate to see the insides of your arteries. You're really going to have to make more effort in the kitchen."

"Darling, I can't," Meg said plaintively. "Not when I'm working."

"Then you're going to have to hire a maid," Valerie said firmly.

Charles Dallas had left his wife and two daughters well provided for. Meg could easily afford the maid.

"Not until I've sold a book." Meg looked at Devon. "You have to set rules or you'll never succeed."

"True," Devon said, grinning at Valerie. "Who knows where you'll end up, Meg. Once you've sold your book and got the maid, you can work your way up to a Rolls-Royce and a mink coat."

"Yeah," Valerie said. "Where's your BMW, Dev? Or did you settle for a Mercedes?"

"Would you believe a Jeep Cherokee?"

"Don't tell me," Valerie said. "It's a four-wheel drive, right? You've packed it full of fishing gear and crab nets, right? There's a fully loaded tackle box in the rear, right? And a cute little ice box designed to keep your bait alive and wriggling."

Meg had fastened rather hazy eyes on her daughter. "Darling, you amaze me. You understand him better than poor Barb ever did."

Valerie hastened to say, "Mama, that doesn't require a great deal of understanding. I remember what he had in the back of that old pickup truck of his."

"It's too bad he didn't fall in love with you instead of Barb." Meg shook her head and rubbed her face in her hands. "I can't understand Barbara myself, and I'm her mother. She married Harry Kilgore just because she thinks he's going to wind up a C.E.O. of some dumb bank or other—not that he isn't a nice man," she added conscientiously. "He's just . . . well, I hate to say it, but he struck me as wet behind the ears."

Valerie's face was flaming once more. Worse, she had no idea how to deflect Meg from a subject that was bound to be painful to Devon.

"Mama," she said, "we were discussing Devon's natural progression from driving a pickup to the successful young entrepreneur's car-of-choice. It has nothing to do with Barbara."

"Doesn't it, dear? I distinctly heard you mention a BMW. That's what Barb is driving."

Valerie gave up. What with Devon's wicked enjoyment of her discomfiture, and Meg's liqueur-induced rambling, things could only get worse.

"Mama," she said, "you've had too much crème de cacao. You'd better lie down and let it wear off."

"No, dear, I think I'll have another look at my story. The way I'm feeling, my right brain should be fully released. Maybe if my creativity is at an all-time high, I can figure out how to fix my story."

Devon was laughing. "I can see it now. Meg Dallas, the great writer, who, like F. Scott Fitzgerald, can only write when she's loaded."

"Shut up, Dev," Valerie said. "Don't you have about six more yards to do before the day is over?"

"Five," Devon said, still laughing. "I'm taking a well-deserved break." He stood. "Don't forget, I'm picking you up tonight at seven."

"You are? What . . .?"

"Jen's party. You should have the house clean by then, right?"

"I don't know , . " Valerie began.

"There isn't a thing wrong with the house," Meg said. "You might as well go, because I'm going to be busy."

"Yes, Mama," Valerie said meekly.

"Walk me to the door, Val," Devon said. "I want you to see the new way I have of edging sidewalks."

Valerie accompanied him to the door and stared at the sidewalk. It was perfectly edged, as befitted a yard Devon had worked on himself, but she noticed nothing new about the method.

"I just wanted you to come outside with me," he said, smiling at her puzzled expression.

"You could have asked."

"I was afraid I'd scare you. Look, Val, for the last time, I'm not mourning Barbara. It's true I was upset when we broke up, but the only thing involved was my pride, if you want to know the truth."

Valerie flushed and said uncomfortably, "Dev, I wish there was something I could do."

"There is, Val. There is. I'll tell you about it tonight, okay? See you at seven."

Valerie nodded and stood watching as Devon climbed in his truck.

She hated what Barbara had done. Of all the reasons for dumping a man, disliking his choice of work surely had to be one of the silliest. Especially when the man was as successful as Devon was.

Valerie was willing to bet Devon collected a bigger salary than Harry Kilgore. The crux of the matter was, Barbara didn't think salary counted over the fact that Devon often liked to help his men with the work. Barb thought a businessman ought to sit in an air-conditioned office wearing a three-piece suit.

Valerie tried to imagine Devon in a three-piece suit and failed.

She watched him drive off, waved, and went back inside.

Surely a man's happiness was worth something. She'd tried talking to Barbara once, pointing out that if Devon was unhappy in his work, he'd take out his unhappiness on his wife.

Barbara had pointed out that if a wife felt ashamed of her husband, she would take out her unhappiness on him.

It was a stalemate, and Barbara had ended it when Devon flatly refused to practice law.

All in all, Valerie thought he was better off. And she should know.

Dev had no idea how tiresome life with Barbara could be.

THREE

Valerie dressed for Jennifer's party while keeping one eye on Meg, who was making regular trips to the kitchen, and another on the clock.

When she'd left Winnie, the scandal of Jonathan Wade had been fresh in everyone's mind. Barbara, always conscious of appearances, hadn't helped by declaring publicly that Valerie had asked for what she got.

Valerie dressed in a tailored white linen dress and braided her shoulder-length hair, pinning it on top of her head. The effect was cool, sophisticated, and definitely not sexy.

Devon did not approve.

"I like your hair down," he said. "You don't look like our Val, does she, Meg?"

Meg, sipping on coffee which Valerie suspected had been surreptitiously exposed to more crème de cacao, replied absently, "She looks like Barbara. I don't like it."

"Neither do I," Devon said.

"Mama, you haven't even looked up from that computer to see what I have on. I'd bet you'd fall over if you did."

Meg glanced around. "Yes, I have, dear. I don't like your hair up like that. It looks—phony. I hate that word, but unfortunately, it describes certain things perfectly."

Devon's long fingers at once burrowed into Valerie's hair, finding and discarding hairpins.

"Dev, cut that out. You're going to make us late."

"Take it down, Val."

Valerie went, grumbling, to unbraid her hair, brushing the pale mass into some semblance of curls.

"That's more like it," Devon said when she re-appeared.

Valerie glowered at him, wishing she could find something to complain of in his appearance. He was casually dressed in slacks, a shirt with no tie, and a sport coat. His sparkling gray eyes contrasted with his darkly tanned face and sun-bleached hair to present an appearance she considered devastating.

"Well?" he asked, leading her to his white Cherokee. "Can't you find something to gripe about? I'm not wearing a tie, you know."

"I'm thinking," Valerie said, with an unwilling grin. "If I didn't think you looked better without a tie, believe me I'd complain."

Devon laughed and helped her in. "Want to check off the contents of the back?"

"What?" She recalled her list of items she was sure he'd stored in the rear of the vehicle and twisted to look over her shoulder. "Never mind. I can see they're all back there, including the cute little ice box. Dev, I hate to say this, but do you think we can give Jen's party a miss?"

Devon had come around and climbed in beside her. "What for? Don't you want to see your old friends? Everyone will be there. Jennifer is looking for a new man, you know."

"I know," Valerie said dryly.

Devon glanced at her with a half-smile. "Don't worry," he said. "She isn't my type. She'd force me into a stuffy law office, and you know how I'd hate that."

Valerie smiled. "A fate worse than death. I never knew how you stuck it through law school."

"Law school was interesting—up to a point." He

started the motor and set the Cherokee in motion. "It's a definite plus when I deal with contracts and so forth."

"For almost two years there, you lost your tan," she said. "I was afraid you were sick."

"Were you? I must have been a pitiful sight."

"You just didn't look like yourself," she said dismissively.

If she didn't watch herself, he'd soon know how closely she'd followed everything he did.

"Barbara told me I looked better without the tan," Devon said.

"She what?"

"That's what she said." Devon laughed. "I think she was trying to coax me into trying one of those downtown Houston glass-box offices."

"Not even Barbara could be that blind," Valerie said.

Devon pulled up at the main traffic light on Highway 124, which ran through the center of Winnie. He smiled at her. "I'm glad you like it. You've never minded the fact that I cut yards for a living, have you?"

"Why should I? It's honest work. Besides, if you want my opinion, you probably make more money running Rayburn Lawn Maintenance than you would if you were another young lawyer just going into practice."

"You're right. I do." Devon sounded oddly satisfied.

The light changed and he concentrated on his driving. Valerie fastened her gaze resolutely on the buildings clustered near the highway and the flat, coastal marshes and rice fields beyond them.

"I'm having a hard time imagining you as a singer," he said. "I never even knew you could sing."

"With Barb singing and competing in beauty pageants, who would have noticed me? My career as a singer was an accident all the way around." Valerie chuckled. "I went to Fort Worth to apply for a job as a music teacher. While I was there, I went to a church service and happened to sit behind a man who toured with a gospel group."

"You're kidding."

"Nope. He was impressed by my operatic voice."

"Barb never told me any of this," he complained.

"Could be because I never told her," Valerie suggested. "Barb wasn't interested in my career. She probably thinks I'm teaching music."

Devon turned the Cherokee into a long, circular drive that was crowded with cars. The house was a brick ranch-style set well back from the street amid a cluster of oak trees.

He parked the car and turned to face her, troubled. "Valerie, are you still . . . angry with Barbara?"

She didn't pretend not to know what he meant. "No, Dev. Barbara has her idea of what life should be, and I have mine. Hopefully, never the twain shall meet."

He looked at her a moment, then came around to help her down.

The sun was setting and cast a golden glow over him. Valerie watched the way the light spilled over his brown hair and colored the sun-bleached parts with gold fire. His shoulders were broad, and she knew his chest would feel as hard and warm as it had two years ago, when he'd held her until the horror of Jonathan Wade had faded and something else began to take its place.

Devon caught her eyes and seemed to freeze. Then he opened the car door and helped her step down, right into his arms.

"Valerie . . ." he said.

She raised her face as naturally as a flower seeking the sun, and he tightened his arms around her as he drew her closer. She closed her eyes, and felt his mouth settle over hers in a gentle, searching kiss.

She opened her eyes when the warm pressure ended and discovered the entire world seemed filled with golden light then realized she was looking directly into the setting sun.

"Dev?" she asked.

Devon was staring at her.

Valerie lowered her eyes and tried to step back.

"I've wanted to do that for a long time," he said quietly. "You'd probably be surprised to know how long."

She looked up quickly and smiled with difficulty. "I guess I did . . . act like I was throwing myself at you that time Jonathan Wade tried to rape me. You looked so strong and comforting, I never thought how you or Barbara might react."

"Valerie, this has nothing to do with that incident or any other in the past. Get that through your head." He set his hands on her shoulders and shook her lightly. "Let's go in and socialize. I have a lot to say to you afterward."

Valerie allowed him to tuck her hand into the crook of his arm and lead her toward the house.

A strange new feeling was growing within her, a feeling composed of hope and the blazing emotion she'd always felt for Devon Rayburn.

She tried to arrange her expression. Until she was sure of Devon's intentions, she'd better not let her face reveal her feelings to the entire world.

Jennifer greeted them at the door, smiling and staring at Valerie speculatively.

"So glad you could come, Dev . . . I didn't know your eyes were green, Val. You look stunning. Come on in and meet everybody. Look who's back, folks."

Valerie fought the urge to back out the door and pull Devon with her. For a woman who made her living singing in front of hundreds of people, she was behaving like the shy high school student she'd been when she'd last seen most of these people.

Pinning her stage smile on her face, she moved forward and nodded politely.

"Val Dallas!" one woman exclaimed.

Valerie stared. Mattie Cloninger had been a curvaceous red-headed cheerleader. Now she was on her way to becoming a plump matron.

Mattie stared back. "Barbara said you were singing with the Shelby Winthrop Quartet. What an exciting life!

You were such a quiet, mousy little thing, and look at you now.''

"I've been very lucky," Valerie agreed.

"Hard work didn't have a thing to do with it," Devon said, grinning.

Jennifer glanced at him. "She doesn't look anything like Barbara, does she? Barbara's hair was perfectly natural. I used to love that pure, golden-blond shade.''

Valerie flushed as she sensed Devon's amused gray eyes focusing on her.

"This unnatural silver-blond looks awfully good to me," Devon said.

Jennifer's wide brown eyes opened further. "Well, for heaven's sake, Dev.''

Valerie could almost hear Jennifer's next ingenuous comment on Devon's fancy for sisters.

Devon cut in with, "Val, let's speak to a few more people, then we'd better be going. We have to be at the club by eight, you know.''

Valerie composed herself in time to close her mouth before she asked him which club.

"You used to wear glasses, didn't you?" Mattie asked before they could move away. "Big, thick ones.''

"I still do, when I'm not wearing contacts," Valerie said.

"Oh. I was wondering about that lovely shade of green. I've never seen pale-green contacts before.''

"That's Val's natural shade," Devon said. "Peridot-green.''

Jennifer stared at Valerie's eyes. "Funny. I never noticed before what color her eyes were. Barbara's eyes are green, also, if I recall.''

Devon's mouth had thinned. "Blond hair and green eyes appear to run in the Dallas family. Come on, Val. Let's get something to eat.''

Urged by his hand at the small of her back, Valerie walked beside him to the dining-room table where plates of sandwiches and chips were waiting.

By the time they had circulated once through the house,

Valerie had endured three more comparisons to Barbara and Devon had smilingly warded off four suggestions that if he couldn't have one sister, he'd go for the other.

Fletcher Morrison, the young rice farmer who had his eye on Jennifer, actually said, "Heck, if I'd known Val looked like this underneath those glasses, I'd have tried for her myself."

It was gratifying in a way, and annoying in another. All her life, Valerie had suffered comparisons to Barbara. It was strange to hear herself described as the prettier of the two.

Devon seemed to know her thoughts.

"You'll get used to it," he said, grinning.

"I don't know . . ." she began. "Besides, beauty is a matter of opinion. Barbara—"

"Val, truer words were never spoken," he interrupted. Valerie subsided.

Mattie Cloninger caught sight of them and gestured. "Val, what's Shelby Winthrop really like? You know her rather well, don't you?"

"She's a lovely person," Valerie responded instantly.

"I adore gospel music," Mattie said, further astounding Valerie. "Do you know, I didn't realize until just now that you're the Rebecca Dallas associated with the Shelby Winthrop Quartet."

"Rebecca is my middle name," Valerie said. "Shelby thought it sounded more . . . biblical."

She became conscious of Devon's interested presence beside her, although he said nothing.

"You have an album out yourself, don't you?" Mattie asked. "I have it. I just love that song you always sing called 'Emanuel.' Gosh, that's so exciting. I'd never have guessed you were Rebecca Dallas. You were always so quiet."

Valerie smiled. With a big sister like Barbara, who'd notice a mousy girl who wore glasses so thick, no one knew what color her eyes were?

"She could talk when she wanted to," Devon said.

Valerie had talked to Devon, but he had taken pains to

draw her out. He had probably known more about Valerie's hopes and troubles than Barbara had.

Jennifer drifted up. "Say, Val, whatever happened with Jonathan Wade? I haven't heard a thing more about him since you claimed he tried to rape you two years back."

"I have no idea," Valerie said, conscious of the tightening of her muscles. "I filed charges against him, but they were dismissed as unfounded."

Beside her, Devon had tensed. "That fellow is a menace to society," he said.

"Did he really rip your dress off you?" Jennifer asked, wide-eyed. "Barbara said—"

Valerie remembered perfectly well what Barbara had said, and cut in with, "Yes, he did, and if you don't mind, Jen, I'd rather not talk about it."

"Well, I don't blame you," Jennifer said. "Did you really throw black pepper in his face?"

"She said she'd rather not talk about it, Jen," Devon said. "We'd better go, Val. It's getting near eight."

Valerie nodded with relief. She'd like to forget her one date with Jonathan Wade, but the ensuing scandal had probably ensured that she would never be allowed to.

She waited while Devon thanked Jennifer for inviting them, then forced herself to walk slowly down the short sidewalk to the circular driveway.

"Does it still upset you to talk about Jonathan Wade?" Devon asked gently.

"It doesn't upset me to talk about him, precisely," Valerie said. "Although he was bad enough. What upsets me is what happened afterward. I got away from him, you know."

"Did you, Val?"

Valerie heard the unspoken question. "Yes, I did. When he hit me and ripped the front of my dress, I had enough presence of mind to get the pepper out and throw it in his face. While he was busy with that, I managed to get control of his car."

"I never got to talk with you much about it," Devon said, guiding her to his car.

Valerie knew why.

"Well, I don't mind telling you, Dev. When I threw that pepper in his eyes, he was blinded, but he still lunged for me. I jumped out of the car, and he tried to chase me. I jumped back in, where he'd fortunately left his keys in the ignition, and took off. I left him in the woods while I drove straight to the Beaumont Police Station."

"I'm surprised you knew where it was," Devon said lightly. He opened the Cherokee's door and helped her in.

"I didn't. I had to ask at three different filling stations." She grinned.

"Really?" He began to laugh. "That must have been almost as traumatic as Jonathan Wade."

"Close. I guess it's a good thing I drove directly there or they'd have really thought I was lying. Can you believe his father filing auto theft charges against me?"

"What gets me is that he'd condone his only son's attempt to rape a young girl. I'm glad I could help you, Valerie."

Devon was standing in the open door looking at her. Night was falling, and the light was fading rapidly.

Valerie looked at him, then at the windshield directly in front of her. "Thank you, Dev. I don't know what I'd have done without you. Mama didn't know what to do, and Barb—I . . . I was too upset to do anything."

"What good is a law degree if you can't use it to help your friends?" Devon asked lightly.

"True." Valerie rallied to smile at him. "I never thought to point out that car thieves are hardly likely to drive said stolen car straight to the police station."

"I think what scared him was my request that he have Jonathan psychoanalyzed. I had the feeling then there'd been trouble before over similar actions on the son's part. Why did you agree to go out with him?"

Valerie felt herself flushing and felt thankful for the dusk. "At the time, I knew nothing about him. He called me every night for two weeks, and all my friends said they wished it'd been them. I thought it was all frightfully romantic."

Devon came around and climbed in beside her, muttering, "Cheez!"

Valerie chuckled. "Well, I did. He was one of the few dates I'd ever had in my young life, and he was rich and handsome, and drove a Camaro. What else could a young girl ask for?"

"Common decency?" Devon asked, in the tones of one seeking information.

"Even Mama will tell you that a romantic young girl isn't quite sure what that means. I didn't start learning until he took me to a movie that was downright pornographic."

"He *what*?"

"Well, it was R-rated, but it was pretty shocking to me. During certain scenes, I couldn't help but see he was getting excited, so I began to get a very bad feeling."

Devon said nothing, but he made no move to switch on the engine. He stared at her in the deepening darkness.

"If I'd had any sense, I'd have refused to leave the movie theater with him. I thought I was being terribly clever when I said I had a headache and wanted to go straight home."

"And he wouldn't take you?"

"He wouldn't take me. He drove to a deserted parking lot in the middle of a wooded area. By then I was frightened, so I got my hand on the pepper canister I'd carried in my pocket just in case."

"He must have planned to rape you," Devon said.

Valerie nodded. "I think he did."

Devon was silent a moment. "I wonder how many others weren't as prepared or as lucky as you were?" he finally asked.

Valerie shivered and said nothing.

"Jonathan Wade is no longer in Beaumont. I've never heard anything more about him, and I tried to keep tabs on him."

Valerie shrugged. "Doesn't his father still own Wade's Appliances?"

"It's like he never had a son. If you want to know what I think . . . he knows Jonathan's a bad apple."

"How horrible," Valerie said in low tones. "When I remember how he tried to railroad me. . . ."

"He'd never have succeeded. You drove directly to the police station, and you could have called those station attendants to testify if necessary." He stopped, then added, with difficulty, "Valerie, that night when you got home and I held you. . . ."

"You don't have to say any more, Dev. I understand. After what I'd been through, you looked so comforting, I wasn't thinking what I was doing."

Devon sighed. "I'm glad you were able to think I looked comforting."

They sat in silence a moment, recalling the night Valerie had returned home to Winnie, driven by a girlfriend who lived in Beaumont.

When she'd phoned home, no one had been there, so she called a friend. By the time she arrived in Winnie, however, Barbara and Devon were home from their date, and Meg had returned from visiting a friend.

Valerie had stepped inside the house and promptly burst into tears. Devon stood directly across the room from her, and Valerie had zeroed in on him like a targeted missile, flinging herself into his arms.

As she did, she released her grip on her torn dress and it fell, revealing her naked breasts for an instant before she landed on Devon's chest.

Nothing was said then, for her friend entered and told the shocked company what had happened, but Barbara had said plenty in the privacy of the room she shared with Valerie.

On top of the horror of what had nearly happened to her, Valerie had been forced to deal with Barbara's accusations that she'd planned the incident to show herself to Devon.

"I've always felt that I left you open for Barbara's nasty remarks," Devon said slowly. "Don't bother telling me she didn't accuse you of trying to seduce me."

Valerie swallowed. "I can understand why she thought that. It must have looked premeditated."

"Val, the last thing it looked was premeditated. Any fool could see you'd had a horrible experience. I'm afraid the real reason Barbara was angry was because she and I were having trouble, and she was looking for a scapegoat."

Valerie stared out the windshield. "I've always felt guilty that the two of you broke up soon afterward. You'd gone together so many years. . . ."

Her voice trailed off. Devon and Barbara had gone together for five years, and everyone had assumed they'd get married. Devon had even attended law school to please Barbara.

"The truth is, Barb and I didn't want the same things out of life. She wanted to manipulate people in the corporate world, and I wanted to work outdoors. We'd been fighting for months before that night. Nothing came to a head as long as she was still in school. The moment she got her M.B.A., everything collapsed."

"I know. I'm sorry, Dev."

"The funny thing is," Devon said, "I'd tried so hard to disguise the fact that I was interested in you. She obviously knew, and used the knowledge to make you leave."

Valerie froze, certain she hadn't heard correctly.

"After you left, the night she and I broke up, she accused me of seeing you on the side."

Valerie turned her head painfully and stared at him. He was a darker outline against the night sky, and he appeared to be watching her intently.

"I'm so sorry, Dev," she murmured.

"Are you? I'm not. Barb and I were great together when we were younger, but we'd have never stayed together in a marriage. I'd realized it was over long before she ended it."

He didn't sound sorry. Valerie peered at him in the darkness.

Devon turned on the motor and flicked on the airconditioner. "If we're going to have this conversation in the car, we might as well be comfortable."

Valerie, suddenly conscious of the tension in her body, relaxed and laughed.

"So you've got an album out," Devon said. "Where can I get a copy?"

"I'll see that you get one. I'll even autograph it for you."

"Mattie thinks you're a big-time gospel star. That's incredible, Val."

"I'm not a big-time star, nor am I likely to become one," she protested. "I leave that to people like Shelby Winthrop and Sandi Patti."

"You're still suffering from the second-sister syndrome."

"There's no such thing. I just don't have as much dedication as the stars have. I enjoy the work, but I think I'm a small-town music teacher at heart."

"Is that so? Do you give piano lessons?"

Valerie suddenly became conscious that Devon had left his position behind the wheel and was moving toward her.

"Of course, I . . . well, I've never had time, but I could give piano lessons. Are you thinking of signing up?"

She was tingling with awareness and delight, and cast him a coquettish glance that he couldn't see.

"How about one o'clock tomorrow afternoon?"

"Fine. I'll start you out on my first piece."

Devon slid both arms around her and held her against him. "I'm sure I'll master it in one lesson."

"I've noticed you were a quick study for anything you could do with your hands," she said breathlessly.

Devon chuckled and ran his hands lightly over her arms. "I learn some things faster than others."

Valerie shivered with anticipation and wondered why he didn't kiss her. Lifting her face, she waited, breathing in the woodsy scent of his cologne with delight.

Devon seemed content to sit beside her, stroking her arms and holding her gently.

Valerie was tired of gentleness from Devon. Placing

both hands on his shoulders, she stretched up and pressed her lips against his. They were warm and hard, and his face was smooth and soft from a recent shave.

At once, his arms tightened around her. He let her kiss him, obligingly parting his lips when she signaled with her own mouth that she was ready for the intimacy.

Valerie had never kissed a man who waited for her to make the moves and to initiate the depth of the contact. She felt incredibly powerful, and the excitement in her began to build.

Since Devon was so responsive to that kiss, she tried another. This time she turned more fully toward him, locking her hands behind his neck as she encouraged him to explore her teeth with his tongue. In turn, she explored his and found them perfect.

Devon sighed his pleasure and let her kiss him as many times and as deeply as she wanted to. She wanted to kiss him all night.

She wanted more than that. For years she'd admired his splendid male body as he stripped to the waist to tackle someone's yard, and she longed to see how it would feel to her touch.

Devon's shirt was open at the neck. Valerie kissed him again and casually stroked his neck with her fingers, then slid them down to tangle with the top button of his shirt. Devon tilted his chin back to give her better access.

Encouraged, Valerie unbuttoned three more buttons, then slid her hands inside his shirt, running her palms lightly across his chest. The thick covering of hair in the center felt springy to her touch, and the skin to the sides was warm and smooth. She leaned forward to kiss the center of his chest and tasted the crisp tang of his skin.

Devon's fingers buried themselves in her hair, and he began a slow massage of her scalp that added to her excitement.

Valerie wondered what the next step should be, then decided to go with her feelings. She strung a line of kisses across his chest, deliberately tasting him with her tongue, then progressed up one side of his neck and kissed his mouth once more.

Devon responded with quickened breathing. Every muscle in his shoulders seemed harder, and his thigh muscles, where she'd propped one hand, were so tense they almost quivered.

He didn't make a move toward her. It was driving Valerie almost crazy.

She brought her hands up to touch his face, exploring with her sensitive fingertips the lean curves of his cheeks, the high cheekbones, and the straight brows as she'd longed to do for years.

Devon closed his eyes and let her explore him as she would, sliding his hands down to clasp her waist lightly.

She discovered his ear and leaned forward to kiss it, tracing the edge with her tongue.

Devon groaned aloud. His hands at her waist trembled, and he pulled her closer, almost crushing her. He leaned over her, kissing her frantically, stroking her tongue with his as his hands slid gently up her sides to cup her breasts.

Valerie had never felt anything like the feeling that invaded her body when Devon used the pads of his thumbs to tease her nipples through the material of her dress and bra. Her hands clutched his shoulders and she whimpered.

They heard a car door slam. Devon whipped his head around and watched a couple walk toward the house. He was breathing as if he'd been running.

Valerie tugged at his shoulders, silently begging for the return of his attention.

Devon hugged her and said, "Lord, I didn't mean for this to happen. At least, not yet, and not in front of Jen Devilier's house."

"You had some other place in mind?" she asked hopefully.

"Remember Livvy and Rex. The first date is where you decide whether or not you want to kiss me."

"I think I've already progressed beyond that decision," Valerie pointed out, her lips inches from his. "What's the next step?"

Devon chuckled and kissed her neck. "We leave here and go someplace public. Otherwise things will progress a lot faster than you're probably ready for."

"That's open for debate," Valerie suggested.

"Val."

"Yes, Dev?"

Her palms were flattened on his chest. Her fingers entwined in his chest hair and tugged gently.

"You'd better cut that out."

"What will you give me if I do?" Her voice was hopeful.

Devon laughed, a delighted, strangled sound. "Val, what I'd like to give you can't be given here. Let's drive to Beaumont and have some dinner. We should have done that in the first place and given this party a miss."

"I told you so," Valerie said, feeling bereft as he slid behind the wheel.

"Never say 'I told you so' to the man who's about to buy you dinner. He might make you starve while he eats."

Valerie sat back and sighed, gazing at his profile. "Go ahead." She recalled a quotation from the Bible and added, "I have food that you know not of."

Devon switched on the overhead light and turned a surprised glance toward her. Then he switched it back off and stared out the windshield a moment. "Val, that's the nicest thing anyone's ever said to me," he finally said. "I'll buy you the biggest steak in the place."

FOUR

When Valerie arose the following morning, she sat down to breakfast with the feeling that the heavens had suddenly opened up and showered favors on her.

Meg, eyeing a bowl of steaming mush doubtfully, picked up a spoon and applied it cautiously to the mush.

She nibbled a spoonful and said plaintively, "Darling, if you mean this to be oatmeal, please refrain from grinding it to a powder."

"It isn't oatmeal, Mama. It's oat bran. I'm worried about your cholesterol. Eat it."

Meg sighed in a long-suffering manner and swallowed the mush. "Yes, darling. You sound like your father. So determined to be as healthy as possible. You haven't noticed any daredevil tendencies beginning to surface, have you?"

Valerie stared. "What on earth do you mean, Mama?"

"Well, the two seem to go together. People who like to be fearfully healthy like to be healthy for a reason—so their bodies will hold up under all the ridiculous stresses they seem to enjoy."

Meg made an effort and took her eyes off the sheaf of pages beside her plate to study her daughter's face.

Valerie finally deciphered this speech and laughed.

"No, Mama. Getting out on stage to sing a solo is the extent of my courage."

"That's enough, dear. I'm very proud of you." Her blue eyes dropped to Valerie's mouth. "Although, I'm not so sure I wouldn't rate kissing Devon as a courageous act. He's exactly my idea of what a man should be." She stared at her pages once more and spooned up more oat bran. "Now, that's an idea. I think I'll write this story calling the hero Devon instead of Blake until I'm ready to do the final printout. Maybe that will make him come alive."

"I'll pretend I didn't hear that," Valerie said, conscious of the blush staining her cheeks. "Devon would faint if he knew you were putting him into one of your books."

"I doubt it, dear. He's obviously got something better on his mind right now."

"Mama . . ."

"A mother isn't blind, Val, even if she is buried beneath an avalanche of manuscript pages. As I've observed before, you'll suit Devon much better than poor Barbara ever did. I tried telling her it's absolutely *fatal* to forbid a man to choose when and how and where he's going to work."

Valerie smiled. "I remember how you packed us all up when Daddy got the job with the crop-dusting company."

"Charles would have gone alone and sent me his paycheck every week if I'd refused to join him," Meg said placidly. "I've never regretted allowing him to follow his heart. He died the way he'd have chosen to die, and we were happy until that day."

"I remember," Valerie said. "He always said he was the happiest man on earth. I think that's worth something, don't you?"

"Darling, it's everything. Which I tried explaining to Barb." Meg pressed her lips together and shook her head, suddenly looking sad and almost forlorn.

Valerie said nothing, recalling that Barbara, in the privacy of their own room, had sobbed into her pillow the day their father died and claimed that Meg had caused his death. Barbara had felt that if Meg had refused to move to Winnie and insisted that Charles accept the salesman's job he'd been offered in Lubbock, he'd still have been alive.

Meg shrugged off her sadness. "She'll have to learn on her own that no good can come of forcing a man into a job he'd hate."

"I know, Mama. Did you know she told Dev he looked better without his tan?"

Her smile invited Meg to join in her amusement.

Meg blinked. "Barb said that? She can't have, dear. Barb doesn't even wear glasses."

At that, Valerie began to laugh helplessly. "You'll have to tell that to Dev, Mama."

"I will, dear. If I remember."

Valerie laughed again and recalled the previous night. After she and Devon had left Jen Devilier's house, they'd driven to Beaumont for dinner, then Devon had taken her straight home, much to her disappointment.

However, he'd sat in the car with her a moment, kissing her with the aggression she'd sensed was carefully banked earlier. It had been very satisfactory.

When she'd walked into the house Meg glanced up from the computer screen, focused on Valerie's mouth, and returned to her work immediately with a vague comment about a good time being had by all.

Meg glanced at the stack of pages beside her plate. "I've decided to completely revise Blake and Pamela. My chief problem seems to be that the book is over in Chapter Eight because Blake has already told Pamela he loves her. Poor Pamela can't help but look like a fool for refusing to marry such a marvelous man."

Valerie had no idea what this signified, but she was willing to be educated. "So what are you going to do, Mama?"

"I've got to come up with a good reason for Blake to keep his mouth shut. Then Pamela can act like an idiot all she wants."

"I had no idea writing was so complicated," Valerie said.

"Few people do," Meg agreed. "I keep on telling myself, this is how you learn."

"Yes, Mama. Eat your oat bran."

Meg finished off the bowl of cereal without once taking her eyes from her manuscript, and Valerie cleared the table while Meg hastened to her computer.

Valerie stood at the window while she washed dishes and smiled at the yard. Meg's crop of pigweed had been reduced to a uniform one-inch height, and Valerie could see the old garden plot in the far corner of the yard.

The plot called to her. Valerie replaced her blouse with a long-sleeved old shirt of her father's and a big hat and sallied forth to inspect it.

The inspection was so successful she repaired to the garage and returned with a shovel. By the time her back began to complain, she'd turned over several square feet of earth.

"Is this intended to be a garden, by any chance?"

Valerie jumped and turned to see Devon standing behind her, watching her with delight. He held a folded square of paper in his hand.

"It will be by this afternoon, I hope," she said, rubbing her lower back. "I haven't gardened in so long, I'm dying to have a shot at it."

Devon took the shovel from her hands and gave her the paper. "Why didn't you call me? You're going to kill yourself, you little idiot. Go clean up and I'll bring a tiller. That's a new hurricane tracking chart for your refrigerator."

Valerie unfolded the chart. "You have a tiller?"

"Of course I have a tiller. Rayburn Lawn Maintenance aims to please, and we have several elderly clients who ask us to prepare their garden plots every year."

"Thanks a lot, Dev."

Devon laughed. "A backache never fails to add about twenty years to your age. Go rest, Val. I'll be back in a few minutes. If you're determined to have a garden, a garden you shall have.''

"Thanks for the chart. Hurricane tracking is one of my favorite late-summer sports.'' She refolded it with satisfaction.

"I guess you haven't had much chance to do that lately,'' he said, walking beside her toward the house.

"Not in two years,'' she said.

Valerie saw Devon off, then went inside and posted the chart on the refrigerator, glad to cease an activity she suspected she was badly out of shape for.

Devon returned with a motor-driven tiller on his trailer. With its aid, he had her garden plot thoroughly turned over within half an hour.

"What are you planting?'' he asked when she brought him a cold drink.

"At this time of year, there's only one thing you can safely plant in this climate that you can count on to grow.''

"Okra?''

"Right.''

"Good luck. I suppose nothing's going to stop you from trying radishes and greens. They should be ready to harvest about the time the really hot weather sets in and everything dries up.''

"I'm pinning my hopes to the okra.''

"You like gardening, don't you? I'll never forget that corn you grew one year. Everyone in town must have eaten it.''

"That was an unusually good year. I'm telling you, Dev, I'll probably single-handedly bring in a hurricane or a flood. Every time my plants get one-inch high, they get drowned.''

"That isn't likely to happen. The spring floods are over. It's time for the hot, dry weather. You're going to have to water every day, if anything.''

"Just wait,'' she predicted. "You'll see. I hope the soybean and rice farmers need rain, because they're going to get it.''

Devon chuckled at her certainty. "It'll be good for me. The grass will grow. Plant away, Val. Shall I drive you to the feed store?"

"Don't you have a few yards lined up for today?"

"I'm taking a day off," he said, smiling in a way that caused her heart to experience that strange surge once more.

"Well, by the time you get through tilling and planting this yard," she said breathlessly, "the bill should be equal to one of those apartment complexes your crews handle."

"Val, you're getting a special rate. Believe me, I'll come out ahead."

Valerie's mouth felt dry, and she reached automatically for the soft drink in Devon's hand. "I hope so," she said fervently.

Valerie had hastily changed into walking shorts and a colorful print blouse while Devon fetched his tiller. Her silver-blond hair was tickling the back of her neck in a ponytail, but Devon didn't seem to mind the ponytail the way he'd minded her chignon, so she left it alone.

The late-June temperature had yet to reach the upper nineties that would let Gulf Coast residents know summer had truly arrived, but it was hot and humid nonetheless.

Valerie rode beside Devon in his pickup, agreeing readily when he asked to drive to his equipment barn to put up the tiller. He drove to the outskirts of town to a big tin building backed by a rice field. Devon had always been particular about his equipment and took no chances on having it stolen.

Valerie remained in the truck while he unloaded the tiller. The rice field was broad and flat, and young rice plants were just coming up green. The field was bordered by levees that sported a line of Chinese tallow trees along them. At intervals, male red-winged blackbirds defended their territories from other blackbirds.

"What are you looking at, Val?" Devon had relocked the barn door and returned to the truck.

"I'm watching a blackbird threaten another blackbird.

What do people do when they don't live in the country, Dev?''

He moved to stand beside her window and followed her gaze to the pair of birds. Each bird was quivering its wings so that the red patches on their shoulders flared angrily.

"I don't know, honey. What do you do?"

She sighed. "I never had time to miss anything. It seemed that we were always on the move. Always late. Always due someplace else. I got to where I never even unpacked my suitcase completely. There wasn't any point in it.''

"Don't you like what you're doing? It sounds rather . . . glamorous.''

"It is, I suppose. It's just me. I like living in a house, with my own possessions and my own plot of ground to work.''

Devon smiled and looked pleased. The noon sun turned portions of his hair to a blaze of white light. His long, sensitive mouth curved upward at the corners.

"Ah, yes, the okra seeds.'' He leaned in at her window and kissed her lips lightly. "No wonder you're hot on the garden. Let's go, honey. You'll feel better as soon as you get the seeds into the ground.''

Valerie agreed and smiled with anticipation as they pulled up at the hardware and feed store. Perhaps some radish and mustard green seeds were still available.

She sighed and put the thought of where she'd be when the garden was ready for harvesting out of her mind. She'd returned home both for a vacation and for serious consideration of her future. So far, all she'd done was refuse to think about the future.

After all, she reminded herself, she'd only been here a couple of days. She had another month. And Devon . . . She resolutely put that thought out of her mind also. It was too soon to think about the impact Devon could have on her decisions.

"What are you thinking so hard about?'' Devon asked, eyeing her pensive face.

"I was hoping Mama will start taking an interest in the

garden once I've got it going. I'd better plant some green onions. She loves green onions.''

"It's a little late in the season for those." He helped her step down and followed her inside. "How long are you planning on being home?''

"I've officially taken a month off. We're supposed to go back on the road in August.''

Devon made a noncommittal murmur and stopped before a display of lawn-mower parts.

Valerie eyed him cautiously. He didn't seem concerned at all.

She watched his minute study of the parts a moment, admiring the way his sun-streaked hair fell attractively across his forehead, then said, "Dev, if you don't look out, that muffler is going to bite you. I'll be over here at the seed display.''

Devon's attention swung back to her and he followed her hastily. "Sorry, Val. I was just thinking.''

"Lawn-mower wheels do require a lot of thought," she agreed, picking packages of seed off the display at random.

"I'll admit they hold a certain fascination for a man who mows a lot of yards.''

"It's a pity I'm not a lawn," Valerie said in her most wistful tones.

Devon grinned. "Am I that bad? Come here, Val. You deserve a kiss for putting up with my bad manners.''

"What bad manners? I realize it's difficult for a woman to compete with grass, but I don't mind trying. Maybe I should have taken off my glasses. Or invested in some grass-scented cologne.''

Devon's arms went around her. He sniffed her neck. "You smell like sunlight. That beats grass any day.''

"Dev, people are looking.''

"So?''

"We're liable to hear all about this little incident in another two hours.''

"I love small towns," Devon said, and kissed her. He turned her fully into his embrace and molded her body to his. This time he held her still and explored her mouth thoroughly while she clutched his shoulders with hands that still clasped several seed packages.

Valerie gasped and began to laugh as soon as she was able.

"Seduced among the seeds," she said.

"Would you prefer among the lawn-mower parts?"

"What the heck? Let's go crazy."

Laughing, they kissed again, and Valerie scattered seed packages wildly about as Devon bent her back over an arm that felt like a steel bar.

"Dev!" she squealed as her feet left the floor.

The remaining seed packages fluttered down as she clutched his neck. Seconds later, her glasses followed. She heard them slide across the floor, but Devon's warm, hard lips were nuzzling the hollow of her neck while she rested on his arm. It prevented her from taking the proper care of her eyewear.

A strange crunch sounded, and a deep, gravelly voice said, "Oh, my God. Who . . . uh . . . Hi, Dev, I think I just totaled somebody's glasses."

Valerie felt her surroundings spin as Devon set her back on her feet.

"Uh-oh. Val, I'm afraid you won't be wearing these again," Devon said.

Valerie gazed at the hazy bulk that indicated an unusually large man standing about ten feet from them and felt something pressed into her palm when she held out her hand.

She brought her hand up before her eyes and a mangled mass of plastic with two lenses that had shattered in a spiderweb pattern came into focus.

"Oh, dear," she said. "Dev, I'm now at your mercy. I can't see anything more than five feet away. At least, not very clearly."

"Ma'am, I'm terribly sorry," the hazy bulk said. "I wasn't looking."

"Don't be silly, Hulk. It's my fault," Devon said. "I made her drop them. Val, I'd like you to meet one of my employees, Donald Murphy, otherwise known as the Hulk.''

"Pleased to meet you, Mr. Murphy," Valerie said. Glasses are always falling off my nose." She felt her proffered hand enveloped by a big, rough hand.

"I hope this means you have another pair at home," Devon said.

"Yes," Valerie said in meaningful tones. "At home."

Devon chuckled. "That bad, huh? Okay, just tell me which seeds you want and I'll find them for you. What's up, Hulk?''

"It's that lady on Shellhammer Road, Boss. She says I'm scaring her kids.''

"What?" Devon sounded exasperated. "Did you tell her you're with the lawn maintenance company her husband hired?''

"Sure, Boss. It isn't that. It's me. She says her kids are scared of me and are hiding under the kitchen table.''

Valerie began to regret the demise of her glasses. Hulk Murphy must have been something to see. His height alone was impressive. In her hazy estimation, Valerie thought him nearly six feet eight.

She fished in her purse for her contact lens case and turned her back to insert them quickly. She couldn't wear contacts for more than a few hours a day, but this was an emergency.

How Mrs. Barlow's children could have feared the man, she didn't know. It was true he was huge compared to normal men, and his brow had a ridge that projected out above his eyes like a small shelf, but the sky-blue eyes were kind, and his touch was gentle.

"I don't think they're scared of you in the least," she said. "They're probably playing at being outlaws hiding in a cave."

Hulk sounded grateful. "I wouldn't know, ma'am, but I can't complete the job. She ran me off.''

"Never mind, Hulk. I'll see if I can borrow a phone and find out where Johnny's crew is. You can take his place and send him to finish up at Mrs. Barlow's.''

"Fine," Hulk Murphy said. He smiled at Valerie. "I'm sorry about your glasses, ma'am."

"It wasn't your fault. It was Dev's. I ought to make him deduct the cost of a new pair of glasses from my lawn bill."

He grinned as if to say it was highly unlikely Rayburn Lawn Maintenance would be sending her a bill and followed Devon.

Valerie knelt on the floor and picked up her scattered seed packages, then searched the rack to be sure she hadn't missed anything exciting.

She carried them to the counter and paid for them, smiling at the clerk happily.

"Fall garden?" the woman asked, eyeing Valerie. "You're Meg Dallas's daughter, aren't you?"

"Yes. Actually, this is a summer garden. With careful nurturing, it will grow. Unless, of course, the flood gets it."

"The flood?"

"Every time I plant a garden, it floods."

The woman was silent a moment. "It's the wrong time of year for that," she offered at last.

"It's the wrong time of year for a garden, too," Valerie pointed out cheerfully.

Devon had commandeered a telephone near the counter and caught sight of her.

"Val, I'm sorry," Devon said. "I shouldn't have gone off and left you with a man who scares the clients." He replaced the telephone receiver. "I can't raise Johnny's crew. Mary says they're somewhere between Pasadena and Houston."

"If you like, you can do Mrs. Barlow's yard yourself," Valerie said.

"Thanks a lot, Val. On my day off, I get stuck with this ditzy female. Hulk, you'd better go on with the next job."

Hulk left, and Devon waited while Valerie paid for her seed and received the bag.

"Oh, Val, dear, there you are."

"Mama?" Valerie turned toward the entrance. "I thought you were deep in the creative process."

"I was, dear, but I got two phone calls that claimed you were being ravished right here in the middle of the gardening aisle, so I thought I'd better come see about it. Hello, Dev. I didn't know you were the kind of man who'd give every busybody in town a vicarious thrill."

Meg's gentle voice was pitched so that everyone in the small hardware store could hear her easily.

Valerie felt her fair skin heating up and tried her best to look nonchalant.

"Neither did I, Meg. I'm discovering new depths to my character."

Valerie could hear Devon's smile in his voice.

"Do you think you could discover them in private, dear? I can't write with the blasted phone ringing off the wall."

Valerie choked. "Mama, you're supposed to be a tigress defending her cub. Telling Dev to ravish me in private is tantamount to throwing me to the wolves."

"He isn't that bad, Val. Buy some more black pepper if you're worried."

"Mama!"

Devon had begun to laugh aloud. "Meg, I think I'll ravish you instead."

"You can't. I'm writing," Meg said.

Devon threw an arm around Valerie. "In that case, I'll continue to seduce Val."

"Good. I've done my motherly duty. Now I can get back to work. Val, dear, when you get home, would you please make a pot of coffee? It's the least you can do after interrupting my best inspiration to date."

They followed Meg out to the parking lot and waited while she climbed into her car and headed back to her computer.

"Want to watch while I give Mrs. Barlow's yard the works?" Devon asked.

"You're lucky I had my contacts," Valerie pointed out,

holding out her hand, the remains of her glasses still resting in it.

"Oh, Lord. Do you need your glasses? You're very near-sighted, aren't you?"

"Very," Valerie agreed. "And my eyes don't take kindly to contacts, which is why I don't wear them for extended periods. They'll do unless this yard turns out to be a football field . . . How could anyone be afraid of Hulk Murphy?"

Devon had helped Valerie into his truck and stood beside it, grinning at her. His mobile mouth curved upward.

"I don't know. He's a very nice fellow," Devon said. "He has a wife and three small children of his own, which is why this whole thing is so annoying."

"Maybe you can add the price of my glasses to Mrs. Barlow's bill. After all, this is basically her fault."

Devon was laughing, and Valerie felt cocooned in his warmth and amusement.

When she accompanied Devon to his equipment barn, then to Mrs. Barlow's property, she recalled her comment about football fields.

"This is quite a spread," she said, staring around Mrs. Barlow's rolling lawn, complete with a swing set and a large wading pool. There were plenty of scrub pecan trees set out to make life difficult for the yardman. A ceramic hen and rooster with five baby chicks occupied the only open stretch of grass.

"Why do they think ceramic chickens make it look like a farm?" Devon grumbled.

"Careful, Dev. It could have been one of those wooden cow silhouettes."

Devon made a rude comment. He drove farther up the driveway and climbed out to unload his tractor.

As he rode his tractor down the loading ramp, Valerie looked toward the house curiously as the front door opened and a woman stepped out on the concrete veranda.

Behind the woman, two little girls peeked around the

doorframe, watching Devon with fascination. The children behaved as though they saw very few people.

Valerie called to Devon and directed his attention to the woman. He shut off the engine, and walked to the veranda, allowing Valerie an admiring view of his easy, confident stride.

The two little girls disappeared from view.

The truck was parked barely fifteen feet from the veranda, so Valerie was able to hear the conversation without straining her ears. Devon apologized that one of his men had frightened the two children, whose heads had reappeared. They watched him with wide eyes.

"I should think so . . ." Mrs. Barlow began in indignant tones. "A great, hulking monster like that. Why, he even scared me. I got a feeling the minute I looked at him. He's probably got a criminal record a mile long, and—"

Devon, sounding irritated, interrupted. "Mrs. Barlow, I can assure you that no employee of Rayburn Lawn Maintenance has a criminal record, and certainly not Donald Murphy."

Mrs. Barlow's gaze transferred to Valerie. "Who's that? Your live-in lover?" Her voice rose. "I won't have those kinds of goings-on around here. I'm trying to raise my daughters to be good Christians—"

Devon's voice took on a definite edge. "Mrs. Barlow, she is not my live-in lover. She—"

"Valerie Dallas!" Mrs. Barlow exclaimed in recognition. Wrath gathered on her brow, and the finger she pointed at Valerie was no doubt intended to be the finger of doom. "Get off my property! Accuser of innocent men! Seducer! Whore!"

Since she'd been on the road with the Shelby Winthrop Quartet, Valerie had run across many people who believed themselves endowed with a holy mission to set the rest of the world straight.

About the only way to deal with them was to pretend unawareness. She gazed out the window as if she were deaf.

Devon was furious. Valerie could detect it in the way his entire body had stiffened, and in the icy tone he used when he spoke.

"I'll be in touch with your husband, Mrs. Barlow. Rayburn Lawn Maintenance is no longer able to service your property."

"That woman was responsible for my cousin's getting kicked out of college," Mrs. Barlow added for good measure. "Ask her where she got the money to buy the bleach for her hair."

There was a good deal more, but Devon was no longer listening. He restarted the motor of his tractor and drove it back to the loading ramp, which effectively drowned out the remainder of Mrs. Barlow's tirade.

She was still standing on the veranda scolding when Devon climbed in the truck and started the motor.

"Believe me, Val, if I'd known about this, I'd never have brought you here."

He was looking at her with concern, Valerie saw with surprise.

"Heavens, Dev, it wasn't your fault. How were you to know she was kin to Jonathan Wade?"

"I should have gotten a bad feeling when she ran Hulk off from finishing his job." He shook his head and laughed. "Can you believe that? She actually thinks Wade was a misunderstood, falsely accused innocent. Cheez."

"I feel sorry for her two little girls," Valerie said. "Imagine having Jonathan Wade as a cousin."

Devon guided the truck back onto the road and glanced in the rearview mirror. "She's still out there shaking her finger and ranting."

Valerie grinned. "She's taking the curse off her yard. This bleached-blond heathen has put a taint in the air."

Devon made another rude comment. "I thought you'd be immune to this sort of thing. Aren't you a singer of contemporary Christian music?"

Valerie looked at him in surprise. "You've been researching. Yes, I am. But Mrs. Barlow probably thinks most gospel music is of the devil, and we singers of it are going straight to hell.''

''Especially the bleached-blond ones,'' Devon added, grinning.

FIVE

Devon unloaded his tractor at his equipment barn and drove Valerie home, grumbling all the way.

"Her husband seemed like a nice enough fellow," he said. "How'd he get tied up with that woman?"

"Now, Dev—to each his own. Maybe he thinks Halloween is satanic also."

"What?"

"She's one of those people who thinks everything is satanic, including Halloween and Christmas. I recognize the choice of words."

"Well, for Pete's sake." Devon looked totally at sea. "Come to think of it, she did sound like an Old Testament prophet." He glanced at her. "I wouldn't have had that happen for the world, Val."

"I'm not upset, Dev. It was all a long time ago, and Jonathan probably never showed his bad side to his relatives."

"Cheez. His cousin!" Devon said, and pulled into the driveway of Valerie's house.

Inside, Meg was busy at her computer. "Don't forget my coffee, dear," she said, barely taking her eyes off the screen.

"Coming right up, Mama."

Valerie went to the kitchen, leaving Devon to converse with the abstracted Meg.

"Meg, do you know a Mrs. Clint Barlow?" he asked. Valerie paused in the kitchen door and looked back.

Meg glanced up and frowned at Devon. "Katie Barlow? With two cute little girls? Poor things. Yes, I do. She was Katie Wilson before she married Clint."

"Did you know she was a cousin of Jonathan Wade's?"

Meg actually turned to face Devon. "So she says, although I wouldn't talk about it if I were her. Such misguided loyalty. She actually confronted me in the grocery store one day. At least she probably thinks that's what she did. She hasn't been haranguing my Val, has she? Because if so, I'll have a few things to say to her the next time I see her in public. At the top of my voice, too."

"Rayburn Lawn Maintenance has just struck her property from its list," Devon said. "Maybe I should be vindictive and inform every other lawn service in the area about the ceramic chickens in her yard."

Meg returned to her computer. "Do that, dear. It would do her good to mow her own grass for a while."

Devon turned toward the kitchen and saw Valerie watching from the door. He didn't speak until they'd entered the kitchen and Valerie had begun washing out the coffeepot.

"I wonder if Katie Barlow knows where Wade is," Devon said thoughtfully. "No one else seems to."

"I don't know why he'd bother letting her know." Valerie set the pot on the counter and spooned in coffee. "She's the sort who'd tell the world."

"True." Devon eyed the refrigerator. "I see you've already got the new chart up."

"A hurricane-tracking chart makes a house a home."

"Actually I think the piano makes your house home. When are you going to tackle the living room?"

Valerie grinned at his careful avoidance of mentioning the stacks of manuscript pages that entirely covered Valerie's piano and piano bench. One would hardly know there was a piano beneath the paper.

"Are you kidding? While she's in there writing? She'd probably shoot me. God forbid that I throw out a single sheet of scratch paper. It might have the most important idea in the whole book scribbled on it."

"That bad, huh?" Devon chuckled. "What about her room?"

"Same story. That's where she keeps one thousand romance novels, all carefully analyzed. I'm telling you, Dev, this is a writer's house. Every stray scrap of paper is sacred."

When she'd carried Meg a cup of coffee, Valerie fetched her seeds and herded Devon back outside to her garden plot. As the sun was still high overhead, he insisted that she watch from beneath the oak tree while he sowed her seeds in the neat rows he'd plowed for her.

Valerie remained under the tree for perhaps five minutes until the call of the damp, fragrant earth became too strong. She joyfully poked her finger into the black dirt in the way she had as a child, then dropped a seed in and covered it. Soon her index finger was black with dirt, and she'd sown three rows of okra seeds on her own.

"Val, you're incredible," he said at last, hauling her under the tree. "No one else would plant a garden this late in the year."

"I don't feel at home unless I have a garden. It might not grow, but I like knowing it's here."

She sat on the thick grass and scrubbed her index finger on the tree trunk.

Devon settled beside her on the grass, leaning back and smiling up at her. His light gray eyes contrasted with the darkly tanned skin of his face, and his teeth suddenly gleamed white as his lips curved upward.

"I'm glad you're home," he said.

"So am I. I didn't realize how much I'd missed this rice-farming country."

He reached for her, and pulled her down beside him. "You're supposed to say you didn't realize how much you missed me. Didn't you think of me at all while you were gone?"

"Of course I did. I thought about all the different women you were probably dating and felt horribly jealous."

Her voice was light and teasing as she lay on the grass watching the dappling of sun over the magnificent male body she'd dreamed of for years. Hopefully, he thought she was joking.

He smiled and leaned up on one elbow to look down at her face. "Good. You'll have to stay in town to make sure I behave myself. What are you doing this evening?"

Valerie pretended to think. "I'm cooking a low-calorie, low-cholesterol supper for Mama. Want to participate?"

"Do you mean help you cook, or help Meg eat?"

"If you want to eat, you have to cook."

Devon leaned over her so that his lips hovered barely an inch above hers. "Didn't anyone ever tell you I'm great at cooking vegetables? I open a can of cheese soup, and boil the vegetable of my choice . . ."

"Dev, you're going to wind up as bad as Mama. She's a big Dairy Queen fan."

"I'll tell you a secret. So am I."

"All that mowing you do helps work it off . . ." she began.

Devon brushed her lips with his, seeming to derive pleasure from the barest of touches.

Valerie sighed and reached up to put her arms around his neck. The scent of grass blended with the scent of Devon's sun-warmed skin created a seduction as powerful as the sight of his tanned face as his thick, dark lashes fell to veil the sparkling gray eyes.

Devon removed her glasses gently and laid them within reach of her hand.

"Now I can do what I want," he said. "You can't see me."

"You can do what you want anyway, but I'll like it even better if I can see you."

"Val, did I ever tell you how much I like your attitude? If not, why not?"

"I don't know," she said, pulling his face down.

He kissed her, savoring her readily parted lips and stroking her tongue with his own. He touched his lips to her eyes, then to her nose and to her cheeks before returning to her mouth for another lingering kiss.

Valerie felt her entire body begin to yearn toward him, and her breasts felt full and heavy even though he hadn't touched them. She turned fully toward him and pressed her chest to his, trying to indicate her desire.

Devon framed her face with both his hands and propped himself on his elbows over her, continuing to kiss her with deep, slow kisses that set her blood singing through her veins. She lifted against him half-consciously, longing to know his touch more fully.

Devon was in no hurry. He explored her face and her arms with his searching hands, then he gently let them travel back up her sides and brush the sides of her breasts.

Valerie sighed her pleasure and tried to entice him back to do it again.

"Val . . ." he whispered.

She opened her eyes to find him looking at her.

"Yes?" she whispered back.

"We'd better go in and join Meg for some coffee. Otherwise I'm liable to start something I can't finish in broad daylight."

"Really?" Valerie asked hopefully. "Would it help if I told you Mama won't surface from her computer for another hour?"

"No."

"And the house next door is vacant. The Broussards moved out a year ago."

"Is that so?"

"We're safe, if you should care to carry on."

"Honey, there's nothing I'd like better. Unfortunately, I'm not equipped to do so."

"Dev, I can't think of any man better equipped than you. You should always let a woman be the judge of your capacity for the job."

"Val, you've turned into a shameless hussy," Devon said, looking delighted.

"I've got news for you. I was born a shameless hussy. It's just that you never paid the proper attention before."

Devon began to laugh, burying his face against her neck. "I don't know what to say. You've taken me by storm, and I have no idea how to handle you."

"Good. I'll be happy to instruct you," she said, reaching for his hands.

Devon jerked his hands away to sit up. He grasped her shoulders and pulled her up to sit beside him.

"Cut that out, Val Dallas. I don't need Meg trying to find a shotgun."

"Mama has no interest in a shotgun unless it's the fictional variety," Valerie said, disappointed.

"You saw how she sizzled up over Katie Barlow. Let me tell you, Val, your mother is one tough woman, and I don't care to be in her way when she goes on the warpath."

"Hah!" Valerie said irritably. "You heard her turn me over to you. So long as you wolf me down in private, she won't say a word."

"That's what you think . . ." he began.

Devon began to look harassed when Valerie gave a disbelieving sniff.

"Dev, can it be that you think I'm going to seduce you?" she said.

"Yes!" he said.

"I thought that was every bachelor's dream."

"Cut that out, Val Dallas. I'm an innocent boy."

Valerie had attempted to kiss him once more, but Devon scooted aside. She shoved her glasses higher on her nose and eyed him.

The beeper at his waist sounded, and Devon's lean, tanned face took on a devoutly thankful expression. He listened closely as the device recited a phone number, then stood and reached for her hand.

"I need to use your phone," he said. "How much do you want to bet it's Clint Barlow, wanting to know why his yard has only been half mowed?"

Valerie let him pull her to her feet. "In that case, I'm surprised you're so eager to talk to him."

"Now, Val, don't be like that."

"Why not? I'm feeling very rejected, and it isn't a pleasant feeling. I'm going to have to have a talk with Mama about what to do when a man refuses your kisses. I must be doing something wrong."

Devon put an arm around her and dragged her along beside him to the house.

"Valerie," he said, "if you were more experienced, you'd realize that I'm trying to be a gentleman, and you're making it damned hard. If I stay out there under that tree with you, I'm liable to be caught with my pants down, literally. Have some decency, for Pete's sake."

Valerie cut her eyes at him. His sparkling gray eyes were warm with laughter, and his mouth had tucked in at the corners.

"You're a real heartbreaker, Devon Rayburn," she said mournfully. "If I'd known how you treat women, I'd have pretended you had the wrong person that day in the store."

"I knew right away I had the right person," Devon said with satisfaction.

He opened the back door and ushered her inside, then went straight to the telephone and dialed the number he'd memorized.

Valerie poured them both a soft drink and went to check on Meg while Devon conducted his conversation. When she returned, he was hanging up the phone and looking mildly irritated.

"I was right," he said. "It was Clint Barlow wanting to know why his yard was only half done. When I told him his wife had run off two different men I'd sent on the job, he wanted to know if I was really stupid enough to regard the opinion of a mere woman. He thought I should have ignored her and mowed the yard anyway. Lord, let him call someone else. I don't need that kind of business."

"I was right. Neither one of them believes in Halloween."

"What has Halloween got to do with this?" Devon wanted to know, looking baffled.

Valerie chuckled. "Not a thing, Dev. Sit down and have something cooling. You need it."

Meg appeared in the doorway with sheets in hand. "Ah, there you are, Dev. You were such a great help to me the other day, I'm sure you won't mind participating again."

Valerie suppressed a giggle at the way Devon rolled his alarmed gray eyes in Meg's direction.

Meg placed some pages in his hand, and a like set in Valerie's hands, then sat down at the table.

"Just read the dialogue," she said. "Skip over the narrative."

Valerie eyed her script. "This looks like all dialogue."

"I'm testing a new technique. One of my books says editors like lots of dialogue." Meg buried her face in her hands and propped her elbows on the table. "Okay. Go."

Valerie read: " 'Blake, please go. I'm not ready for this.' "

Devon responded with, " 'Pamela, you can't leave me like this. You're mine. You belong to me.' "

" 'I don't belong to any man. Let me go.' "

" 'No, Pamela. Let me love you, darling. Let me show you how good it can be between us.' "

" 'You promised you wouldn't put me on the spot like this, Blake. Let me up. I didn't mean for things to go this far.' "

" 'Darling, I can't. You're mine, and I want you.' "

" 'Blake!' "

" 'Pamela!' "

"Cut!" Meg said. She raised her eyes and glared at her daughter. "Val, I don't mind you finding my work amusing, but I'd appreciate a little cooperation."

"Muma, you have it all backward. Ask Dev. All you have to do to fix it is reverse the speakers. If you have Pamela say Blake's stuff, and Blake say Pamela's stuff, you'll be right in line with the nineties woman."

Meg stared at her manuscript, arrested. "Do you think so? I never thought of that."

Devon eyed Valerie and wisely kept his mouth shut.

"Trust me, Mama. The nineties woman knows what she wants and doesn't mind going after it. Isn't that right, Dev?"

"You're the nineties woman," Devon said. "You tell us."

"I'm trying, but, like Mama, I need some cooperation."

Devon swallowed a sip of cola the wrong way and coughed until Meg patted him on the back.

"Dev, that sounds like the kind of suggestion that would make me very nervous if I were a man," Meg said.

"It does, believe me." Devon's coughing faded into choked laughter. "You try to be a gentleman and the nineties woman insults your manly dignity."

Devon's beeper went off again, and he stepped to the counter to use the phone.

"Val, do you really think it should be the other way around?" Meg said.

"Why not, Mama? If a woman likes a man, she has nothing to lose by letting him know it."

"Except her pride," Meg warned, shooting a glance at Valerie.

"What's a little pride?" Valerie said. "The same thing happens to a man all the time. He can't know ahead of time whether he'll be accepted or rejected."

"True, dear." Meg thought a moment. "I'll have to give that serious consideration. Of course, if I go with it, I'll have to rewrite from the beginning. Pamela will have to become an entirely different kind of person." She sighed and raised her eyes from her manuscript to eye her daughter wistfully. "You remind me more and more of your father every day. He had exactly the same attitude toward life."

"Really, Mama? What attitude is that?"

"He never minded taking a chance. When I met him, you know, I was engaged to another man, and had a diamond as big as you please on my finger. But Charles didn't let that stop him from making a play for me. I've never been sorry."

"That's an idea, Mama. Imagine a woman with Daddy's personality. Editors should love a female cropduster."

Meg's face took on an arrested expression. "Valerie, you may have solved my problem. Pamela is a secretary, because I just can't see her as a C.E.O. Editors these days want interesting professions."

"If Pamela were Daddy in drag, you could—"

"Have some respect, dear. Certain aspects of your father's personality would not do in a romance, believe me."

It was too much. Valerie dissolved into laughter, and Meg soon joined in. By the time Devon rejoined them, they were engaged in drawing up a personality profile of one Pamela Carlisle, age twenty-six, who resembled Charles Dallas in looks and in attitude.

"Walk me to the door, Val," Devon said. "I have to go straighten out a complaint. It seems one of my men ran over a set of concrete ducklings buried in the grass."

"A set of antique concrete ducklings, no doubt," Meg said, rubbing her chin thoughtfully. "I haven't read any romances with a hero in the lawn-care business. Blake can quit being a lawyer and start being the C.E.O. of a lawn-care company."

"A yard man," Devon supplied, grinning.

"A very sexy yard man," Meg agreed, shuffling her pages.

Valerie crowed with joyful laughter.

Devon didn't redden, since his tan was too deep to allow it, but he hunched his shoulders with embarrassment and edged quickly out of the kitchen.

"I'll be back for supper," he said when ho reached the front door

"Sure, Dev. Mama's going to want to interview you about every detail of the lawn-maintenance business. Don't be surprised if she dedicates this book to you."

"Oh, Lord." He leaned over to kiss her lightly. "I just hope these concrete ducklings aren't antique."

Valerie returned to the kitchen and found Meg still adding to the personality profile.

"This book is going to sell," Meg said. "I just know it is."

"If you have a really good heroine, it probably will. You can dedicate the book to Daddy's memory."

This suggestion found favor with Meg. She scribbled a few more notes and headed for her computer.

The telephone rang and Valerie reached for it automatically. Perhaps it was Devon, calling to tell her he'd be late.

Instead, when she spoke into the phone, there was silence.

"Hello?" she repeated, annoyed.

"You whore!" a voice whispered.

Valerie slammed the receiver down. The voice could have been either male or female, but she was willing to bet it was female and belonged to Katie Barlow.

Devon arrived just as Valerie put the chicken breasts on to broil and began cutting up fresh squash.

Meg snagged him before he could follow Valerie to the kitchen.

"I need to know what a typical day is like in the life of a lawn-maintenance professional," she announced. "Just speak into this."

She waved a tape-recorder microphone in his direction and pushed the "record" button.

Devon stared at Valerie with the most pleading expression she'd ever been privileged to see on a man's face.

"Grin and bear it," she told him.

By the time he reached the kitchen, he was looking harried.

"Can't you talk her into letting her hero be a junior banking executive?" he said.

"I wouldn't dream of trying. A junior banking executive just doesn't sound sexy. On the other hand, remember Lady Chatterley. There's something magnetic about a man who's into the earth."

Devon made a rude sound.

"You just don't understand women. Most women," she qualified, remembering Barbara.

Devon leaned against the cabinet and watched her. Valerie had put on a pair of white pants and a soft green blouse, was wearing her contacts and her silver-blond hair loose to her shoulders.

"Tell me about women," he said. "Especially nineties women."

"The nineties woman knows what she wants in a man."

"Is that so?"

"And she doesn't mind letting the nineties man know her demands."

"Uh-oh."

"Which are small."

"I'll be the judge of that."

The telephone rang once more and Valerie reached for it automatically, her attention still on Devon.

"Hello?"

She listened a moment while the caller spoke his or her mind on her morals, then hung up without comment when the caller became obscene.

"Well?" Devon said. "Who was it?"

"A crank caller," Valerie said, and began tearing lettuce. "I'm afraid Mrs. Barlow has taken exception to my presence here in town and hopes to run me off."

Devon's face hardened. "Are you saying someone is making threatening phone calls to you?"

"It wasn't a threatening call, precisely. It was a moral-judgment call."

"What did she say?"

"He or she," Valerie said scrupulously, "wished to inform me that I was a bitch and whore, and that if I thought I could wreck lives, I had another think coming."

"Dammit," Devon said, scowling. "Maybe you should get an answering machine."

"If I get any more calls, I will. Want to help with the salad?"

Devon refused to be diverted. He took the head of lettuce she held out to him and began tearing it.

"Do you think it's Katie Barlow?"

"It must be someone connected with her. Unless it was someone who saw you kissing me in the hardware store." She turned away to get plates down from the cabinet. "We were discussing the nineties woman and her demands."

"I don't like this," Devon said.

"You don't?"

"I'm not talking about the nineties woman, Val. I'm talking about these phone calls. When did they start? How many have you had?"

"This is the second. The other one came right after you left. What happened with the concrete ducks, by the way?"

"We deducted the cost of replacement from his bill, although why we should pay for a bunch of stupid ornaments that are so overgrown they can't be seen is beyond me. What did the first caller say?"

"Dev, can't we talk about something other than these calls? Believe me, it brings back memories I'd rather forget."

Devon resembled a bird dog scenting quail. "Are you telling me you got these calls two years ago?"

Valerie closed her mouth, wondering how he had deduced that.

"Dammit, Valerie, why didn't you tell me? This could be dangerous."

Valerie shrugged. "It didn't seem important. Two years ago I had worse troubles than a few obscene phone calls."

"I'm going to bring you a recording machine. Every time you get a phone call, I want you to record it. That way, you'll have a record to show the sheriff."

Valerie eyed him.

Devon dropped the lettuce. "I'm going now. This won't wait. If the calls are starting again, it could be anyone who knows you're back in town."

"Dev, can't it wait until tomorrow?"

"How many calls have you had today?"

"Two."

"No."

There was nothing she could say that would change his mind. He stalked through the living room and out the front door while Valerie stood in the kitchen door watching him.

Meg looked up from her computer screen. "What's wrong, dear? Did you and Dev have a fight?"

"No, Mama. Dev is doing the protective male bit, and it's interfering with my plans for his body."

Meg brightened. "Is that so? Would you mind sharing your plans with me? Research, you know. I need to know more about how the nineties woman regards the male of the species."

"Your job as a mother is to keep me chaste until I walk down the aisle looking like an upside-down ice-cream cone. Telling you my plans for Dev's body would cause a conflict between your mother's heart and your writer's heart."

"What?"

"I couldn't do that to you," Valerie added.

"I don't have the faintest idea what you're talking about," Meg complained.

"Good."

Valerie withdrew to the kitchen, wondering how long it would take Devon to locate the promised recording machine and return with it. Her chicken would be done in half an hour, and she'd like to serve it at its best.

Before he returned, she answered the phone once more and received another barrage of foul talk telling her what should be done to women like herself. Feelings of gratitude toward Devon arose in her. Perhaps recording a few of the calls wouldn't be a bad idea.

"I just got another call," she announced baldly when Devon knocked at the front door.

He carried a tape recorder and some wires and a small black box in his hands.

Scowling, he said, "I don't like this."

"Neither do I. Would you mind answering the phone if it rings while you're here?"

"You're going to answer it and test out your recorder," he said, indicating the objects in his hands. "Let's get this installed so I can eat some of whatever you're cooking that smells so good."

Valerie watched as he attached the black box between the telephone and the wall, plugging and unplugging connections until he was satisfied. He showed her how to see if the device was working correctly and how to turn it off if the caller was legitimate.

"What's that, dear?" Meg appeared in the door with an empty coffee cup in her hand. "Is it time for supper? If not, can I have some more coffee?"

"Supper's ready," Valerie said, experimenting with the recorder. "This is a machine to record the obscene phone calls I've been getting."

"Obscene phone calls? But you've only been here two days." Meg looked totally baffled. "I haven't gotten any obscene phone calls."

"We think it may have to do with Katie Barlow. The callers are saying things similar to what she said to Val this afternoon."

Meg appeared to swell. "She *what*? Just wait until I see her in the grocery store. I have a few things to say to her about all that phony religion and Clint Barlow. Can you believe it? The silly cluck doesn't know Clint's been seeing Patricia Dubois on the side for the past year. And who can blame him? It's high time she worried about her own household instead of everyone else's."

"Get 'em, Meg." Devon lifted the telephone receiver and watched the tape inside the recorder begin to move. "This is just a precaution. I want Val to record a few of the calls so she'll have something to give the sheriff if necessary."

"Ha!" Meg said. "Let me answer the phone!"

"Later," Devon said, and pulled out a chair at the table. "Come sit down, Meg. Val's been to all kinds of trouble over supper, and you'd better do it justice."

Meg settled at the table, muttering, "Sick minds" and glaring toward the phone.

Valerie served up broiled chicken and vegetables and salad. Meg, as usual, approached her food enthusiastically but without the least idea what she was eating. Devon, however, complimented her on each dish, even though it was simple cooking for the sake of Meg's arteries, and took second helpings of everything.

"Dev, you're a cook's dream," Valerie said.

"Considering how long it's been since I've had a home-cooked meal . . ." he began.

"Nonsense," Meg said, surfacing from her abstraction. "Your mother recently moved from Houston to Austin, didn't she? When was the last time you visited her?"

"That's what I mean," Devon said, grinning. "I haven't been home since Christmas. That was the last time I had a home-cooked meal."

Meg came to attention. "Does this mean the nineties woman no longer tries to catch her man by cooking him delicious meals?"

Devon broke into delighted laughter. "Meg, the nineties woman is usually too busy moving up the corporate ladder to do more than microwave one of those low calorie frozen dinners."

Meg looked oddly satisfied. "I'm glad to hear that."

Valerie looked up. "Why, Mama?"

"You haven't gone totally nineties on me, dear. I was getting worried."

SIX

Devon's recording machine had an opportunity to work within minutes of finishing the meal. The telephone rang, and Valerie, prompted by Devon, answered.

Her silence after saying "Hello" was enough to alert the others, and Devon made signals to indicate that she keep the caller talking. Valerie made no effort to do so, merely standing and listening while the tape turned, then hanging up in equal silence.

"Well?" Devon asked, scanning her still face with concern.

"It was him. Or her. Whichever."

"I'll listen to that tape," Meg said militantly. "I'm not having anyone threaten my daughter on my own telephone."

Devon stood and put an arm around Valerie. "Are you all right, Val? What did he say . . . ? Never mind. We'll find out soon enough."

He kept one arm around Valerie, hugging her lightly against his side while he rewound the tape, switched the device to the playback mode, and turned it on.

The caller, whose voice obviously had been disguised, accused Valerie of leading astray every honest man in Chambers County, of sleeping with three-quarters of them, and of being in strong need of correction.

Devon stiffened, frowning.

The caller then described in obscene detail the kind of correction Valerie needed.

"That isn't Katie Barlow," Meg said. "Such things aren't in her vocabulary. She's too self-righteous to know about them."

"I think it's a man," Devon said, in cold tones. "I don't like this, Meg."

"Neither do I," Meg said. "He isn't going to get away with this."

"Good. If he calls back, record him the way I showed you, Val. We'll give this tape to the sheriff."

Valerie straightened. "I don't like it, either. I also don't like having to listen to this guy while he tells me everything he'd like to do to straighten me out. Is it okay if I just put the phone down and let him talk?"

"Fine," Devon said. "He doesn't seem to require any response from you."

Valerie sighed with relief. It was one thing to record an obscene phone call. It was another thing to have to listen to it.

Devon set up the device to record once more and reached for Valerie's hand.

"Let's go out and have some ice cream," he said. "I can see Meg is itching to get back to work, and you could probably stand to get out of the house for a while."

Valerie, who earlier had been overjoyed to be back in this house after two years on the road, agreed. Suddenly the small wooden house seemed unbearably small and confining.

When they'd finished their ice cream, Devon drove back to her house and parked in the driveway, then released his seat belt and turned to her,

"Want to go fishing tomorrow?" he asked.

"Don't you have to work? I thought June was your busiest month."

Devon chuckled. "It is. Do you know how long it's been since I've had a vacation?"

"Never?"

"Never. Fortunately, I have a staff that understands the work, and Mary to dispatch everyone efficiently."

"You're liable to set a bad example. Where are we going?"

"Meacom's Pier, if you have no objections. You can run the crab traps. We'll feast on whatever we catch."

Valerie smiled at him. "I hope you're good at this, because I've always been afraid of crabs."

She watched him hopefully. Devon wasn't making a move to kiss her, and she wondered if a nineties woman should take matters into her own hands.

"Val, you're an intrepid woman. I feel certain you can master the art of grabbing a crab from behind."

"All the crabs I've ever caught have had it in for me, and they've all had extra-long claws."

"Then I'll bring along a pair of channel locks. Ever grabbed a crab with channel locks?"

"So long as I grab them with something other than my hand."

She unfastened her seat belt and waited. He made no move either toward her or to get out of the Cherokee. It was most frustrating.

Devon suddenly grinned at her and opened his door. "If we don't go inside, Meg is liable to decide we're out here necking."

"I wish," Valerie murmured, watching his tall, muscular silhouette circle the hood of the vehicle.

He opened the door and helped her down. "Val, you have a most remarkable look of discontent on your normally smiling face. Didn't I buy you enough ice cream?"

Devon was watching her with such a knowing look on his face that Valerie flushed with irritation and felt absurdly thankful Meg hadn't left the porch light on.

She might as well be bold.

"I was hoping for something better than ice cream," she said.

"Oh? Like what?"

She faced him, effectively blocking his attempt to reach

for the front doorknob. "Like a passionate kiss or two on a lonely road in the middle of the rice fields."

Devon sounded delighted. "Be reasonable, Val. It's June. Hear that high-pitched whine? Those are rice-field mosquitoes, and they're starving. If they're that bad here, just think what they'd be like in the rice fields."

Valerie sniffed and turned to open the door herself. "That's why they invented air conditioners."

Laughing, Devon pulled her into his arms before she could get a grip on the doorknob. "If you want a kiss, why don't you just grab me and take one?"

"That's a little difficult."

"Yes? Do you care to explain why? I thought I was projecting an attitude of hope."

He was standing with his legs slightly spread so that she fit precisely between them and was able to lean against the entire warm length of his body. She wrapped her arms around his waist and tilted her head back, enjoying his male strength and the hard feel of his body.

"I guess I'm not as much a nineties woman as I'd thought," she said. "Perhaps I should attend an assertiveness seminar or two."

"Val, if you did that, you'd terrify me."

He kissed her twice—hard, quick kisses that did nothing to satisfy the hunger she constantly felt in his presence, then opened the door.

Valerie went inside reluctantly and discovered Meg on the floor with several sheets of paper spread out on the floor before her.

Meg looked up. "I've replotted my story," she said. "This time, I know it's going to work."

"That's wonderful, Mama," Valerie said automatically. She wondered what it would take to get Devon to kiss her again as he had the previous night outside Jen Devilier's house.

"Have there been any more calls?" Devon said.

"One," Meg said. "He hung up when I answered."

"He knows Val's voice. I don't like this," Devon said.

Valerie didn't, either, but other than let Meg answer the

phone, there was nothing she could do about it at the moment.

Meg pointed to a stack of letters. "I've read all my rejection letters and identified another problem. My heroines haven't been growing or learning anything about themselves as the story progresses."

This was beyond Valerie. "Does that mean falling in love isn't growth or learning?"

"Of course not," Meg said, tapping the letters. "It just means poor Pamela is going to have to realize before the story is over that her independence is keeping Blake from proposing. She's going to have to realize she *needs* him, and that it isn't weakness to need another person."

"I didn't know she thought it was," Valerie said. "I thought she was a female version of Daddy. He was always going on about how he couldn't get along without you."

"That's because I trained him, dear," Meg said placidly.

Devon laughed and cast Valerie a meaningful glance.

Valerie grinned back and said, "Careful, Dev. You could use a little training."

"I'm doing the training around here," Devon said, reaching for her hand. "Let's go check the recorder."

Devon left, after reviewing her on the recorder's use, promising to come for her early the next morning.

The telephone rang a grand total of five times during the night, and each time, Meg answered. Each time, the caller hung up. Valerie cringed each time she heard a ring from the phone.

When Devon appeared the following morning, Valerie was looking and feeling somewhat worse for the wear. She'd dressed in a pair of soft, old jeans and a long-sleeved work shirt in preparation for pier fishing, and carried a big hat in her hand.

Devon eyed her with concern. "You look worn out. Did you stay up cleaning the house all night?"

"The phone rang all night," she said dryly.

He looked thoughtful. "It did, eh? I hate to say this,

Val, but you'd better talk to the sheriff. It won't hurt to have him aware of what's going on.''

During the night, Valerie had begun to feel that she'd like every law officer in the town of Winnie and the county of Chambers to know about it.

"Whenever you're ready, Dev," she said.

Devon used the phone to call the sheriff's office, then drove her directly there.

The sheriff's deputy, when presented with the tape, merely played it without comment. When pressed by Devon, he said, "There isn't much we can do unless the harassment continues and you get a tap on your line. You'll need to speak to the telephone company.''

They left the office feeling unsatisfied, but the deputy's statements were easily understood. Until she knew who the caller was, there wasn't much the sheriff or his deputies could do.

Devon headed the Cherokee south toward the beach.

"I don't like the tone of these calls at all," he said. "It'll be two weeks before the phone company will put a tap on your line. In the meantime, the caller will just keep on working himself up.''

Valerie shivered, even though the day was hot and sunny. She found little comfort in the familiar coastal marshes lining the beach road, failing even to count scissor-tailed flycatchers on the power lines along the road as she once had.

Instead, she looked at the tall walls of cattails lining the highway and felt as if she were boxed in. When they drove over the bridge spanning the Intracoastal Canal, she took no interest in the barge passing beneath them. Upon reaching the beach, she took little notice of the state of the tide or the height of the surf.

Devon parked his Cherokee on the sand in front of Meacom's Pier. They walked onto the pier carting an ice chest, fishing poles, crab nets, and two lawn chairs, and staked out an area near the end of the pier.

"You get the crab nets," Devon said.

"Thanks a lot, Dev," Valerie returned, settling on the

wooden floor of the pier so she could watch the calming roll of the ocean between the cracks in the planks.

She cut pieces of twine and used them to secure a chicken neck in the center of each crab net, then lowered the net on a long piece of twine over the side of the pier until it disappeared beneath the water.

The whole operation was unexpectedly soothing. By the time she had baited and tied each of the five crab nets Devon had given her to the pier railing, Valerie had forgotten all about the obscene caller in her rediscovery of the pleasures of being on the pier.

Valerie had taken the precaution of tying her silver-blond hair beneath a scarf, then tying the big hat over the scarf to keep the steady wind blowing off the Gulf from whipping her hair into her face.

She loved the brisk coolness that contrasted with the heat of the sun on her back and the salty tang of the air. Even the odor of fish that clung to various parts of the pier was a pleasure that brought back pleasant memories of nights spent on this same pier as a child.

Devon had baited the hooks of the two fishing poles he'd brought and handed her one as he settled into one of the lawn chairs. Valerie took the pole and sat beside him, suddenly feeling weary enough to nap.

"Go ahead," Devon said. "I can tell you didn't sleep much last night."

He had to raise his voice to be heard over the steady Gulf wind.

Valerie yawned. "Every time I fell asleep, the telephone rang and jolted me awake. Poor Mama had to get up and answer it. I don't like having to live in fear of answering my own telephone, Dev."

"Let's think about an answering machine," he said, smiling at her.

Valerie hated to waste a minute of the precious time she could spend with Devon in sleep. It seemed criminal, but what could she do when her eyelids kept drifting shut so inexorably?

A strange sound awakened her. Her eyes popped open

and she sat up until she located the sound's origin. It came from the ice chest sitting beside her.

She reached out a cautious hand and thumped the chest. A frantic scrabbling rewarded her.

She looked around and saw Devon approaching with a large crab, pincers waving, in one hand. He opened the ice chest and dropped it in, and the scrabbling began again.

"You've caught some crabs," she said, sitting up. "How long was I out?"

"Two hours," Devon said.

Her scarf and hat had slipped during her nap, and Valerie pulled them off. Devon reached down and lifted her glasses off her nose.

Valerie looked up at the blur his crisp features had suddenly become. Suddenly they cleared, and she realized he had leaned toward her.

He smiled. "That's better. Your eyes definitely look more rested."

"Is that so? How about letting me have my glasses back so I can see the rest of the world?"

"I'm your world at the moment," he said, and kissed her.

Valerie sighed and reached up to slip her arms around his neck. He had no idea how true that was. His lips were warm and hard, and she wished he'd kiss her more deeply.

Devon drew back and set her glasses back on her nose.

She blinked as her surroundings came back into focus. "I liked it better when you were the world," she told him.

"Val, you always know the right thing to say to build up a man's ego."

His pole chose that moment to jerk and bend. He grabbed for it and began reeling.

Valerie got to her feet, disappointed, and watched as he fought the fish at the other end. It was a vigorous contest, but Devon won out and hauled a small shark, about two feet long, onto the pier.

Unnoticed by them, other people on the pier took an

interest in Devon's fish and gathered around to watch as the gray hammerhead flopped on the pier.

"Throw him back," a man suggested.

"Kill him," a woman insisted. "My kids swim on this beach."

"He's too skinny to eat," an old man said.

Devon's gray eyes widened in surprise when his shark landed amid a circle of people, including several children.

"I'm throwing him back," he said, and proceeded to remove the hook from the still-flopping shark.

"Can I have him?" one of the children asked.

There was a cacophony of sound from the adults, which Devon ignored as he leaned over the pier railing and dropped the shark back into the water some twelve feet below.

Valerie removed her glasses a moment to remove several drops of water that had flown off the shark's moving tail. The wind fluffed her silver-blond hair around her face, and her pale-green eyes were large and dewy.

"Say, I know her," one woman said. "Don't you sing with the Shelby Winthrop Quartet?"

Valerie replaced her glasses and looked at the woman, a plain, plump country matron in her mid-fifties.

"Yes, I do," she began.

"Rebecca Dallas! That's the name," the woman said triumphantly. "I heard you sing last year in Atlanta when I went to visit my daughter. Can I have your autograph?"

Embarrassed, Valerie wrote, "With Best Wishes From Rebecca Dallas," on a sheet in a bedraggled notebook the woman produced.

"Is she a rock star?" one of the small boys asked.

"No, dummy," a girl of about eleven said. "She's better than those creeps."

"Better than Madonna?"

"Give me a break!"

With Valerie's status thus established, the children, backed by the adults, clamored for a song. She looked helplessly at Devon. He was leaning on the rail with his arms folded across his chest, and he seemed to find the situation amusing.

It looked as though she was going to have to sing, or disappoint what seemed like half her fans.

Glancing down, Valerie saw the channel locks Devon had placed for her use and was seized by inspiration.

"I'll tell you what," she said to the children. "I'll teach you my song. Then you can go home and sing it for your Sunday school. How's that?"

"I'd rather hear you," the girl said.

"You will. I have to sing it to teach it, you know."

The children agreed that this might be fun, especially when Valerie suggested they call themselves the Crab Pier Six.

Valerie picked up the channel locks and arranged the children, in double rows of three facing her. "This is my baton. Here's the first verse."

Her vibrant soprano voice flowed easily as she sang for the children, beating time and indicating with the channel locks where the tune went up and where it went down.

"When I think of those who face the world
    unaided by His love;
Who fight for things the world holds dear
    and think that it's enough.
Will they ever know the peace and joy
    the Gift that holds me up.
The promise of God-With-Us-Now
    Jesus, Emanuel."

Her voice was strong and clear, and carried well despite the steady wind that seemed to blow her words toward the shore.

The small crowd, including Devon, listened raptly.

"Now it's your turn," she told her choir, and led them through the verse, line by line.

After fifteen minutes and as many repetitions, when the Crab Pier Six had mastered the entire verse, she swung into the chorus.

"Emanuel, Emanuel,
  In Spirit and in Truth.
Emanuel, Emanuel,
  In my life,
  In me."

Barely aware of the parents watching and commenting, Valerie concentrated on the five squabbling boys and one dedicated girl. They were a challenge, one she'd much rather face than the ordeal of singing for even this small crowd.

The children learned the chorus quickly. Valerie soon appointed the girl, who had a strong, high voice, as assistant choir director. The boy who wished she'd been a rock star, she appointed choir master. All insubordination within the ranks halted at once.

There were two more verses to the song, but Valerie wisely stopped while she was ahead. Any moment, the fish were liable to start biting.

She ran them through the song twice more while their parents looked on, then dismissed them. The children were all eager to get to the end of the pier and send their voices out over the water as Valerie had suggested.

Their parents accompanied them, loud in their praises of Valerie.

"If they don't forget it in the next few days," one mother said, "we'll have them perform that song in church Sunday."

Devon, still leaning on the pier rail, said, "I didn't know you were such a big star that part of the populace recognizes you."

"Neither did I," Valerie said dryly. "Maybe I'd better check on the status of my album."

She laid the channel locks on the ice chest and put her scarf and hat back on.

"I want a copy of that album. You're very good." He smiled. "Where did you learn to control a handful of rowdy kids like that?"

"I told you. I'm a small-town music teacher at heart. That's the kind of thing music teachers excel at."

"Why didn't you just sing for them and get it over with?" he said, grinning.

"Come on, Dev. That wouldn't have been nearly as much fun."

She turned away, embarrassed, and leaned over the wooden rail to haul up a crab trap containing a single large crab.

Devon watched as she landed the net trap on the pier and reached for the crab.

The crab sensed her approach and waved its claws.

Valerie jerked her hand back.

"Come at him from the rear."

"I did come at him from the rear," Valerie said irritably. "Look at the length of those claws. He's determined to get me."

Devon was grinning, so she gingerly reached for the crab's tailpiece. She succeeded in grasping it and lifted the crab triumphantly from the net.

The crab reached back with one wildly waving claw, discovered her fingers, and closed on one of them.

Valerie yelped and dropped the crab, which scuttled sideways toward the edge of the pier.

"I've never seen one do that before." Devon leaped after the crustacean and scooped it up.

Although the claws waved as wildly as ever, Valerie noted with resentment that they couldn't reach Devon's fingers. She popped her pinched finger in her mouth and glared.

"I told you," she said. "Crabs have it in for me."

Devon, laughing, leaned down, picked up the channel locks, and handed them to her.

They left the pier late in the afternoon with two trout and an ice chest full of crabs. Valerie was tired and happy because Devon had seemed to enjoy her efforts at taming the crabs she caught.

For a moment she'd thought she detected a certain cautious reserve when people had asked for her autograph and begged her to sing "Emanuel."

"We're going to eat like kings tonight," Devon said, turning the Cherokee into her driveway.

Meg's car had been parked at the curb in front of the house. Peering at it curiously, Valerie noted the presence of Meg's favorite dress hanging on the hook beside the backseat.

"Mama must be giving a talk somewhere," she said.

"Meg gives talks? On what?"

"Writing, of course. She did sell that one romantic novel, so that makes her an author."

Devon helped Valerie down and they each grabbed a handle on the ice chest, from which arose the loud clatter of scrambling crabs.

As they reached the front door, it burst open and Meg issued forth with a stack of books and notebooks in her hands.

"Val!" she exclaimed. "Thank heavens you're back. I'm leaving on a research trip to Arkansas. I didn't want to leave until you got home."

"A research trip!" Valerie stared. "What on earth are you talking about, Mama? I thought all your stories took place in Beaumont or Houston."

"Not this one," Meg said with considerable satisfaction. "I've decided my own locale is too familiar to me. I need a place I'm familiar with, but not so familiar I can't see the interesting things about it. So, I thought, why not Camden?"

"Camden? Oh, Lord."

When Valerie was five years old, the family had lived briefly in Camden, Arkansas. Meg had loved it, considering the climate perfect, the air clean, and the people friendly.

"I still have friends there," Meg said.

"I hope the Camdenites appreciate what you're going to do for them, Mama. Can you eat some crabs and trout before you go?"

"Of course, dear. I'm not leaving until tomorrow morning. I wanted to wait until you got home."

Valerie blinked, then decided not to question Meg's assumption that she wouldn't be coming home that night.

Devon's shoulders were quivering with silent laughter. She shoved the ice chest toward him and made him stagger, but he remained unrepentant.

The moment they set the ice chest down on the kitchen floor, Devon tested his tape recorder and went in search of Meg, who was carrying a suitcase to her car.

He returned, frowning. "Meg says the phone has rung three times since you left. If he phones while I'm here, go ahead and answer it."

Valerie stared at the telephone. It was hard not to consider it her enemy.

Even while she and Devon cleaned crabs and cooked them in Meg's large stock pot, she prayed the telephone would remain silent. Perhaps the caller had given up. She hadn't answered since the previous evening. Maybe he'd think she had left town once more.

Meg entered the kitchen, radiant with creative forces. "Dev, you're an angel. Once I imagined you as my hero, he really came alive for me."

Devon looked startled. "Meg, if you're telling me you cast me as a romantic hero . . ."

He clearly didn't know how to ask Meg to cease and desist.

"Of course not, dear. You're simply the prototype. I've made my hero into what I *imagine* you to be."

This clearly made as much sense to Devon as it made to Valerie, but neither cared to ask Meg to elaborate on it.

"As long as no one knows it's me," Devon said, in resigned tones.

Valerie bit back laughter.

"Blake still looks like a surfer," Meg informed them happily. "Come to think of it, so do you, Dev. It's his personality that needed work. I've got him now."

Valerie took pity on Devon. "Good, Mama. What's Pamela like?"

"Oh, Pamela." Meg's voice took on a rapt overtone. "She's just perfect for Blake—so adventurous and daring. She needs that shot of adrenaline every day to keep her feeling alive, which is why she became a crop-duster."

"Do they dust crops around Camden, Mama?"

"They must," Meg said firmly. "That's one of the things I intend to find out. When we lived there, your father was flying for that private air cargo service." She paused thoughtfully. "If Camden doesn't work out, I'll go on to El Dorado and a few other places. There's got to be someplace in southwest Arkansas where they employ crop-dusters."

Valerie dropped crab-boil, a cheesecloth sack filled with spices, into the vat of boiling water. "Camden sounds great, Mama. How long will you be gone?"

It was good to know Meg had plans to get away from Winnie. In the two years Valerie had been gone, Meg had hardly left her computer. A fact-finding trip was bound to be helpful to both her mind and her body.

Devon, however, cast a doubtful glance at Meg, and a second glance at the tape recorder sitting on the kitchen cabinet.

"Valerie will be here alone while you're gone . . ." he began.

"I doubt I'll be gone more than a week," Meg said cheerfully. "Surely you can keep Val entertained while I'm gone, Dev."

"It isn't a question of entertainment. Val, maybe you should consider going with Meg. I don't like the idea of your being alone in the house."

"Dev, I've been on the road two years, and I'll be darned if I'll spend a single night I don't have to in a motel room. Besides, I've just planted a garden. Unless Rayburn Lawn Maintenance plans to add my garden to its lengthy list, I'm not leaving." She paused. "I'm not leaving, period. I just got here. Besides, I've already been to Arkansas this year."

On cue, the telephone rang. Devon jerked away from his position at the sink where he was cleaning the fish.

"Answer it, Val," he commanded.

"Do I have to?"

He gestured with the knife.

Valerie reached reluctantly for the receiver. "Hello?"

Her subsequent silence confirmed the caller's identity. She listened for several minutes without comment, then quietly held out the receiver to Devon.

Devon took it, listened a moment, then said, "Oh, yeah? You and what army?"

He winced and jerked the instrument away from his ear.

"He's getting worse," Devon said grimly. "I really don't like this, Val."

"No problem, Dev," Meg said cheerfully. "While I'm gone, you can have my bedroom. With you in the house, Valerie should be quite safe."

"That's right, Mama," Valerie said dryly. "Throw me to the wolves."

"Valerie Dallas, I'm surprised at you," Meg said, content now that she'd solved the problem of her daughter's safety. "I'm sure Devon has always behaved like a perfect gentleman. Blake would never take advantage of a situation like this, so I'm sure Devon wouldn't."

"I'd like to meet this Blake," Devon said. "He sounds too good to be true."

"You can't, dear. He's you. More or less."

Devon groaned. "Meg, if you ever tell anyone that, I'll turn into a wolf and devour Valerie."

"Puh-leeze do," Valerie said in hopeful tones.

SEVEN

During the night the telephone rang twice, and Meg finally took it off the hook after it awakened them the second time.

After that, they both slept soundly, and Meg arose early, breakfasted on the oat bran cereal Valerie prepared for her, and went happily out to her car.

"Call me when you get there," Valerie instructed, leaning into the car window to kiss her mother one more time.

"Let Devon answer the telephone," Meg said. "That should discourage this sicko."

Valerie grinned and nodded, wondering how Devon was taking the news that Meg expected him to move in and protect her daughter.

It was Devon's habit to get an early start in the morning since afternoon thunderstorms often interrupted his business later in the day. He drove up in his pickup truck soon after Meg left and asked cheerfully if there was anything in the house for breakfast.

"Of course there is," Valerie said. "I've got the oat bran cereal I've been feeding Mama. How's your cholesterol, Dev?"

"Normal," he replied, making a beeline for the kitchen to check his recording machine. "At least it will be if you add some bacon and eggs to that cereal."

Valerie scrambled eggs and made toast, which she served with the cereal while Devon checked his crews' schedules for the day and scowled out the window at the two or three fluffy clouds that marred the pure blue of the early-summer sky.

"Those clouds are innocent," she told him.

"I'm hoping they hold off until sundown, although I doubt they will. We're backed up already from the afternoon showers we had last week."

"Must be tough, being at the mercy of the weather."

"You have no idea." He appreciatively eyed the food she set before him.

The telephone rang, and Valerie stiffened.

"Want me to get it?" Devon asked, eyeing her with concern.

"Please."

He stood and reached for the telephone, then conducted a grim-voiced conversation that made Valerie stiffen even more. By the time he replaced the receiver, she was white-faced and weak in the knees.

Devon turned to face her. "The Houston Police Department would like to talk with you about your date with Jonathan Wade two years ago, and they'd appreciate a copy of the taped phone calls you've been receiving."

"Why?" Valerie whispered.

"It seems the sheriff is taking action after all. Friend Jonathan has surfaced at last, and the police have connected him to the rape-murders of two Houston women. He's implicated in several more in Louisiana and New Mexico. Anything you can tell them about the way he operates will be appreciated."

"But, Dev!" Valerie wailed. "I don't know anything about the way he operates."

"Hush, Val. Your episode may suggest something to them. At least they can warn women what to look out for."

Valerie shuddered. "Do I have to?"

"The detectives will be here in thirty minutes. If we're

lucky, maybe they'll get something done about these phone calls.''

''Dev, do you think it's possible the obscene caller is Jonathan Wade?''

''I've thought so from the first,'' Devon said.

Somehow, Valerie wasn't surprised. She wrapped her arms around herself and shivered, despite the fact that the day promised to be dry and hot.

Devon's beeper went off, and he spent the next few minutes on the telephone. Valerie left the dishes in the sink and went to her bedroom, where she changed from the white shorts and loose cotton blouse to a pair of tailored trousers and a silk blouse. Perhaps it would help if she looked cool and collected.

She looked at herself in the mirror and felt much better about the upcoming interview. Operating on the theory that she'd do better if she projected an image of cool sophistication, she took the rubber band out of her hair, fluffed it around her shoulders, and inserted her contacts.

When she returned to the kitchen, Devon had washed the dishes and was drying his hands on paper towels.

''Is this an example of drawing courage from your personal appearance?'' he asked, smiling.

''I hope so,'' Valerie said gloomily. ''Dev, I really hate having to go over all this again. I thought I'd almost forgotten about it, and now they want me to remember all the gory details.''

''You'll do fine,'' Devon said. ''Let's make a pot of coffee. Would you like me to doctor yours with Meg's creme de cacao?''

''God forbid. I'd probably fall out during the questioning.''

The detectives turned out to be two ordinary-looking men in plainclothes, which comforted Valerie considerably. Two years ago, she'd had to explain her ordeal to a group of uniformed policemen while clutching the shreds of her dress bodice, and the memory still disturbed her.

She introduced Devon as the lawyer who had helped

get the senior Wade off her back, and the detectives eyed Devon with interest.

"Miss Dallas," said one. "Two years ago the Beaumont Police recorded the incident you reported, although they were inclined to believe it was unfounded. Unfounded doesn't mean you weren't attacked. It simply means the case would have been difficult to prosecute successfully. We now have reason to believe Jonathan Wade is a very sick and dangerous man. That's why we'd like to know anything you can tell us about your experience with him."

Valerie complied, describing how Jonathan, a fellow student, had called her every night until she went out with him. She then described the events of the evening as well as she could recall them, and told of her fear when he parked in the woods outside Beaumont.

"What was in the backseat of the automobile?" one of the men asked.

Valerie thought back. "There was a blanket. At least I think it was a blanket. There was a roll of some silver-looking stuff, like masking tape, only a lot bigger."

"Duct tape," the detective said, in tones that chilled Valerie to the marrow.

"What about it?" Devon said sharply.

"It appears to be part of Wade's current strategy. Once he gets the woman isolated, he knocks her out and secures her with duct tape."

Valerie clenched her teeth. She'd known she was lucky two years ago, but it was terrifying to realize just how lucky.

"What happened next, Miss Dallas?"

Valerie described how Jonathan had driven a fist toward her jaw, but she'd been frightened and already had her hand on the pepper canister in her pocket, thanks to her training in self-defense at the Beaumont Karate and Judo Studios.

The two detectives regarded her with admiration, and Devon smiled at her encouragingly.

She went on, telling how she'd leaped from the car,

followed by Jonathan, then how she'd leaped back in while he was still suffering the effects of the pepper.

Devon broke in impatiently. "I don't like the sound of any of this. Val has only been home three days, and she's already started getting threatening, obscene phone calls."

"I told you I'd like a tape of those phone calls," one of the detectives said.

"I have one for you," Devon said, producing it. "What I want to know is, what are you going to do about it?"

"Do you have a tape recorder?"

Devon went to the kitchen and returned with his tape recorder. He slid in the tape he'd just given the detectives and let it play.

The two detectives looked at each other.

"Could be," one said.

"We'd like your permission to tap your phone line, Miss Dallas. We'd like to trace these calls."

"It's high time," Devon said. "Val's been getting several calls a night. I should mention that they started after Wade's cousin, Katie Barlow, recognized Valerie and accused her of plotting to seduce and ruin innocent men."

"I see." The detective produced a notebook and thumbed through it. "That would be Mrs. Katie Wilson Barlow on Shellhammer Road?"

"It would," Devon said with satisfaction. "Either she's behind the calls or she's in touch with Wade."

The two detectives looked at him sharply, but Valerie noted that neither man argued with him.

When the detectives left, hopefully to call on Katie Barlow, Valerie felt almost lonely. The more people in the house, the better she felt.

Devon came to stand beside her as she watched the detectives go to their car and slipped an arm around her waist.

"Cheer up," he said softly. "I'm not leaving you alone."

"Please don't. Dev, do you think you could take me with you if you go to check on your crews? I don't even care to be around the house alone in broad daylight."

"Remember that job I offered you," he said. "You get to ride with me."

"I'll take it. Why on earth did Mama have to pick now to research Arkansas?"

She changed into jeans and a loose cotton blouse to ride with Devon to check on several of his job sites. It was a relief to replace her contacts with glasses. Stress made her rub her eyes twice as much.

"Want to stay and help out the crew?" he asked when they arrived at a Houston apartment complex.

Devon believed in hiring women as well as men, and had learned that on larger maintenance jobs, crews of three were most efficient.

Valerie glanced at the three busy workers. Two of them were women, and they all seemed happy to look up from their work and recognize Devon. It gave her a strange feeling akin to jealousy.

"Where are you going?" she asked.

"To talk to the owner of this complex. He has something I want to rent for a few weeks. I shouldn't be gone long. Susan is the head of this crew. Tell her I said you were an expert on hedges."

He pointed out a tall brunette who was using a gasoline-powered blower to clean the sidewalks.

"Take this cap," he added, handing her a battered baseball cap that had been crushed on the seat between them.

Valerie climbed out slowly and walked toward Susan, who looked up with a friendly smile and shut off the blower.

"I'm supposed to help with the hedges," Valerie said.

"Great. The clippers are on the trailer." Susan waved toward the truck bearing the logo, "Rayburn Lawn Maintenance." "Is this your first day working for Devon Rayburn?" she asked.

"Not exactly. I . . . uh . . . did some work for him several years ago, when he was first getting started. I'm in town for a vacation . . ."

She trailed off, not knowing how to approach the subject of the obscene calls that had driven her from her home.

"I understand," Susan said quickly. Most of the women Devon had hired were supporting children with little help from their ex-spouses. "Earn every dollar you can when you can. Are you sure you don't need a bigger hat? Your skin is awfully fair."

"I need to get a little sun."

"You don't want to work so hard, you get sick," Susan said. "How long have you known Devon?"

"About eight years," Valerie said, thinking back.

"Oh, wow. You have known him a long time. That must have been when he first started Rayburn Lawn Maintenance."

"It was." Valerie walked beside the friendly Susan to the company truck and reached into the trailer behind the truck for a gasoline-powered hedge clipper after glancing at the length of the hedge. "He started out with a lawn mower, one pair of hand-operated hedge clippers, and a weed trimmer."

"That was back when he was dating that girl from Winnie. Everyone is dying to find out more about her. She married someone else right after they broke up."

Valerie nodded noncommittally and wondered how to introduce herself as the girl-from-Winnie's sister.

"It's a shame, isn't it?" Susan went on. "He's such a nice guy. Maybe his heart was broken or something. He ought to be married by now."

"I'm glad he isn't," Valerie said devoutly, then flushed with embarrassment.

"Oh, it's like that, is it?" Susan's grin was kind and knowing. "Look out, honey. He's very careful about dating employees. Several have tried, including one on this team who shall remain nameless." Her laughing brown eyes singled out a petite woman with short dark curls clustered around her face. "It was a waste of her time all the way around."

Valerie studied the petite brunette and decided to say nothing about her relationship to Barbara. Devon mightn't like it, and, besides, in a month she'd probably be on the road again.

She sighed, wishing she felt more enthusiastic about her career as a singer. That was one of the reasons she'd taken this vacation. She needed time to think over her reasons for continuing to sing professionally.

"Go ahead and get started," Susan said, smiling kindly. "You do know how to clip a hedge, don't you?"

"Oh, yes." Valerie manipulated the clipper and checked the gasoline level. "Dev taught me years ago."

"Say, you *are* an old friend of his, aren't you?"

Valerie supposed she shouldn't have called him Dev. "I've known him a long time," she said truthfully, and headed for the long row of ligustrum bushes that bordered the apartment complex.

The unaccustomed exercise in the heat of the day was invigorating to a woman used to riding all day in air-conditioned vehicles. She was like Devon about yardwork in that she found tremendous satisfaction in looking back where she had been and seeing results from her work.

She had worked almost an hour before Devon reappeared with a tanned, fit-looking blond man beside him. He came over to her at once, and she switched off the clipper.

"Val, I'm going to be gone several hours. Will you stay with the crew until I get back? Wherever they move, I'll find you. You'll be safe with them."

Valerie studied him. He looked hard and anxious, and his gray eyes searched hers with an intensity that made her cautious.

"I'll be fine, Dev. I'm enjoying myself." She pointed her clipper at the expanse of perfectly trimmed hedge.

"You haven't forgotten a thing about hedges," he said, grinning at her. "You're a good sport, Val. I'll be back as soon as I can, I promise."

"I'm not in any hurry," Valerie informed him. She shoved her glasses higher on her nose and caught a glimpse of the petite brunette watching them while she edged a sidewalk. "Do you give your slaves a lunch break?"

Devon chuckled. "That may be a problem. Most of them bring a lunch, but you didn't have any warning."

Valerie looked beyond him. "No problem. I see a Burger King a block away."

"I don't want you going alone. I'll pick you up something and put it in the truck for you, okay?"

"You take care of everything, Dev. Make it a cheeseburger with mustard and onion."

"Oh, Lord. Not onion." He turned away, laughing.

"I love onion," she yelled after him.

Devon rejoined the blond man, still laughing, and the pair drove away in Devon's pickup.

She was so busy on the hedge, she didn't notice when Devon dropped off her cheeseburger, but when the workers broke for lunch, a sack from Burger King was waiting in the truck with the other lunches.

Apparently Devon's return had been noted.

"I see the boss dropped you off something," the small brunette said.

Now that she saw the woman up close, Valerie was reminded forcefully of Barbara.

"Yes, I didn't have a chance to prepare a lunch, and he didn't want me wasting time going to Burger King," she said diplomatically.

"He usually doesn't care where we go for lunch," Susan said.

"What's your name?" the brunette asked. "I'm Karen. If you're going to be joining our crew, we might as well get to know each other."

The girl was friendly, outgoing, and lively. Just like Barbara, Valerie observed as she introduced herself. Much as she'd love to hate someone who was interested in Devon, she found Karen likable.

"I don't blame you for making a play for him," Karen said. "Devon Rayburn is a real dreamboat, and he doesn't even seem to know it."

Valerie didn't bother to deny making a play for Devon. That was what she was doing, all right.

"I've been working for him for three years now." Susan said. "If you want to know what I think, that girl he was engaged to soured him on women."

"God, what a stupid woman!" Karen said, groaning.

They grabbed for their lunches and walked to a shady area and sat on the curb. Another man who had been working at the rear of the complex joined them.

The members of the crew were good friends, Valerie discovered, and all were curious about her but too polite to question her much.

They were also fond of, and curious about, Devon.

"You said you've known Devon for eight years," Susan reminded her. "That's a lot longer than any of us. Did you know the girl he was engaged to?"

"Yes," Valerie began.

"What was she like?" Karen asked eagerly.

"She was a lot like you, believe it or not," Valerie said. "Petite, pretty, and outgoing."

"Oh." Karen sounded disappointed. "No wonder he didn't like me. Wasn't she a blonde?"

"Yes."

"How sickening. You saw her a few times, didn't you, Pete?"

Pete Martinez, a quiet, lanky man, was munching a roast beef sandwich with supreme disinterest in anything except his food. "Yeah, I saw her," he said. "Dizzy broad. He was well rid of that one."

"Pete, you're so sickening," Karen said. "Here we are perishing for gossip, and you're full of it and you won't give." She fished in her lunch bag. "Are you susceptible to bribery? It just so happens I have a homemade eclair in here someplace . . ."

Pete's eyes fastened on the lunch sack.

"Well?"

"What do you want to know?" Pete asked, grinning and holding out his hand.

"Why do you say Devon was well rid of his girl-friend?"

"She was a status-hungry bitch," Pete said succinctly.

Valerie flushed, realizing it was too late now to reveal her relationship to Barbara without embarrassing everyone present. She unwrapped her cheeseburger and tried to hide behind the wrapper.

"What about you, Val?" Karen's interest swung to Valerie. "Would you agree with that?"

Valerie cleared her throat. She'd never thought of Barbara as status hungry. To her, Barbara had seemed to care too much about how other people saw her.

"She was very interested in being a successful, professional woman, and she wanted to marry a successful, professional man, which is why she pushed Dev into going to law school," she said slowly.

"Why do you say she was a bitch, Pete?"

Karen had discovered a way to extract the most information possible, Valerie saw with amusement. By playing Valerie and Pete off each other, she'd soon arrive at a more accurate assessment of Barbara's character.

"Heard her arguing with the boss one day," Pete said laconically.

"Pete!"

Susan and Karen spoke together.

Valerie said nothing. She bit into the cheeseburger and discovered it had no onions.

"She was giving him hell," Pete said. "About the company. Seemed to think he'd do better as a lawyer. He shouted back that if she didn't like his job, she could stuff it."

"And then?"

"When she saw she wasn't getting anywhere, she accused him of having the hots for her little sister."

"Oh, wow!" Karen said.

Valerie choked on a bite and stayed behind the cheese-burger. It was a stunning shock to learn Barbara hadn't confined her accusations to Valerie.

"Are you all right, Val?" Susan said. "You're awfully red. Here. Have a cold drink."

Valerie grabbed for the drink and gulped it.

"You should eat slower," Karen told her. "Go on, Pete. What happened then?"

"He told her she ought to be ashamed of her nasty tongue, and she said she saw the way he looked at her little sister's breasts. That's when I got the hell away from there."

"Pete, you're so sickening," Karen said again.

"Val, are you sure you're okay?" Susan asked. "You look like you're about to be sick."

"I'm fine, thank you," Valerie managed. "I choked on a piece of cheeseburger."

"Oh, gosh, we're embarrassing her," Karen said. "You'll get used to us, hon. We love gossiping about Devon Rayburn. It never hurts to dream."

"No," Valerie agreed fervently as soon as she was able. "It doesn't."

Karen returned immediately to the subject of interest. "So what happened to the little sister? If he really was looking at her, where is she?"

Pete shrugged. "Never met her."

"What's her name?"

"Never knew." Pete started on the eclair.

Karen's interest swung to Valerie. "Did you know the little sister?"

At this point, Valerie had no idea who would be embarrassed the most by revealing her identity.

"Yes," she said. "She was tall and lanky and mousy blonde, and she wore glasses and was quiet."

"That's more like it," Susan said wisely. "At least she wouldn't have the big head."

"I wonder what happened to her," Karen said.

"She graduated from college and left town," Valerie said simply.

"You don't think Devon is waiting for her to come back or anything, do you?" Karen asked the group at large.

"The Hulk said she's back," Pete said suddenly. "The boss was kissing a blonde in a hardware store in Winnie yesterday."

Valerie wondered if it was possible to sink through the concrete and vanish from sight. Fortunately, no one seemed to connect the blonde with her.

"I hope the Hulk gets assigned to our crew sometime soon," Karen said intensely. "I'd like to find out more about her."

Valerie's cheeseburger tasted more and more like cardboard. She couldn't possibly eat another bite of it, she decided.

"Did he say what she looked like?" Susan asked.

"Sort of pale blonde with pretty, light-green eyes. At least, that was the Hulk's impression." Pete finished off the eclair and licked his fingers.

Valerie could only be thankful for the thick glasses that hid her eye color. She kept her eyelids lowered just in case.

"I love romance, don't you?" Karen asked the group at large. Karen looked at Valerie, who was still cowering behind the cheeseburger. "I think Devon Rayburn would make a fabulous husband. Look how sweet he was to Val, making sure she had a lunch and everything."

"I wouldn't mind testing that out," Valerie muttered, and smiled when the rest of the crew laughed.

"If you aren't going to finish that cheeseburger . . ." Pete began, eyeing it.

Valerie gave it to him with alacrity.

It was late in the afternoon when Devon came for her, and by then the crew had moved to another apartment complex. Valerie had been accepted as a member of the crew and was trimming back a row of pyracantha bushes with a pair of hand-held clippers when Devon approached from behind.

When his arms came around her waist, Valerie swung around with the clippers, ready to bash him over the head.

Devon leaped back. "Hey!" he cried.

"Sorry, Dev," she said, grinning. "You scared me half to death. You shouldn't sneak up on a woman who's receiving calls from a probable rape-murderer."

"He hasn't got a prayer if he comes around you," Devon said, eyeing the clippers. "You're a dangerous woman." He stepped nearer and took the clippers away from her, then slipped an arm around her waist. "I've got everything set up. I'll take you home so you can pack."

"Pack?" Valerie balked. "I'm not through with this hedge. Are you trying to upset my already disturbed nerves?"

"I'll explain it all to you on the way home." He held the clippers out of her reach when she grabbed for them. "Someone else can finish the hedge. You're through for the day."

"I was just getting into the job," Valerie protested.

It was true. She had forgotten how soothing yardwork was to overwrought nerves, and how much time there was to clear one's mind and think.

Devon tightened his grip around her waist and walked her along beside him.

"Tough," he said. "You're supposed to be my helper, and besides, I'm the boss around here. Move it along there, slave."

Valerie shoved at him. "Let go of me, Devon Rayburn. How do you think you're going to look with a pair of hedge clippers attached to your ear?"

"Horrible. Let me rephrase that. *Please* move it along there, slave."

"Dev . . ."

"I'm in a hurry, Val. You don't want everyone to think I'm kidnapping you, do you?"

Valerie brightened. "I can see it now 'Boss of Yard Crew Flips Out.' "

They had reached the crew's truck, where Devon replaced Valerie's hedge clippers. He turned to study her face.

"You were having a good time, weren't you?" he asked quietly.

"Well, of course I was. This is the first chance I've had to do some real thinking since I've been home." She smiled and indicated the almost-finished bushes. "There's something about mowing and clipping that gets you back to zero."

Devon leaned against the truck. "What were you thinking about?"

The sun glinted off his sun-streaked hair and highlighted the muscles of his tanned forearms. He looked so beautiful to Valerie, she had to turn her eyes away.

She shrugged and watched Karen, who was busy with the blower. "I was thinking about . . . about what I've been doing the past two years, and what I want to do with the next two."

"Did you reach any conclusions?" He studied her.

"No. I told you, I've just gotten started. Maybe I can join the crew again tomorrow. I need a really long hedge before I reach any conclusions."

"Forget it. You have something else to do tomorrow."

"I do?"

"I'll tell you about it later. Come on, Val. I want to get going while it's still daylight."

Valerie allowed him to pull her along by the hand while she stared at the afternoon sun and checked her watch. It was barely four o'clock, and the sun wouldn't set until eight.

They arrived at Devon's pickup, and Valerie balked once more.

"I'm not taking one more step until you tell me what this is all about."

"Hop in, honey. Remember how you once told me you'd love to take a few days off and go cruising on a yacht?"

Valerie regarded him suspiciously. "What about it?"

"I rented a yacht. We're going cruising."

Valerie allowed him to help her into the pickup. What else could she do, when her brain was reeling with shock?

"Dev, do you know anything about boats?"

He looked hurt. "Would I risk life and reputation going out on the Gulf if I didn't?"

"Probably, if you thought a yacht was enough like your bass boat."

Devon grinned. "It is."

"Are you sure you don't want to think about this?"

"I have thought," he said, looking at her with satisfaction. "That's what I like about you, Val. You're an intrepid spirit."

"Is that the same thing as a good sport?"

"More or less. Come here."

She reared back her head and peered at him through her glasses. "Dev, I hate being called a good sport."

Devon reached in and got his hands around her slender waist. He pulled her out effortlessly and set her on the ground before him.

"After all the trouble you went through to get me in there, I'm surprised at your hauling me back out," she grumbled, conscious of both Karen and Susan's interested gazes.

Devon laughed and used both hands to turn her face up to his. "I'll get you back in," he said, and kissed her.

Valerie clutched his shoulders. "I'll never be able to show my face around here again . . ." she began.

"Yes, you will," he said, and wrapped both arms around her. "Everyone will be deeply interested in whether or not you'll be joining the crew permanently."

Valerie planted both hands on his chest, but it did no good to try to shove him away. He merely let her bend back over his arms, then he leaned forward to kiss her once more until her legs threatened to give way.

Valerie kissed him back enthusiastically until her glasses began to slide.

"Dev, I'm warning you. This is my last pair of glasses, and they're about to go."

Devon lifted her erect at once. "That should give the crew something to talk about for the entire time we're gone."

"Somehow that doesn't comfort me," Valerie said.

EIGHT

"I can't believe you did this," Valerie murmured as Devon helped her climb a ladder from the pier to the deck of a large, blue and white motor yacht.

A dock official was standing nearby, which was why she didn't say it louder. She glanced over her shoulder and wondered if she should mention something about Devon's lack of experience with any boat larger than a bass boat.

Devon had hurried her home, instructing her on the way as to what to pack, then drove her back to his apartment in a western suburb of Houston, where he flung a few items into a duffel bag.

The next thing Valerie knew, they were on the Gulf Freeway heading for Galveston.

Once in Galveston, they headed for a marina where many boats were berthed. Valerie wasn't sure what to expect, unless it was a boat a little larger than an ordinary fishing boat. The yacht Devon pointed out looked intimidating to Valerie.

When they went down the companionway into the cabin, she was stunned to see what looked to her dazzled eyes like a well-furnished house. The galley was a regular kitchen, complete with a refrigerator, an electric coffee percolator, and a microwave oven. The sitting room was elegantly furnished in teak and pale-blue leather. There were two staterooms, one fore and one aft. Each had a double bed, two bedside tables, and a head with the luxury of a shower.

Valerie wondered again if Devon knew what he was doing, but he seemed to. He was out on deck doing what he called "casting off."

"Come on up," he said. "You can criticize my skippering." He fished a pair of sunglasses from his pocket and put them on.

"Criticize your what?"

She followed him to the cockpit, took the chair beside him, and stared with disbelief at the course he intended to steer out of the yacht basin.

"Dev, why are you doing this?" She gripped the sides of her chair as he turned the key in the ignition and the powerful motor began to vibrate the craft.

Devon grinned at her reaction. "You need a vacation, and so do I. I can't rest if I'm worried that some nut is going to break in and rape you."

It still hadn't become real to her that Devon intended to take her and this fantasy of a boat out on the Gulf.

"How long are you intending this vacation to last?"

"A couple of weeks," Devon said. "I spoke to the Houston police, and they have some leads. *And* a policewoman to answer your phone a couple of days until they can trace your obscene caller."

"What?"

"I gave them permission. I want this guy caught, Val."

Her heart was warmed, even as she protested, "I've always read where the callers hardly ever proceed to action."

"Don't you believe it," Devon said. "This guy means business. Especially if it's Wade. I think he's developed some sort of fixation on you because you escaped him."

Valerie had arrived at this conclusion herself, but she still shivered when Devon said it aloud. Only by refusing to think about it could she maintain a facade of normalcy.

The boat began to move forward slowly, and Valerie clutched the seat, staring rigidly ahead.

Devon guided the big boat carefully out of the yacht basin toward the open Gulf. He seemed familiar with all the protocol, yielding the right of way readily to sailboats and smaller craft. Long before they reached the Gulf, Valerie had begun to relax.

"Want a cold drink?" Devon asked, smiling at her.

"No."

"Would you mind getting me one?" He was laughing now, having sensed her reluctance to move.

"This is not funny. You neglected to find out if I'm susceptible to seasickness before hauling me out here."

"Well? Are you?"

"I'm not sure yet. The fact that I'm not sure yet is not a good sign."

"A good test of your sea legs would be to fetch me a cold drink from the refrigerator."

"I hope Shelby Winthrop doesn't hear about this," Valerie muttered, sliding off her chair.

"She hates boats?"

"Putting out to sea with a man one isn't married to is not the behavior expected of one of the Shelby Winthrop Quartet. Shelby is very adamant about appearances."

Valerie made her cautious way down the ladder and the companion way. Devon's laughter followed her, and she couldn't help but grin also.

"Maybe a reporter with one of those telephoto lenses is following us," he called down.

"Thanks a lot, Dev." She disappeared into the cabin and emerged a moment later with two cold drinks. "Before you know it, you'll be coerced into marrying me to save my reputation."

"Or mine," he said.

She climbed back up. "I just want to know one thing."

"Yes?"

"What are we going to *do* out on the Gulf for two weeks?"

She thought he might fall off the chair, he laughed so hard.

"We'll think of something," he said when he was able to speak.

"I hope this boat packs a game of Scrabble."

"There's a deck of cards," Devon offered, straight-faced.

"I hate checkers," Valerie went on.

"How about strip poker?"

Valerie sighed with mock-boredom. "It may come to that."

They rode in the cockpit for an hour, which was all the time they had before the sun set. By then, they had reached the open Gulf and saw few other vessels on the horizon. Devon went to the deck and set the anchor with a skill that surprised Valerie.

"Where did you learn all this?" she asked.

"This boat belongs to a friend of mine from law school, Flynn Sutherland. I've been on several fishing trips with him."

"He's been giving you yacht lessons?"

"You could say that. I had him give me a few more lessons this afternoon, when I decided to get you out of Winnie."

"You could have moved me to your apartment," she pointed out.

"Come on, Val. Doesn't a vacation on a luxury trawler count as relaxation anymore?"

"I'm not sure. It depends on how calm the Gulf is."

Devon straightened and came toward her. "Want to take a swim?"

She bent to stare over the rail at the stretch of deep-green water surrounding them. "Is it safe? Don't sharks live out here?"

"Do you have any open wounds?"

Valerie's gaze switched back to Devon and she regarded him in alarm.

"Do you plan on slashing your wrists while swimming?'' he went on, in the manner of one seeking information.

"It's becoming clearer and clearer that I may be in far more serious trouble than I'd thought," Valerie said thoughtfully.

"Go put on your bathing suit," Devon said, grinning. "If it'll make you feel better, I'll swim with a knife tucked in my trunks.''

Valerie feigned disappointment. "Isn't this a situation where we take advantage of the isolation and go skinny-dipping?''

"Then I'd have no place to put the knife," Devon pointed out, and dodged when she aimed a mock punch at his chin.

Devon had placed her gear in the forward cabin, and she went swiftly down the stairs of the companionway and through the galley and sitting room, glancing about her with awe. The next few days should be close to heaven.

Valerie owned a single bathing suit that she'd hardly worn in the two years she had been touring with Shelby Winthrop. She put it on, scowling at the way it covered her slender figure. If she'd had advance warning, she could have bought a sexy bikini. A black tank suit that had been purchased because it was the least sexy item on the rack didn't cut it in this situation.

She went back on deck and found Devon putting a swimming ladder into place on the deck. Untying the strap that bound the two pieces together, he dropped the lower section of the ladder into the water.

He looked up, and his eyes scanned her body with approval. "Want to go first? Or would you rather make a grand entrance?''

"What's a grand entrance?" she asked, regarding him suspiciously.

He stood and came toward her. Valerie backed off, but not fast enough. He grabbed her around the waist and swung her off her feet.

She shrieked and grabbed for her glasses, which were threatening to tumble off her nose. "Devon Rayburn, if you lose my last pair of glasses, your life will be miserable, I promise you.''

"Then drop them here on the towel."

He had hoisted her over his shoulder. Turning, he aligned her with a towel he'd placed ready on the deck and waited while she reached down to drop her glasses carefully onto the center of the towel. Then he walked to the deck rail with her and tossed her into the water.

Valerie landed with a great splash and allowed herself to sink like a stone. Perhaps if she didn't come up at once he'd come looking for her and she could get a grip on him.

Seconds later, she felt the turbulence created by the entry of a second body into the water and grabbed for it. Her searching fingers closed around his ankle. Grasping strongly, she attempted to drag him deeper.

He didn't resist, and Valerie pulled him down to face her. In the dusky light of the setting sun, with her vision hampered by the saltwater, Valerie could see only a blurred shadow where Devon was.

Now was the moment to kiss him, but her breath ran out and Valerie had to surface.

Devon surfaced beside her. "You had me fair and square," he said, shaking his hair back from his eyes. "What were you planning on doing with me?"

"I had all kinds of plans, but I needed more air to carry them out, unfortunately." She blinked water off her eyelashes and tried to focus on him. "It would also help if I could see better."

"Val, you're a treasure. Come here."

"Where's here?" she asked humorously, reaching for the blur treading water just outside her focusing range.

He suddenly came into focus about six inches from her face. "Never mind. I'll come to you," he said.

She felt his arms go around her and stopped moving her legs so she could mold her entire body to his. They both sank as Devon's warm mouth touched hers in the preliminary advance of a kiss that demanded all the territory she had to surrender.

Devon's legs moved in a powerful kick that propelled them both back to the surface. He kept an arm around her and moved toward the swimming ladder, where he hooked an arm over one of the rungs and let her dangle in his embrace.

"I don't want to drown you," he said, gray eyes gleaming with laughter.

Valerie stared, devouring the way the red setting sun highlighted the planes of his face and made the drops of water clinging to his lashes glow like red jewels.

"Can you see me?" he asked, concerned.

"Yes. Very well."

Devon looked back at her. "Do I have a weird new growth on my face or something? You keep staring."

"It's so rare to get anything into focus," she lied. "I thought I'd better memorize you while I can."

Devon threw back his head and laughed, then drew her close, letting her chin rest on his shoulder. "You liar. Confess. I'm growing a third eye and you don't want to embarrass me."

Valerie relaxed in his arms and sighed her contentment. "Actually, I was checking out your weight by the sharpness of your chin. You look like you've been missing a meal here or there."

"You'll have to do something about it. We seem to have this nice galley, and it's loaded with food."

Devon's hand had flattened on her back and was moving gently up and down, spreading warmth and soft tingles of sensation. Valerie leaned back to put her arms around his neck and lifted her chin invitingly.

"Val," he whispered. "I don't think you know what you're asking for."

"Yes, I do. I'm asking for a kiss. Are you going to hold out on me?"

"I probably ought to," he said on a long sigh. "As it is, I wouldn't want to hurt your feelings."

"Good."

He held her tightly with one arm, letting his lips seek hers and teasing her into parting hers with his tongue.

Valerie opened to him readily, and slid one hand up to nestle against the back of his sleek, wet head and hold him against her. The cool water surrounding her contrasted with the warmth of his body in the spots where her skin came into contact with him.

"We'd better cut this out," he said, lifting his head to smile at her. "I'm not made of stone, you know."

"I know," Valerie said, clutching his shoulders. She ran her hands down his brown arms to test the strength of the muscles in his arms. "Thank goodness you're not."

"That isn't what I mean," he said with mock sternness. "What I'm trying to say is that I have you in a position where I can take advantage of you, and now you're trying to encourage me to do so. Have you no shame?"

"No," Valerie said. "Nor any compassion for a male in a weakened condition, either."

"That was my next line of defense." He shifted position so that her body no longer rested against his. "Val, you aren't helping."

"I don't want to help. I want to be kissed. Taken advantage of. Seduced. All those lovely words that sound like such fun."

She tried to pull his head down for another kiss, but Devon quickly let go of her and forced her to grab for the ladder.

"Dev, this is not gentlemanly behavior on your part."

He gave her a slightly shame-faced grin before he moved out of her focus. "Sorry. In another minute, I won't be capable of gentlemanly behavior at all."

Valerie held on to the ladder and turned her head in the direction of his voice. The sun had set, and the sky was darkening rapidly. She couldn't locate him, so she let go of the ladder and reached forth blindly.

"Who wants a gentleman when she can have a seductive rake?" Valerie asked reasonably.

She heard the splash as Devon moved out of her grasp. "Tell you what," he said. "If you can catch me, I'm yours to do with as you please."

Valerie lunged through the water toward his voice, but

he remained just beyond her reach. Encouraged by her near-success, she chased him around the boat several times, almost catching his foot twice.

She caught the ladder, panting, and glared at the blurred dark shape she figured was Devon's head. "I can't go another stroke, you fiend. You planned this. You're trying to wear me out."

He chuckled. "I've heard it said that exercise and cold showers—"

She made one more try for him, and was rewarded by his shout of alarm as she latched onto his arm. He jerked out of her hold and swam beyond her.

"Caught you fair and square!" she called.

"No, you didn't. You tricked me, and you let me get away."

"You only said I had to catch you. Come on, Dev. Surrender yourself."

"No way," he said.

"All right. Be like that. I'm going to stay right here and guard the ladder. You can just stay out there shriveling up until you decide to give in."

"Valerie."

"Yes, Dev?"

"That's evil."

"No, it isn't. It's logical."

"Valerie." He swam closer.

She hoisted herself part way up the ladder and peered over the dark water nearby.

"Have you no mercy?" he asked plaintively.

She homed in on the blurred shape that had come within leaping distance.

"Valerie?"

She threw herself off the ladder and landed with her arms around him. She wrapped her legs around him for good measure, and held on while he reached for the ladder.

"Are you going to make me climb the ladder like this?" he asked, laughing. "If you aren't careful, you're going to drown us both."

Valerie clung with all her might while Devon climbed

the swimming ladder bearing her attached like a koala bear to his chest. Pretending collapse, he staggered onto the deck and dropped down beside their towels.

Valerie remained attached.

"Val, you can let go now. There are no more sharks."

"I don't think I will. You might come up with another excuse."

"Excuse!" he exclaimed, hurt. "Be reasonable, Val. Meg is my good friend. What would she say if I seduced her youngest daughter within three days of meeting her again?"

"After she told you to move in while she was gone? She wouldn't dare say a word."

Valerie laid her head on his shoulder and sighed with pleasure. His wet skin was sleek and cool to her touch, with warmth beneath the surface.

"Val."

"Yes, Dev?"

"You'd better sit up. I'm not ready for what you seem to be asking for."

His voice was light and teasing, but Valerie let go of him and sat up. Suddenly, everything became all too clear to her, and she wondered how she could have been so blind.

Devon still wasn't over Barbara. He was probably having an attack of conscience from the thought of making love to Barbara's little sister.

It was the only explanation of his behavior over the past two days. Surely if he felt something for her, he would have taken advantage of all these opportunities by now.

She struggled to laugh naturally and reached for her glasses. "Let me know when you are," she said.

Devon appeared unaware of her withdrawal and began drying off with the towel lying beside him. "Let's go inside and shower off the saltwater," he suggested. "I don't suppose you've ever had the experience of cooking on a boat, have you? Well, you're in for a treat. Wait until you see the groceries."

Valerie pretended enthusiasm for the galley. Perhaps

she'd better develop an interest in the boat and ocean-related acticities rather than placing all her attention on Devon Rayburn.

"Come on down," Devon said, and reached for her hand.

Valerie let him lead her down the companionway to the galley. Together they opened cabinets and inspected the groceries, then investigated the contents of the refrigerator.

"You really outdid yourself, Dev," she murmured, staring at the steaks and ground meat in the refrigerator. "We don't even have to depend on fish."

Devon chuckled. "I followed Flynn's advice on the groceries to the letter. Modern boats are wonderful."

"I'll say." Valerie opened the vegetable bins and discovered fresh celery, parsley, and green onions, among other things. "I'd assume I was in a regular kitchen if it weren't for the water sounds."

"Tomorrow we'll try our hands at fishing." Devon gestured toward the deep, narrow galley sink, with its two faucets, one for fresh water from the boat's stores, and the other for raw water from the Gulf. "In the meantime, we can toss a coin to see who cooks and who washes."

Valerie smiled and closed the refrigerator door, not quite meeting his eyes. "I'll cook. You're the one who knows all about those little pedals on the sink."

"I'll show you how they work," he promised. "Go rinse off, Val. I need to make a couple of phone calls."

Valerie went gratefully, closing her cabin door behind her as she gave way to the two tears that had been swimming in her eyes since they had left the water.

How could she have been so stupid? she wondered. It just went to show—the nineties woman wasn't as smart or as liberated as she'd like to think.

Still, she had managed to hang on to her dignity, and Devon had no idea she realized he didn't really want her. That ought to be worth something over the next few days. Surely he didn't intend to stay out here with her for much longer. At least she hoped not. Torture wouldn't be the word to describe it.

She stripped off her bathing suit and stepped into the small shower, where she rinsed her hair carefully. No telling what salt water would do to her bleached hair. It wouldn't do to turn up for Shelby's next tour with green hair.

After the shower, Valerie dressed in a loose cotton blouse and a pair of old jeans. There was even a blow dryer on the small dressing table, which helped her outlook considerably. She'd face Devon looking as together as she possibly could.

Devon had no idea he had to be faced. He had showered and dressed in a pair of jeans and a T-shirt, and was standing before the open refrigerator.

He looked up and smiled when she entered the galley. "Come help decide what to eat first," he invited.

"I'll cook you a steak," she said, reaching for the package of sirloin steaks.

Devon dropped a kiss on the top of her head as she leaned down. "How about broccoli and my favorite cheese sauce."

"Fine," Valerie said in strangled tones.

If he kept doing things like that, her new resolve to treat him in a friendly, sisterly manner would never last.

Devon grabbed a bunch of broccoli and took it to the sink. "Want to see how to operate it?"

"What's the little pedal for?"

"That's for pumping in seawater from the Gulf. We use it for washing dishes and almost any other task except the final rinse. I'm going to use it to wash the broccoli."

She watched as he operated the small hand pedal beside the tap. Fortunately, everything else in the galley had its equivalent in her kitchen at home. Valerie wasn't at all sure she'd remember when to use raw water and when to use the boat's stores of water.

Valerie broiled the steaks in the galley stove, which operated like a regular oven. It was easier to behave normally while engaging in everyday tasks like cooking.

Devon reached into the cabinet and brought out a can of cheese soup.

"What are those little bars across the bottom of the cabinets?" she asked.

"They're called fiddles. They keep the groceries in place if we hit rough weather." He opened another cabinet and showed her an elastic cord stretching across that held some tall items in place. "That's a shock cord, and it does the same thing."

"I don't like the sound of that," she said, expertly flipping the steaks.

"Don't worry. According to the weather reports, the Gulf is behaving just the way a vacationing couple on a luxury yacht would have it."

"I can hardly tell I'm on a boat," Valerie agreed.

They ate a meal of salad, steak, and broccoli with Devon's special cheese sauce at the dinette beside the galley, and Valerie kept staring out the dark windows at the points of light on the horizon that identified other boats.

"I can't believe this is a boat," she said again. "I feel as though I'm in a luxury trailer house."

"Flynn loves the water. He bought this boat so he and his wife could get away regularly."

"Must have cost the earth," Valerie observed.

"It did. Old Flynn could afford it, fortunately."

Valerie grinned at him. "Confess, Dev. You're thinking about buying one yourself."

"Rayburn Lawn Maintenance will have to quadruple its size before I can afford one of these."

"Trade up," Valerie suggested.

"You have great faith in my trading abilities." He laughed suddenly. "I'd forgotten about the time you put me onto that tractor. I was desperate in those days. I don't know if I'm up to that kind of negotiating anymore."

"Sure you are, Dev," she said in comforting tones. She stood and took his empty plate. "All you need is the proper mental attitude of wanting something badly enough. After a few days on this boat, we'll see how you feel about offering your bass boat as a trade-in on a forty-foot motor yacht."

Valerie carried the plates to the galley and stared doubtfully at the deep, narrow sink.

"You broiled the steaks so I'll wash up," Devon said.

Valerie obligingly stepped aside and watched as he used the raw-water pedal to wash the dishes. She seized a towel and dried the dishes, fighting the longing to wrap her arms around him and beg for his kisses.

A nineties woman didn't mind letting a man know she was interested, but she drew the line at making a pest of herself.

Valerie sighed and wondered if she should consider making one more bold effort at switching Devon's affection from Barbara to herself.

"What's wrong, Val?"

She looked up to find Devon's concerned gray eyes studying her face.

"Not a thing." She forced a smile. "I was just thinking about Mama and wondering if everything was okay with her. We left so suddenly, I forgot that I wouldn't be home when she arrived in Arkansas."

"There's a policewoman there to answer the phone. I've already checked with her. Your mother arrived safe and sound and has a room at the Hotel Camden if you'd like to call her."

"May I?"

"Of course. This boat has everything, including a television set if you're interested."

She wasn't, but it was nice to know entertainment was available if she got to mooning too much over Devon.

Devon showed her how to use the ship-to-shore telephone, and Valerie spent a few minutes talking to Meg, who didn't seem to realize Valerie wasn't at home. Valerie decided against telling Meg she was alone on a yacht with Devon. After all, it looked as though nothing would come of that circumstance.

When she replaced the telephone receiver, Devon had gone on deck. She debated a moment, then went up in search of him.

"Come sit down," he said.

He was sitting in one of the comfortable chairs in the boat's stern, which looked to Valerie like a patio. She took the chair beside him and stared out over the water.

It was a clear night, and without the interference of city lights or the moon, the sky seemed crowded with stars. Manmade lights dotted the horizon, pinpointing the locations of other boats, and the only sounds were from the lapping of the water against the boat.

"How do you like your first evening on a boat?" Devon asked.

Valerie injected her voice with enthusiasm. "It's wonderful, Dev. So quiet. Thank you for bringing me."

"What's wrong, Val?" he said quietly.

"Nothing," she said, too quickly. "I'm having a great time. I can't wait to try some fishing tomorrow."

"Valerie."

She didn't like the quiet, inflexible tone. She'd heard it before when he'd been determined to find out which of his employees had damaged one of his mowing machines.

Well, she wasn't an employee.

"Yes, Dev?"

"What's wrong?"

"Nothing's wrong," she said patiently. "Why should anything be wrong?"

"That's what I intend to find out. Are you worried about Meg?"

"Mama's having a great time. She's already got lunch and breakfast dates lined up with some of her old friends in Camden."

"Are you afraid of Jonathan Wade?"

"Well . . ." she said cautiously. "I'm not exactly thrilled to be the target of his obscene phone calls."

"That's why you're here," Devon said. "You won't be going home until he's caught."

"That could be a while. I don't think any boat is equipped to stay out that long."

"Oh, we can always put in for supplies," he said. His smile was in his voice. "So what's bothering you, Val?"

She had no intention of answering that. "It must be

subliminal. I can detect nothing on a conscious level that's causing me any concern.''

''Valerie.''

''Yes, Dev?''

''What's wrong?''

He had injected his voice with all the caring and concern that had grown between them over the years, and Valerie found that harder to resist than anything else he could have said.

''Nothing, Dev. Maybe I'm a little tired or something. I think I'll go lie down.''

If she didn't get away, she'd break down and tell him the truth.

Devon stood with her and slipped an arm around her waist. ''Let's have a look at the stars,'' he said, and guided her to the stern.

They stood staring up at the glittering arch of the galaxy, and Valerie focused all her attention on it in order not to read too much into Devon's warm hand at her waist.

She felt his other hand at her temple, fumbling with her glasses. He removed them, folded them, and tucked them into her hand.

''They're in the way,'' he whispered, and kissed her.

Valerie clutched her glasses and hoped she wouldn't crush them. With Devon's warm, mobile mouth exploring hers, his hair blowing in her face, and the woodsy scent of his aftershave surrounding her, she felt as close to heaven as she was capable of feeling on earth.

She wrapped her arms around him and held him close, letting him kiss her as he pleased without making any move to invite further attentions. The restraint needed was so great, she wondered how long she could hold out.

Devon's arms tightened around her, and he turned her so the wind would carry his hair to the side and out of her face.

He kissed her eyelids and both brows gently. ''You're so sweet, Valerie.''

Valerie could have screamed with frustration, but she controlled her tongue firmly. ''Thank you.''

Devon was silent a moment. "Do I detect sarcasm in that mellow voice?" he asked.

"I hope not," she said sincerely.

There was another silence while he tried to work this out. At last he said, "Val, you're enough to drive a man to swim fifty laps around this boat."

She forgot her resolve and retorted, "You're enough to drive a woman to do double that."

NINE

"Valerie, you still don't understand, do you?" Devon said softly.

"No, Dev, but I'd sure like to."

He sighed. "Come sit down."

"I was just beginning to really enjoy myself," she protested.

Devon grabbed her hand and pulled her toward the two chairs. "I'm beginning to see this boat idea was a big mistake," he said. "It's hard enough keeping my hands off you without all the encouragement you keep giving me."

"Has Mama threatened to shoot you or something if I wind up in your bed? Is that what all this noble restraint is about?" Valerie was inclined to be indignant.

"Look, Val, this isn't the way I wanted to do things, but with Wade running loose and terrorizing you, and Meg packing up and running off to Arkansas, I can't leave you home alone. My place is too accessible, and I can't make you clip hedges all day whether you like doing it or not."

Valerie followed him with difficulty, fastening at once on his first statement. "What are you trying to do, Dev?"

He was silent a moment. "I'm trying to keep you safe, both from Wade and from myself."

"Do I get to choose which of you I'd rather be safe

from?'' She leaned back in her chair and stared at the dark water surrounding them.

''While I was in Houston today, I stopped in at a gospel bookstore and picked up a copy of your album.''

She turned her head to look at him. All she could see were the planes of his face. His eyes and the position of his mouth were shadowed.

''And?'' she asked.

''I mentioned you to the clerk. Did you know almost everyone in that store knows of you?''

Baffled, she said, ''Well, I expect they have. Anyone frequenting a gospel store is most likely into gospel music.''

''Is that it?'' His smile was in his voice. ''Here I was thinking you were a big celebrity. Are you trying to tell me you aren't?''

''What if I were?'' She studied his relaxed posture and longed to leave her own chair to sit in his lap. ''Is that the point of whatever you're trying to say?''

''The only point I'm making is that you are obviously getting to be well known. Correct me if I'm wrong, but it seems to me that you're on the verge of having your career really take off.''

''I think so,'' she said cautiously. ''That's one of the reasons I came home for a month. I wanted time to think it over and see if this is really what I want.''

''And is it?''

''Dev, I need to clip a few more extra-long hedges, and maybe mow a yard or two before I can answer that. I've only been home three days, and clipped two hedges.''

Devon chuckled. ''It's a good thing I'm in a position to furnish you with hedges.''

''So what has my career, or lack thereof, got to do with your irritating restraint?''

''Irritating restraint,'' he repeated, and laughed. ''I have a feeling that anything I say will be used against me. I hereby refuse to answer that question.''

''Dev.''

''Val, I'm tremendously attracted to you, but it wouldn't

be fair to take advantage of this situation to make love to you.''

''Who says?''

''I do. So just relax and let me kiss you every now and then. If I kiss you too much, I'll forget all my good resolutions.''

''Am I being too pushy for you?'' she asked, with deceptive meekness.

''Actually, I love the nineties woman,'' he said. ''It's just that this is an unusual situation.''

Valerie didn't see that it was at all. ''What you mean, I suppose, is that I'm Barb's little sister,'' she said.

''That is not what I mean,'' Devon said, an edge to his voice. ''Get it through your head that Barb has nothing to do with this.''

''I know she accused you of . . . of having the hots for me,'' she said, eyeing the light on the horizon.

''Who told you that? Never mind. It's true she accused me of wanting you. Didn't she accuse you of making a bold play for me?''

''Yes.''

''Was it true?''

''No. At least it wasn't true that I was deliberately trying to let you see my breasts.'' She added scrupulously, ''But it is true that I did everything I could to further your business and learned to clip hedges so I could impress you.''

''Barbara was striking out blindly. She was furious with me, and she had the feeling that if she didn't break up with me first, I was going to break up with her.''

Valerie clasped her hands in her lap and kept her eyes on the horizon. ''Would you have?''

''Yes. I'd realized I could never be happy with her. She wanted me to be something I didn't want to be. I was fed up with her constant criticism of my business and let her know it. That's when she laid into me about you.''

''I went to Fort Worth because I knew I had to get out of her way,'' Valerie said in a low voice. ''Whatever happened between you had to happen without my complicating things.''

"Believe me when I say it would have happened despite your presence. At any rate, Barb has nothing to do with us now. I haven't seen her in two years.''

Valerie was silent a moment, staring at the water. She turned to face him. "I suppose you're asking me to cool it, right?'' she asked.

He laughed. "That's crudely put, but, yes.''

"Dev, you ought to win some kind of award for your behavior. When I decide what it is, I'll let you know.''

She deliberately kept her voice light and humorous. It was too humiliating to confess to herself that she was guilty of chasing a man who didn't want to be chased.

Devon chuckled, and she heard the relief in his voice.

"Make it the Gentleman of the Year award,'' he said, which was extremely polite of him. He wanted to let her think he was avoiding her for her sake, but she wasn't fooled. She obligingly began talking about her garden and sat chatting lightly with him until she began to yawn.

"You'd better go to bed,'' he said, smiling at her. "We can get an early start in the morning and catch a few fish for lunch.''

Valerie went below deck to her cabin and shut the door behind her with relief. How she was going to project friendliness and sexual disinterest during the next few days toward the man she was so eager to seduce, she had no idea.

She changed into her nightgown and turned down the covers on the double bed. Sleep would probably elude her. At least her surroundings were perfect to stay awake in.

During the night, she awakened from a dream and left her bed, disturbed. Pulling on her robe, she settled her glasses on her nose and went through the sitting room and galley and climbed the stairs to the deck.

The moon had risen and laid a silver path across the water to the boat. It gave the illusion she could climb over the deck rail and start walking.

"Don't try it,'' Devon said from behind her.

"Why not?" she said dreamily.

"Because I don't want to have to get the dinghy out to fish you from the water."

"Don't be so matter-of-fact. It's depressing."

"What aren't you asleep?"

"I was. Bad dreams."

"Of Jonathan Wade?"

She couldn't think of a good way to tell him she'd dreamed of him kissing Barbara while she watched.

"I don't remember," she said. "It was just bad. Did I wake you?"

"No, I was awake and heard you stumble in the companionway."

Great. That underscored her clumsiness.

"It's very soothing out here, isn't it?"

Devon slipped an arm around her waist and pulled her against him. "I wouldn't say that, precisely."

Valerie shut her mouth firmly on the words she wanted to utter. She'd take anything he offered, she decided, and damn her pride. Perhaps if she made no moves toward him, she wouldn't scare him off.

Devon was rubbing her upper back soothingly while cradling her head in the hollow of his shoulder. Valerie sighed and accepted his comfort in the spirit it was offered.

She opened her eyes to find him staring at her in the pale light of the moon. She stared back and made no movement toward him

"Val, have I hurt your feelings?" he asked wistfully.

"No, Dev." She let her lashes drift shut, so as not to reveal herself.

She felt his lips brush hers lightly and forced herself to remain still. This was when the nineties woman would lock her arms around his neck and kiss him for all she was worth, she reflected with humor. Well, she'd try imitating a sixties woman. Perhaps Devon would prefer that.

It seemed he did. He pulled her deeper into his embrace and kissed her in earnest, parting her lips gently and pressing her breasts against his chest. Valerie sighed and relaxed, letting him do as he pleased.

"I have hurt your feelings," he said.

She opened her eyes. "I promise, you haven't."

"Val, you liar. Take this, and this."

He kissed her again, then once more, and Valerie, delighted, rested in his arms and took it.

The nineties woman would have said, "Can I take some more?" Valerie cast around in her mind for what the sixties woman would say.

She settled for, "Dev, you're mean," and shoving in a halfhearted way at his chest.

That should have resulted in an attempt on his part to kiss her some more. Instead, Devon burst into laughter and backed off when she aimed a fist in his direction.

"I never know what you're up to," he complained. "It's getting very nerve-wracking."

"I don't know what you're talking about," Valerie said with dignity.

"You appear to have switched tactics," he said.

Valerie sniffed, shrugged, and turned back to the rail to stare once more at the moon. Admit nothing, she adjured herself.

Devon stepped close once more, swept her hair aside, and kissed the back of her neck.

"Someday you'll appreciate my efforts," he said.

She couldn't stop herself. The words popped out before she could restrain them.

"No time soon, Dev," she snapped.

Devon broke into unrestrained laughter, and Valerie seized the opportunity to flee back to her cabin, fuming. Sixties womanhood was fine, but a nineties woman had a tough time maintaining the act for any length of time. Apparently you had to be reared during the appropriate period in order to perform naturally.

She arose the following morning with new resolve and marched militantly to the galley. The sun was just moving above the horizon, and Devon had long been an early riser.

He was on deck, dressed only in a pair of shorts. Valerie paused in the companionway and admired him. His shoulders were broad and well muscled, and his tan was dark and uniform, showing each muscle as he leaned on the deck rail. Even his legs were tanned and muscular, and the dark hair covering them served only to make her want to run her hands over every inch of his body.

"Listen, Dev," she announced when he turned and saw her. "This is the way it is."

Devon grinned. "Uh-oh."

"I want you, okay?"

"Okay."

"But for whatever reason, you don't want me."

"Val—"

"Just shut up and listen, Dev . . . Therefore, I have decided to stop encouraging you to kiss me or . . . or anything else. I hate rejection, and I don't see why I should keep on asking for it. For the remainder of the time we stay out here, we're going to behave like the good friends we are. Got that?"

"Am I allowed to say a word on my own behalf?" he asked meekly.

Valerie considered. "I probably shouldn't allow it, but go ahead. It won't change anything, unless you intend to give in."

She looked hopefully at him.

Devon shook his head. "I don't mean to tease you, Val. It's just that I can't resist kissing you."

Valerie rolled her eyes. "I'm going to have to remember this conversation so I can tell Mama. It'll go perfectly in her new book."

"Do I sound that idiotic?"

Valerie nodded, grinning. "Mama told me how girls used to be called teases."

Devon eyed her. "If you call me a tease . . ."

Valerie shook her head with silent amusement.

"Look, Val, let's just have a good time on this boat

until Jonathan Wade is caught, okay? You need a vacation and I need a vacation, so let's have one.''

"That's what I came to tell you, Dev." She smiled and turned to go back to the galley. "So what do you want for breakfast?"

Devon followed her to the galley, but he wisely swallowed whatever he'd been about to say.

He watched as she fried bacon and eggs. He showed her how to use the pyramidal metal structure that served as a toaster, then sat with her at the breakfast table chatting lightly.

After he had washed the dishes while she dried, he showed her how the sockets at the stern of the boat worked to hold fishing poles.

"Want a morning swim before we do some fishing?" he asked.

Valerie decided on the swim. Heavy exercise, she reflected with grim humor, had been the antidote for sexual frustration for centuries.

She began at once to swim laps around the boat.

"What do you think you're doing?" Devon asked, trying to keep up with her.

"Laps," she said. "I figure fifty should do it."

"Fifty!" He stared and laughed. "Maybe I should do a hundred."

He swam beside her, and his words couldn't help but bring a warm glow to her heart. She swam until she was utterly worn out.

It didn't work.

She climbed back aboard and tested herself by putting on her glasses and scrutinizing Devon's tanned physique. She still longed to run her hands over every inch of his smooth, warm skin and to follow her hands with her tongue.

Devon appeared unaware of her regard. He dried himself off and smiled at her.

"Let's do some fishing," he said.

That was the way things went for the next three days. They awakened early every morning and swam laps around the boat. Valerie ceased teasing him or chasing him, since she might catch him. Then Devon retracted the anchor and she baited the poles, and they trolled for fish. When they caught something, she watched while Devon cleaned and dressed it, then she wrapped it in tin foil and cooked it.

During the afternoon they swam, lay on the deck in the sun, or talked. After supper, they sat on deck and watched the stars as they talked. Being Devon's companion was sweet, and she almost felt ashamed of wanting something more.

Valerie was more and more conscious of an almost unbearable longing to lie in Devon's arms and savor his kisses while she touched him and felt him touching her.

She had discovered a box of books and magazines in her cabin, which helped when she couldn't sleep. Not sleeping, despite the soothing sounds of the water and the gentle rocking of the boat, was becoming a nuisance.

If she left her cabin to go on deck, Devon often heard her and joined her, and that made everything worse. When she returned to her cabin, she was tense with the desire he aroused in her by simply being there.

On their fifth night out, Valerie awakened from a light doze and sighed with frustration. She was wide awake, and knew it would be several hours before she returned to sleep. She tied her robe about her and went on deck quietly. Perhaps by going barefoot, she could sneak past Devon.

"Val?"

He stood waiting for her at the boat's stern, wearing a pair of jeans and nothing else. Valerie checked, then walked toward him and stood looking at the lights of an ocean-going vessel headed for Galveston. Overhead, the moon had set and the stars were like glitter spread across black velvet with a heavy hand.

"I suppose this boat is so restful, I can't use any more sleep," she said.

"Maybe that's it. I can't sleep, either," he said. He turned from the rail and leaned against it, looking at her.

Valerie tilted her head back, enjoying the way the breeze lifted her long blond hair and ruffled it around her face. She closed her eyes, savoring the gentle tickle of the wind on her scalp.

Devon apparently figured out what she was doing, because she next felt his fingers at the back of her scalp. He massaged the back of her head and neck with the tips of his fingers, causing her to lean forward to give him greater access.

"Dev, you're wonderful. If I could fall asleep right now, I believe I'd sleep forever."

"Would you? I wouldn't."

She felt his fingers pluck her glasses off her nose and tuck them in one of the big pockets on her robe. Then he cradled her in his arms and stood there just holding her, making no move to kiss her.

Valerie scarcely dared to move. She brought one hand up cautiously and rested it on his chest, sighing her pleasure, and tested the resilience of the springy mat of hair covering his chest.

"To heck with it!" Devon said, and took her face between his palms.

She blinked at him. "To heck with what . . . ?" she began, but her words were stopped by the sudden descent of his lips.

Valerie allowed him instant access to as much of her body as he wanted. She felt his arms around her tremble and tried to move closer.

Beneath her fingers, his shoulders were warm and strong and smooth with muscle, and after testing them thoroughly, she moved on to explore the muscles of his back. They were hard and tight, moving as he moved, and she flattened her palms to better feel his actions.

His body pressed against hers so that she could feel the heat radiating from him, and a shift in his position caused the breeze to waft the scent of his favorite aftershave to her nostrils. Everything added up to inform her that the man in her arms was Devon, whom she loved, and she promptly forgot her resolve to let him set the pace.

She dug her fingernails into his back and kissed him for all she was worth, whimpering when he responded with a shudder and an answering groan.

"Valerie," Devon whispered, and slipped his hands around to cover her breasts, massaging them through the light fabric of her robe and nightgown.

When she leaned back slightly to give him better access, he unbelted the robe and slipped it off her shoulders. It fell unheeded to the deck, and he stared at her, shivering.

Valerie stared back. He was well within her focus, and she studied the taut face and blazing gray eyes, visible in the light from the companionway. His expression awakened something in her as fierce as what she saw in his face.

She ran both her hands down his chest and let her nails trail lightly over him.

The touch was incendiary. Devon shuddered, groaned, and lifted her off her feet to lay her on the deck. He stretched out beside her, cradling her head in one hand and smoothing the other down the nylon fabric of her nightgown.

Valerie locked her hands behind his head and pulled him down for another kiss. At last it was happening, she thought dizzily, riding on waves of desire. Devon was hers, and he was responding to her in all the ways she'd dreamed of for the past few nights.

He stroked his hand up and down her body while she kissed him, and she welcomed his touch.

When the kiss ended, he looked almost like a man undergoing torture. He raised his head and stared at her. Whatever he saw drove him on. He took his hand from beneath her head and used both hands to ease the nightgown down over her shoulders, baring her breasts to his gaze.

Valerie lay still and let him look his fill, pleased that he obviously found her beautiful.

She had never known anything like the incredible pleasure that flooded her when he touched her with exquisite tenderness, then let his lips taste where his hands had been. She gasped and moaned, an animal sound that caused him to intensify his caresses until she thought she would go mad with pleasure.

Her nails dug into his shoulders and her back arched almost involuntarily as she tried desperately to hold him in place so he'd continue the exquisite torment.

Devon was trembling also, and feeling his desire caused hers to increase to almost unbearable limits. His entire body was hard and taut. She lifted toward him, begging him silently to bring his caresses to their natural conclusion.

"Valerie, you're so beautiful," he was whispering, raising his head to stare at her.

Valerie opened her eyes and stared at his face. He was partially in the shadows, but she could see the intense blaze of his eyes. The pale light from below highlighted the planes of his face to make him look as taut as he felt to her.

She gasped and managed to say, "So are you, Dev."

She had managed to free her arms from the nightgown, but it had bunched up around her waist. She struggled to ease it from beneath her hips.

"Oh, don't, Valerie," he said, and suddenly buried his face against her neck.

He trapped her hands with his and held them, shaking all over.

Valerie stilled. "It's bunched up and annoying me," she said softly.

"Better let it keep on annoying you," he said, on a choked laugh. "Maybe it will take your mind off killing me."

Valerie sighed, knowing he was trying to ease the tension between them.

"Kiss me again, Dev," she invited, without much hope.

"I don't dare kiss you again. If I do, I'll wind up making love to you."

"What's wrong with that?" she asked reasonably. "Are you afraid I won't respect you in the morning?"

The tumult in her body was making her irritable, and

she wondered what he would do if she simply rolled him over and began doing to him what he'd just been doing to her.

She made a movement to try it, but Devon flung one leg over hers and held her still.

"Don't, Val."

He said nothing else, merely holding her until his shivering began to ease.

Valerie longed to jerk a handful of his hair out for a moment.

"Now I see why high school boys used to get so mad at their girlfriends," she said.

"I'm sorry, Val. I didn't mean for this to happen."

"Dev, I hate to say this, but you're driving me crazy. I want to go home."

"Don't talk. Just lie still and let me hold you. You'll feel better in the morning."

"I doubt it," she muttered. "I'll probably feel like a damn fool."

But she continued to lie in his arms, savoring his warmth and scent and the fact that it was Devon in her arms. She wrapped both arms around him and wished she could melt her body into his.

Later, he helped her sit up and drew the nightgown gently back up over her shoulders. She'd begun to feel chilly as her heated body cooled down, and she actually welcomed the comforting warmth of her robe as he withdrew his touch.

"I'd better go to bed," she muttered, not looking at him as she set her glasses on her nose.

"I'll tuck you in," he said firmly, and followed her down the companionway.

Valerie said nothing. She shrugged off her robe, laid her glasses on the bedside table, and climbed back into bed. Devon became a blur, which at the moment suited her perfectly. The sight of his chest and arms reminded her too vividly of the way they'd felt beneath her curious fingers just minutes before.

Devon sat on the side of the bed and smoothed her tumbled hair back from her face.

"Go to sleep, Valerie," he said softly. "We'll talk in the morning."

Valerie gazed up at his hazy image and decided to make one last effort.

"You can climb in with me, you know," she said, smiling faintly.

Devon laughed. "I know. Don't tempt me."

Valerie sighed and closed her eyes to block him out. "Go away, Dev. You're torturing me."

He chuckled and kissed her mouth lightly. "Go to sleep. Tomorrow you can swim a hundred laps and make me cook all the meals."

She heard him leave the room, switching off the light as he went, then opened her eyes to stare at the porthole on the wall of her cabin. The sky had lightened, which meant dawn was on its way. Surprisingly, she fell asleep within minutes of closing her eyes.

Valerie awakened late in the morning and arose swiftly, feeling almost guilty.

Devon was waiting for her. "Are you still mad at me?"

"You are now number one on my kill-on-sight list," she informed him. "Better watch turning your back on me today."

He laughed and grabbed her around the waist. "Good. In that case, I may as well be shot for a sheep as for a lamb."

With that, he tossed her overboard, ignoring her indignant shriek as she clutched her glasses.

She hit the water with a loud splash and yelled up at him, "Dev, if my glasses sink to the bottom of the Gulf, guess who gets to get out the scuba gear and find them?"

Devon leaned over the deck rail and laughed at her. "I'm giving you a head start on your hundred laps today. Give me your glasses and get going."

Valerie made a face at him and handed up her glasses. Then she took off around the boat, swimming for all she was worth.

Devon had been right. She felt much better this morning than she'd thought possible after last night, but she knew it wouldn't take more than a kiss to bring all her desire to the surface once more.

Several laps later, Devon followed her into the water and swiftly caught up to her.

"Slow down," he called. "I can't keep up with you."

Valerie attempted to speed her pace. That was a laugh. He was in ten times better shape than she was.

He caught her foot and brought her to a seething halt.

"Dev, that isn't a good idea just now," she warned.

He retained his hold on her foot. "I just caught a bulletin on the weather station," he said. "A tropical depression just popped up in the middle of the Gulf."

Valerie stared around them. The sky was clear on all sides. The only clouds visible were the white, fluffy ones that promised a hot, clear afternoon.

"They're making it up," she said cheerfully. "This is June. We don't have hurricanes in June."

"Valerie, there's one brewing, and it doesn't care whether this is June or September."

"So, what are we supposed to do about it?" she asked, resigned.

Just when she'd gotten somewhat used to life on the boat, Devon was planning to return them to land.

"Do?" he repeated. "We're going to turn this boat around and make a run for shore, what else? Conditions are favorable for further strengthening, and you know what that means."

She did, as did anyone who lived on the Gulf Coast. In a day or two, the storm could be a full-fledged hurricane.

A thought struck her and she laughed. "I told you what would happen if I planted a garden. The plants will be drowned just as they're coming up."

Devon laughed with her. "You're a menace to the Gulf Coast."

"I suppose you want me to climb aboard and start packing, right?"

"Right."

She jerked her foot from his hold. "*After* I finish my laps," she called back, swimming strongly.

She felt better for the small act of defiance. She'd need those laps if this was truly the end of their idyllic vacation.

By the time she climbed aboard, Devon had prepared to retract the anchor. She located her glasses lying atop her towel, set them on her nose, and went to watch him.

"Aren't we running a little scared here, Dev?"

"I don't like the sound of those reports. It's just to the south of us, and could make landfall in a couple of days. I've already put in a call to Flynn. He'll meet us at the marina so he can see to securing the boat."

"Cheez," Valerie muttered, and headed down the companionway to her cabin.

On the way, she stopped off at the nook in the sitting room where all the radio equipment was kept and listened to the reports that were constantly playing.

Devon was right. They didn't sound promising.

She prepared breakfast while Devon got the boat underway, and carried a plate of bacon, eggs, and toast up to the cockpit. At his urging, she gingerly took the wheel while he ate, and soon was enjoying the feel of the powerful boat transmitted through the wheel to her hands.

They arrived at the marina before noon, and a tall, blond man met them at the dock.

Valerie tossed him a line, and he secured it, calling, "I see now why Dev was so eager to rent my yacht at any price. Why didn't you simply take off for Bermuda, old buddy?"

Devon had cut the motor and descended rapidly from the cockpit. "The damn thing would follow me for spite," he said, joining Valerie on deck. "Do you want me to toss the other lines, or are you going to move the boat."

"I'm going to move the boat," the blond man said, grinning at them. "I can't take chances with my yacht, you know."

"Yeah, sure," Devon said. "Val, this is the owner of this luxury yacht, Flynn Sutherland."

Valerie enjoyed her brief meeting with Flynn Sutherland, but all too soon she and Devon were heading back to Winnie. The interlude had been nice, but it hadn't led to anything, and she was no closer to Devon than she'd been before they left. The thought was most depressing.

When they pulled into the drive, a strange car was parked in the garage. Valerie regarded it suspiciously.

"It's the police, probably," Devon said. "They were going to monitor your phone."

"I thought you said they traced the calls to various pay phones in Houston."

Devon shrugged. "That's what they said this morning when I called in. Pack what you need for a stay at my apartment. I don't want you here alone."

More frustration, Valerie thought, with inward humor.

But when they unlocked the front door and walked into the house, it wasn't a policewoman who greeted them.

"It's about time someone showed up," a lilting soprano voice said. "Where the hell have you been, Val?"

The woman who appeared from the kitchen was small, blonde, green-eyed, and beautiful.

"Hello, Barb," Valerie said, without surprise. "Fancy meeting you here."

TEN

Barbara was wearing her favorite at-home outfit, a pair of khaki trousers, a starched, plaid shirt, and polished loafers. As usual, Valerie began to feel slightly creased and uncombed within a few minutes of greeting her sister.

Barbara's emerald eyes had gone immediately to Devon while Valerie was dutifully kissing her cheek.

"Well, Dev," Barbara said, "its nice to see you again. You look as fit and handsome as ever. Val, you'd better do something about that hair color. It doesn't look natural at all."

"It isn't supposed to," Valerie said, but Barbara had already lost interest.

Devon was standing politely near the door and made no move to come further into the room. Barbara came to him and put her arms around his neck, kissing him on the cheek when he swiftly turned his face aside.

"Hello, Barb," he said calmly. "Is this a banking holiday or something?"

"Oh, no! I'm just taking a leave of absence. After all, I haven't seen my little sister in two years, so I thought I'd spend a few days at home visiting." She appeared to remember she had a little sister and turned to Valerie. "Where's Mama?"

Valerie was toting the canvas bag she'd carried aboard

the boat. She set it on the floor. "She's in Arkansas researching locales for her book."

"That's the most ridiculous thing I ever heard of," Barbara said. "She wastes more money on those ridiculous books, and she hasn't made a cent beyond what she made on that one she sold years ago. It seems as though she'd realize it just isn't cost-effective—"

"What it does for her is far more important than any money she might ever make from it," Valerie interrupted. "It gives her purpose and a lot of pleasure."

Barbara's cupid-bow mouth tightened, but she said nothing. Valerie knew that expression.

Devon glanced at Valerie. "True," he said. "Everyone should love her job that much."

Valerie had no idea whether he meant that for Barbara or for herself.

Barbara had always been quick to adapt herself to circumstances.

"I'll go along with that," she said. "Mama loves her writing the way I love banking. Val, I'd have never guessed you'd go into singing on stage. After that time Daddy talked you into singing a solo at church—"

Valerie shrugged and interjected quickly, "That was a long time ago."

Barbara actually looked respectful. "I'd overcome a lot of terror for that salary myself."

Valerie grinned, recalling Barbara's youthful speculations about the starting salaries of various jobs. "It was quite an inducement," she said.

"There's a woman at the bank who has every album Shelby Winthrop ever did. She thinks I'm almost a saint because you're my sister," Barbara said. "Isn't that a laugh?"

It was. Valerie headed to the kitchen, almost doubled over with laughter.

Barbara stood in the doorway and watched her. "What's so funny?"

"I was just remembering how my seventh-grade teacher,

Mrs. McBride, was absolutely determined that I was a person of some kind of talent because I was your sister.''

"Well, of course you were," Barbara said. "No one knew it because you refused to participate in the stage stuff.''

Devon appeared behind Barbara, and his eyes went at once to the tape recorder still sitting on the cabinet. It was turned off, and he edged around Barbara to check it.

"What's that?" Barbara followed him.

"Val has been getting some threatening phone calls. The police think it may be Jonathan Wade.''

"Jonathan Wade? Well, for Pete's sake.'' Barbara looked stunned. "There was a piece on him in the *Chronicle* the other day. He's a suspect in a killing. God, Val, just think of that date you had with him!''

"I'm trying not to.''

Valerie opened the refrigerator after scowling at the new hurricane-tracking chart posted on the door. If it weren't for this stupid storm, she'd be back on the Gulf with Devon right now instead of standing in the kitchen with Barbara, feeling inadequate.

"Gosh, you were so lucky to get away. The others have all died.''

Barbara's lilting voice dramatized everything, Valerie thought, casting a sour glare at her sister.

"Oh, don't be so tiresome," Barbara said. "You know I didn't mean any of that stuff I said. I was just upset at the time and wanted to think you were up to something.''

"She was damn lucky to escape," Devon said grimly. "What has me worried is that Wade may think he has something to prove by killing Val. I'll call the police and see if they got anything on the caller.''

He dialed while Valerie extracted several cold drinks from the refrigerator. She gave one to Devon and offered another to Barbara.

Barbara took the can thoughtfully. "That's incredible. What makes Dev think Wade would do anything so stupid? It's bound to get him caught by the law.''

"Dev thinks Wade is beyond rational thinking," Valerie

said, repressing a shudder. "Wade is so disturbed that I got away and made such a fool of him, so to speak, that he feels he has to destroy me."

"Lord, Val! What an exciting life you lead." Barbara shrugged and turned away. "Well, you were always the brave one in the family, eager for new experiences."

Valerie stared, wondering where on earth Barbara had come by that idea.

Devon hung up the phone. "The police traced the calls to three pay phones in the same general area of Houston. Now they're concentrating on showing pictures of Wade to businesses in the area in hopes of finding where he's staying."

"So what am I supposed to do?" Valerie asked.

"They also said the caller figured out the policewoman they had answering the phone wasn't you. He's quit calling for the time being."

"Good," Valerie said, with heartfelt relief.

They wandered into the living room, where Barbara suddenly took note of the canvas bag Valerie had dropped there.

"Where have you been, Val?" she asked. "I got in last night, and there wasn't a soul around who knew where you were."

Valerie hesitated.

Devon answered quickly. "I borrowed a friend's boat and took her cruising on the Gulf. With Meg in Arkansas, she'd have been alone in the house."

Barbara didn't question how long they'd been gone. "Thanks, Dev," she said. "That was awfully sweet of you."

Valerie bit back a grin and debated making a caustic remark about her sister's sudden concern

Devon caught her eye and smiled faintly.

Barbara eyed them both narrowly. "Well, well," she said. "It took you long enough to make a play for my little sister, Dev."

Devon said nothing. He raised his brows and smiled as he sat on the sofa.

Valerie started toward the sofa, but Barbara was there first, so Valerie took the big arm chair across from the sofa. Barbara didn't sit touching Devon, but when she extended her arm along the sofa's back and tucked one perfect foot beneath her, the effect was one of closeness.

Valerie watched her sister, puzzled. Barbara was supposed to be happily married, but something in her attitude alerted Valerie.

Barbara, she soon realized, was trying to get Devon alone in a perfectly natural, friendly way.

Valerie sighed and sipped her soft drink. How did one compete with a beautiful, vivacious, socially perfect sister like Barbara?

Not on Barbara's terms that was for sure.

Valerie rose politely. "Dev, it's past time for lunch," she said. "I'll put something on to cook."

Devon rose also, although Valerie couldn't detect any sign of relief in his bearing. "We'll come to the kitchen with you."

Valerie took celery, green onions, bell peppers, and parsley from the refrigerator and chopped them swiftly, then sautéed them in oil. Barbara sat at the table and tried to engage Devon in conversation about his business.

After a moment's silence, Valerie asked, "How's your husband doing? I'm sorry I forgot to ask earlier."

Barbara gave a noncommittal reply, but Valerie realized at once that Barbara had no desire to discuss her husband. That meant poor old Harry was in the doghouse. Valerie recalled instances in the past when Barbara had behaved the same way when Devon's name was mentioned.

Valerie added ground meat, water, and chili powder, and shook her head when Devon offered to help. She'd have to trust that Devon knew what he wanted in a woman. If she tried to compete with Barbara, she'd only look foolish.

Barbara transferred her attention to Valerie. "Val, do you remember when Dev first started his business? How undercapitalized he was?"

Valerie glanced at Devon, who had propped his chin in his hand and was regarding Valerie thoughtfully.

"I remember when he started his business, but I didn't know he was undercapitalized," she said. She shrugged and sought for a way to avoid confessing she had no idea what undercapitalized meant. "I thought he did just fine."

"He did. That isn't the point. Dev, what you should have done was go to the bank and present a plan—"

"I tried that," Devon interrupted, grinning. "No reputable bank wanted anything to do with me. Then."

"You probably didn't prepare your plan correctly. I wish I'd known then what I know now. I'll bet I could have gotten you that loan."

"Dev was better off without a loan," Valerie stated. "Who could sleep at night knowing he owed all that money?"

Barbara clearly considered this not worthy of reply. She turned back to Devon and said, "What you need is a study to identify your competition. It will enable you to market your services—"

"I know my competition," Devon interrupted. "It's all those guys out there with lawn mowers."

"That's right," Valerie chimed in, stirring her stew. "The reason people hire a professional is that they don't want to have to worry every week about how the yard looks."

Barbara plunged into a discussion of the new IRS rules for the amortization of equipment. Had Dev taken full advantage of the IRS allowances?

It appeared he had. Barbara went on to point out certain other tax advantages he should investigate.

"I have an accountant who deals with all that," Devon said, in dismissive tones.

"Dev, you can't let an accountant do everything for you," Barbara said earnestly. "You're at the point now where you should consider investing your money."

"Is that so?" Devon asked. "Need some help with the food, Val?"

"It'll be done in a few more minutes."

"Dev, you really need to consider some investments," Barbara said.

"Why? Are you looking for new clients?"

"Of course I am. You'd be a big coup for me."

"Really? A guy who mows lawns for a living?"

This gentle mockery passed right over Barbara's head. Or, she was clever enough to ignore it. Valerie watched her sister's animated face, noting the sophisticated touches that had been added since Valerie saw her last.

The telephone rang, and Valerie cut slices of bread diligently. Barbara glanced expectantly at her, then went to the telephone herself.

"How do you like that?" Barbara said, replacing the receiver. "They hung up on me."

Devon stiffened. "That could have been him."

"Oh, don't be ridiculous, Dev. It was probably some lazy idiot who can't be bothered to check the number before he dials. Now, about your portfolio."

"What portfolio?" Devon glanced at Valerie, frowning. "Next time it rings, you'd better get it, Val. The line is still tapped. If it's Wade, he'll talk to you."

Valerie shivered. "I don't want him talking to me."

"I don't blame you," Barbara said. "Now, Dev, it's time you gave some thought to investing in the stock market. In the past two years, you've done very well with your company. You should be pulling in a tidy profit without having to turn much back into the business."

Valerie smiled. It looked as though what Barbara had once referred to as "unskilled labor," and "unfit for a man with brains," had now become dignified as "the business."

"Let me get some paper. I can show you how to invest your excess to get the best possible return. It's criminal to let your money sit in a savings account or even CD's these days. Wait till you see this."

"Wait until after lunch," Valerie said.

She turned to the cabinets and took out three plates, plunking them loudly on the table.

"This won't wait," Barbara insisted, heading for the living room.

Valerie shook her head. "Sorry, Dev. I tried."

Devon grinned. "Maybe I should listen to her and get rich. I have a feeling she knows all the tricks."

"I have a feeling she does," Valerie said grimly as Devon rose to help her set out silverware.

Barbara enlivened the entire lunch with her enthusiastic discussion of something called "return on assets," then launched into reasons why Devon should give some thought to incorporating. She remained at the table figuring on a scratch pad while Devon helped Valerie with the dishes.

Devon's pager sounded, and he went to dial the telephone while Valerie turned on the radio and acquired the latest coordinates of Tropical Storm Allie, the disturbance which had made it to tropical storm status and acquired a name in the process.

As Devon hung up the phone, she said thoughtfully, "It looks like this storm is going to turn into something after all. Conditions are favorable for further strengthening."

Devon came to look at the spot Valerie had plotted in red ink. "What direction is it moving?"

"North-northwest."

"Oh, Lord." He followed the projected track. "If it keeps on like that, it'll hit between Galveston and High Island. That means we'll get it. When do they predict landfall?"

"They don't, yet. They seem to think it's going to slow down and strengthen. If it should keep moving at this pace, it'll make landfall tomorrow night. Isn't that sickening?"

Devon straightened. "Worse than that. I'd better go to the office and start preparing."

Valerie looked at him hopefully, but he didn't offer to take her with him.

"You'll want to visit with Barbara," he said. "I'll be back tonight."

He left, and Valerie watched him drive off, suddenly feeling bereft.

"I suppose you realize I've left Harry," Barbara said.

"You've left him?" Valerie questioned, surprised.

Barbara shrugged and stared intently at the floor. "What else can I do? I found out he was having an affair."

"Oh, Barb. I'm so sorry," Valerie said, with genuine regret.

"Don't be," Barbara said angrily. "You'd say it was my own fault. I suppose it was."

Valerie glanced at her tense face and said nothing.

"You and Mama both warned me about trying to force a man into something he doesn't want to do. Well, it's too late now."

"Does this mean you're trying to get Devon back?" Valerie said quietly.

Barbara shot her a searching glance. "Would you let me have him? Don't answer that." She followed Valerie into the living room and threw herself on the sofa. "So you're now a big-time gospel singer. Don't those two conflicting ideas ever bump head-on in your mind?"

"What conflicting ideas?"

"Getting cozy with Devon and maintaining chastity. If you haven't been to bed with Dev yet, you'd sure like to," Barbara added shrewdly.

Valerie turned away. "I've always believed love is the greatest force in the universe," she said quietly, and went to the kitchen.

Barbara followed. "Val, I want to apologize for all those horrible accusations I made two years ago. I knew better all the time. It was just that I knew I was about to lose Devon, and I wanted somebody to blame."

"It's all right, Barb. It was a long time ago."

Barbara shrugged. "Don't be so forgiving. I was a bitch, and you know it. I had no right to accuse you of showing yourself to Dev after you'd just undergone such a terrifying experience."

Valerie nodded. "It was horrible, and you didn't help. At the time, Devon had no idea how I felt about him. I had hoped you didn't, either."

"A sister always knows, baby," Barbara said lightly.

"I didn't know, actually, but my subconscious mind sure picked up on all the signals and brought it forth when you threw yourself at Dev and he caught you."

Valerie smiled. "Did he catch me?"

"My conscious mind picked up on that," Barbara said dryly. "Give me a hug. That's better. I'm going to visit Mattie Cloninger. Can you believe the weight she's gained?"

When Barbara left, Valerie wandered over to the multi-band radio Meg kept on the kitchen counter and tuned it to the weather station. Since Devon had supplied her with the new tracking chart, she might as well keep up with the storm that had run them in off the Gulf.

She went out to her garden and inspected the tiny plants that were just beginning to appear above the soil, then went back and listened to the radio once more. It looked as though her garden was due for a more thorough soaking than it needed.

Barbara returned later in the afternoon, having discovered more town gossip in a few hours than Valerie had in all the time she'd been home. She spent the remainder of the evening catching Valerie up on the latest marriages and divorces of their friends.

Devon returned that night and stayed until nearly midnight, entertaining Barbara and making her laugh. When he left, he instructed them to lock themselves in the bedroom. Valerie considered asking him to sleep on the sofa, then decided against it. Clearly, he considered Barbara protection enough, although he called the sheriff for good measure and requested a regular patrol of the area.

He arrived the following morning and scanned the storm's latest position on the tracking chart with disgust. Allie had increased to nearly sixty-five miles per hour, and had temporarily slowed its forward motion. That meant it was likely to become a hurricane later in the afternoon.

"What are the two of you planning on doing this morning?" he asked.

"I'm visiting a few friends," Barbara said.

Devon nodded. "I'm a person short on one of my crews, Val. Want to trim some more hedges?"

Valerie changed into jeans and a cotton work shirt with alacrity. Hanging around the house alone wasn't her idea of a vacation, especially with Jonathan Wade still loose.

When she arrived back in the living room, Barbara was standing near Devon and leaning eagerly toward him.

Instantly Valerie's heart contracted. How many times in the past had she seen Barbara standing before Devon in that same way?

Devon's head was inclined toward Barbara, and Valerie wondered if his pose still held the old tenderness.

Barbara had said no more about the situation with her husband, nor had she said anything about making a play for Devon.

Valerie looked at Devon, devastating even in his jeans and plaid shirt, and wondered how any woman could resist making a play for him.

"Val, if you wouldn't mind, I'll drop you off in Fannett. You can join the same crew you were with a few days ago."

Valerie groaned mentally, then. "That'll be fine. I hope there are lots of hedges."

Devon chuckled. "There are. Karen came down with a summer cold the other day, which is why I'm short a person. Want to make a few extra dollars, Barb?"

"Running one of your mowers? Are you kidding? I'm a financial consultant. I'd mow my own foot or something."

"What does Mary say the storm is doing?" Valerie asked.

"She has her own sources of hurricane information," Devon said grimly. "It's her opinion that every time one of these little guys pops up in the middle of the Gulf, it makes a beeline for the Southeast Texas coastline. So far, she's never been wrong."

"I was wondering why you suddenly leaped into action," Barbara said brightly. "You never used to hang around the house when there were yards to be mowed."

"I *was* taking a short vacation," Devon said.

"You? A vacation?" Barbara exclaimed.

Valerie eyed her sister's profile with its charming, uptilted nose thoughtfully. If Barbara's husband was having an affair, perhaps Barbara was interested in having one with Devon.

She wondered if she was wise in allowing Devon to drop her off in Fannett at the large ranch with spreading, finickingly well-kept lawn. Perhaps she ought to insist on remaining with him. She wouldn't have put it past Barbara to follow Devon.

Devon was clearly counting on her help in speeding up his crew, however, so she climbed out and went at once to the truck for a gasoline-powered hedge trimmer. The long hedges would give her plenty of time to contemplate her stupidity, she reflected.

"Glad to see you again," the crew boss, Susan, said cheerfully. "We could sure use your help today. Karen's sick and Allie's on her way, so we're in deep trouble if we don't get ahead of schedule."

Valerie nodded. "According to my tracking chart, it's coming right this way. It's all my fault for planting a summer garden."

Susan spent a few minutes talking to Valerie, telling her the jobs that needed to be completed before the crew could move on to the next site. Valerie noted thankfully that nothing was said about her relationship with Devon. She was accepted as simply another member of the crew.

Her day was a busy one. She worked as rapidly as possible, since the entire crew seemed fired by the realization that a hurricane was likely to interrupt their schedule for the next few days.

"The boss is going to be proud of us," Pete Martinez said, as the sun set. "We completed every job lined up for today, plus all the last-minute jobs. Let's get started on something from tomorrow's list."

"Forget tomorrow's list," Susan said. "We've had it for the day."

Valerie recalled Devon's chief gripe about hurricanes, that everyone called and wanted his yard done *before* the storm hit. She smiled and said, "Maybe the storm won't come this way and we'll all make overtime."

"It'll come. Mary is always right." Pete rubbed the back of his head and looked thoughtfully at Valerie.

She sensed the comments he wanted to make and was thankful for his restraint. At present, she wasn't sure herself just where her relationship with Devon stood.

"You're mighty handy with that hedge clipper, Val, Pete said. "Where'd you learn to handle it?"

"Dev taught me years ago, when he first went into business," she said, hefting the machine into the trailer.

She climbed into the double cab of the big pickup truck with the two other workers. The sun was setting and they were all tired from the extra push they'd put into their work that day. Conversation lagged, as Pete and Susan seemed to be minding their tongues around Valerie.

Valerie was too tired to care. Despite the exercise she'd been getting from her laps around the yacht, she still wasn't conditioned to the work the way the others were.

She sighed and wondered whether Barbara could be induced to cook supper for a change.

"You look tired, Val," Susan observed.

"I am. All I need tonight is a hot shower, a supper I don't have to cook, and a soft bed."

"I understand old Dev's a good cook," Pete said slyly.

Valerie looked up and smiled. "Yes, he is."

Susan and Pete smiled back.

Valerie wondered what the night would bring. Devon had apparently abandoned his idea of taking her to his apartment. Now that Barbara had arrived, he seemed to be relying on her to protect Valerie.

"Valerie, would you mind taking off your glasses?" Susan said softly. "I'd like to see your eyes."

Valerie removed her glasses and looked toward Susan, who was now a colorful blur in the center of her vision.

"Pale green," Pete said. "Unusual."

"How lovely," Susan agreed. "No wonder the boss is taken. Poor Karen couldn't believe her eyes when he kissed you last week. She was going crazy until she found out you were the legendary little sister."

Valerie put her glasses back on and the world returned to focus. She had no idea what to say to this.

Pete grinned lazily and stretched out his legs. "She could bear it once she knew you were the boss's lost love."

"I'm not Dev's lost love," Valerie said. She felt the heat rising in her face. "I'm not so sure I'm his love, period. It's too soon for that."

"Time will tell," Susan intoned. "I'd say you're off to a good start."

When the truck pulled up at Devon's office, a small, tin building on the outskirts of the western suburbs of Houston, Valerie was feeling less tired. She noted Devon's Cherokee parked in the small, shell-covered lot at the rear of the building.

They piled out of the truck and went to the office, where the regular employees received instructions for the next day's work from Mary, the dispatcher and Devon's right-hand-woman.

"Assuming Allie goes to Corpus or Louisiana," Mary qualified. "It won't, so don't bother listening too closely to anything I'm saying."

Valerie listened, and wondered if she'd be trimming hedges again tomorrow.

The big painting of mallard ducks on the wall was the only decorative touch in the crowded, threadbare room, but to Valerie it had the grace of timelessness. Everything was exactly the same as she remembered, from Mary's home-style desk of ratty-looking books that nevertheless kept track of every job and every client, to the big, cork hurricane tracking chart Mary kept on the wall beside her.

The others dispersed, and Valerie went toward Devon's small office. A smaller painting of shoveler ducks hung on the wall opposite Devon's neat desk.

He wasn't there, and she turned away, baffled, until she remembered the small shed behind the building where he kept his pickup truck parked.

Stepping to the small window, she peered out. Two more vehicles had pulled in beside Devon's Cherokee.

Devon stood beside his truck as if he'd just slammed the door shut, and Barbara stood close beside him. Her BMW was parked next to Devon's pickup. As Valerie watched, Barbara appeared to be pleading with him.

Devon shook his head and turned away, but Barbara was insistent. Finally Devon turned back and spoke at length, still looking adamant.

Barbara moved close and wrapped her arms around his neck, pulling his face down for a kiss.

Valerie froze, conscious of a pain in the vicinity of her heart that seemed likely to double her over. How many times in the past had she caught glimpses of Devon and Barbara in just that pose?

Devon's hands clasped Barbara's waist, and he leaned back out of her reach. He said something, looking stern, and Barbara stretched out her hands, pleading with him.

Devon suddenly grinned and threw an arm around Barbara's shoulders, hugging her lightly as he marched her toward the front of the building.

Valerie stepped back from the window with a gasp and slipped her hands beneath her glasses to press them against her eyes.

It did her no good to lecture herself that Devon hadn't kissed Barbara.

He had also refused all Valerie's best efforts to make love to him.

Valerie had come to know Devon well over the years, and one thing she knew was that he had a rigid code of honor. If he still cared for Barbara, but had been passing time with Valerie, he would first break with Valerie before he pursued Barbara.

No wonder Devon had resisted making love to her. He probably couldn't go quite that far in substituting her for Barbara.

ELEVEN

For once Valerie was thankful for the thick glasses that hid the pain in her eyes. She went quickly back into the dispatcher's office and seated herself in one of the chairs.

She had pride! she lectured herself. She'd never let on that Devon had broken her heart and made a fool of her.

She had dignity!

She had—nothing, she realized suddenly. She'd be lucky if she wasn't in tears before the evening was over. If she was wise, she'd get on the phone to Shelby and join the group again as soon as possible.

To heck with vacations.

She gripped her hands in her lap and clenched her teeth as the door opened and Barbara entered, followed by Devon.

"There you are, Val," Barbara said. "Are you ready?"

"Hold your horses, Barb." Devon headed for his office. "I still have a few things to check out."

Devon looked faintly cross and irritable. And why not? Valerie wondered. He now faced the unpleasant task of trying to let her down gently.

Barbara gave a long-suffering sigh and plopped down in a chair beside Valerie.

"What's the storm doing, Mary?" she asked.

"They're predicting a northeasterly turn because of high

pressure building to the west," the dispatcher said. "Mark my words, it's coming."

"A northeasterly turn would take it to Louisiana," Valerie managed, surprised that her voice came out sounding normal.

"*If* it turns northeast," Mary said. "It won't."

"Well, I think all this preparation for a storm that probably isn't coming is absurd," Barbara said. "I waited while Dev mowed five yards in Hamshire-Fannett."

Valerie pressed her lips together and lowered her eyelids to keep back the tears. Barbara wasn't even trying to pretend she hadn't followed Devon.

Devon came out with a sheaf of papers and bent over Mary's desk.

Valerie stared at his well-shaped backside and thought about what might have been. Once more, she had to squeeze back tears.

"Dev, poor Val is worn out," Barbara said impatiently, "and so am I, for that matter."

Devon glanced over his shoulder. "I'll be through in a moment." He smiled at Valerie. "How'd it go, Val?"

"Fine, Dev." She added, as a preparatory statement, "I had time to do lots of thinking."

He straightened, his gray eyes scanning her closely. "Are you all right? You didn't try to do too much, did you? I told Susan to see that you didn't overdo things."

"No, I did not," Valerie said irritably.

Devon eyed her sharply. "I'll take you home in a few minutes."

"I'll take you home now," Barbara offered.

Valerie discovered her pride was nonexistent. Given the choice, she'd ride with Devon any day just to be near him.

"I'll wait for Dev," Valerie said. "This chair is comfortable."

Devon eyed her. "Thank you. I'll try not to be long."

He still wasn't satisfied, Valerie saw. Every so often, she felt his eyes on her, checking her for any signs of exhaustion, but Valerie avoided catching his gaze by leaning back and feigning total relaxation.

Beside her, Barbara fidgeted and stared around the small office with the sort of bright interest that conveyed contempt.

Devon had gone back inside his office when Barbara said suddenly, "I'd have thought Dev would have a better office by now. This place looks as unprofessional as ever."

Valerie caught Mary's sidelong glance and recalled that Mary had been with Devon from the beginning and remembered Barbara's attitude toward Devon's business.

"What else does he need?" Valerie asked. "Dev likes to work with the men, you know. He spends so little time in that office, a mahogany desk would be wasted on him."

Barbara hunched an impatient shoulder. "He should have a good office for appearances. If he goes public, he'll have to look and act like a businessman."

Mary and Valerie exchanged glances.

"Is he going public?" Valerie asked.

"Yes!" Barbara said militantly. "He's ready to expand."

Valerie looked again at Mary and shook her head slightly. Mary turned away, satisfied. Barbara's insistence probably meant Devon was treating the matter exactly as he had Barbara's assertions that he was going into law practice.

Barbara was on her feet glaring at the large painting of ducks that graced one wall of the small office when Devon closed the door to his office and told Mary to go home.

Mary stood and picked up her purse. "I was just catching the latest coordinates," she said. "It's just sitting there. The winds are now up to seventy miles an hour." She stuck a push-pin carefully into the cork at the specified latitude and longitude.

Valerie got slowly to her feet. The storm aroused a slight bit of interest in her, and she asked Mary to write the coordinates down so she could plot them on her chart.

"Are you still keeping that stupid chart?" Barbara

asked. "Just turn on the radio. They'll tell you where it is. Radio stations love a hurricane."

"I like to plot them," Valerie said quietly, accepting the slip of paper from Mary.

She went back to her chair, sensing Devon's eyes on her but refusing to let him catch her eye.

"I was just thinking, Dev . . ." Barbara said slowly. "Do you know, these two duck paintings are the only decent furnishings in this office."

"Every furnishing in my office is decent," Devon said absently. He stared at Valerie.

"I'll look around for you," Barbara said, with great firmness. "If you want to make a good impression on investors, the office is everything in a business like yours. You should relocate—"

Devon snapped impatiently, "For the last time, Barb, I am not going public, and I am not relocating. For one thing, I don't need the money or the headache. For another, this office is located perfectly."

Barbara ignored him. "You haven't seen the deal I'll put together for you," she said. "Are you ready to go?"

Devon turned back to Mary. "In a minute."

"That man is impossible," Barbara said, sitting back down beside Valerie. "He could be a millionaire in five more years if he listens to me."

Valerie sighed. "You'll have to work on him."

"You bet I will," Barbara said, determined.

Valerie wondered how much leverage Barbara would be able to apply from a position in Devon's arms. To do him justice, Devon seemed as adamant about having Barbara interfere in his business as he ever had, but who knew how he'd react with his old lover back in his arms?

Valerie propped her chin on her hand and closed her eyes, suddenly depressed.

"You're tired, Val," Devon said, concerned. "I'll get you home right away."

Valerie started to protest, then gave it up. With Barbara leaping up at once, agreeing eagerly that poor Val was exhausted, who'd listen to her.

She caught Mary's sympathetic eyes on her and forced a smile. If she got through the next half hour, she'd be okay.

Devon hustled her out to his Cherokee and helped her in beside him. Barbara climbed into her own car without help. No doubt she was biding her time, giving Devon a chance to do things decently and with honor.

Valerie unlocked the door to her own house and sighed with relief. Perhaps she could claim total collapse and go to bed early. Devon showed signs of a man determined to find out what was troubling her.

Barbara headed at once for the bedroom, but Devon followed Valerie into the kitchen.

"Val . . ." he began softly. "What's wrong?"

She glanced up to find his gray eyes intent on her, and knew suddenly he wouldn't be satisfied with her story of extraordinary fatigue. Devon knew something had gone seriously wrong in her world, and he intended to find out what it was.

"Want a cold drink?" she asked and opened the refrigerator.

"No."

She turned and had to fight the urge to crawl into the refrigerator. He had come so close, he was crowding her. For once, Valerie didn't regard it as a golden opportunity.

When the telephone rang, she actually regarded it as a lifesaver and slid quickly around him to grab for it.

"Why, Shelby!" she exclaimed. "What on earth . . . ? Because I haven't been here, that's why. In an hour? I can't possibly make it. I have to have a shower, and my hair's a mess, and I haven't rehearsed, and—"

She fell silent, listening while Shelby pleaded with her to come instantly to a church in Houston, where a big gospel concert was in progress.

Valerie glanced at her watch, frowning. If she leaped in the shower, flung on a dress, and ran into no traffic trouble, she could just make it.

If she chose to do the concert, she could have a reprieve

from Devon's questions, at least for a few more hours. She wasn't ready to face him yet.

"All right, Shelby. I'll do it. Just don't say a word about my hair or makeup. Okay, okay, I'll be there."

She hung up and said, "Shelby's doing a concert in Houston, and she goes on in one hour, and both her replacement singers didn't come through."

Devon watched her. "Are you going?"

"Yes. Shelby's been a good friend to me, Dev. I can't let her down."

"Then go get ready. I'll drive you."

Valerie was in the shower before the reality of what he'd said hit her. If he was going to drive her, he'd have plenty of time to talk to her.

She dressed hurriedly in a plain white dress and stuffed her contact lenses into her purse. She twisted her hair up, pinned it, and dabbed on blusher.

Within ten minutes, Valerie was in the living room.

"I'm coming with you," Barbara said. "I've never been to a gospel concert before. It should be interesting."

"It'll be a whole new experience for you," Valerie said, detached.

Now that she was ready, it still didn't seem real to her, to be heading for a concert when her mind had been prepared for a vacation. Numb, she walked out of the house, scarcely aware of Devon's hand at her elbow or his concerned gray gaze fixed on her face.

"Are you sure you aren't too tired for this?" he asked.

"Yes."

"You worked hard today on those hedges . . ." he began.

"I enjoyed it," Valerie said, like an automaton.

Devon helped her into his Cherokee and stood looking at her, ignoring Barbara, who waited impatiently behind him.

"Val, you don't look right."

"Yes, I do. If Shelby wants long gowns, she's just going to have to provide one. I didn't bring anything home."

"That isn't what I meant." Devon gave it up and helped Barbara in.

Valerie rode in silence, hardly speaking unless spoken to, and then she had to have the remark repeated. She supposed that she was in shock. Two powerful emotions, betrayal and fear, must have canceled each other out.

Devon reached for her hand as he drove. "Your hands are like ice," he observed. "Val? I said, your hands are cold. What's wrong?"

"I have to sing," she replied, as if that explained everything.

"I know you have to sing," he said patiently. "That's why we're on the road to Houston after mowing every yard between Winnie and Beaumont today. What's wrong?"

"Val, are you trying to say you're still afraid to sing in front of an audience?" Barbara said suddenly. "Well, I'll be!" She leaned forward and addressed Devon. "When we were kids, she'd never sing in the choir, even though the choir director begged her to. She had a beautiful voice, but she was terrified of getting up in front of people."

"Val?" Devon said.

Valerie said nothing. She withdrew her hand from his and clasped both hands in her lap.

"One day Daddy talked her into singing a solo at church," Barbara went on. "She was deathly sick, but she made Mama drive her to church anyway."

"She was sick? With what?" Devon's voice was incredulous.

"Fear," Barbara said succinctly. "The poor kid was absolutely petrified. Daddy was fearfully upset with himself about it, but of course he praised her to high heaven for having done it after all."

"Good God," Devon said, almost whispering.

Valerie registered the conversation with a mind that was capable of registering without participating.

"Val?" Devon waited until her attention gradually focused on him. "Are you still afraid of going onstage?"

"I don't care for it much," Valerie said slowly, "but I manage."

"I'll bet you do," he said.

He sounded angry. Valerie wondered what she had said to bring about that reaction.

"I thought she had gotten over it," Barbara said, sounding astonished.

Devon knew where the church was and drove her straight there. Once the security men recognized Valerie as one of the Shelby Winthrop Quartet, they had no trouble getting to the hall where Sunday school classrooms had been converted to temporary dressing rooms for the singers.

"Rebecca! Thank God you made it! I was at the absolute end." A lovely brown-haired woman rushed up and wrapped Valerie in an enthusiastic embrace. "I'll never forget this."

Valerie tried to smile and return the hug without betraying her stiff numbness. "I'm glad to help out, Shelby. This is my sister, Barbara Kilgore, and our friend, Devon Rayburn. They helped rush me here on time."

"Go on in and get ready," Shelby said. "I'll make sure they get the best seats in the house. We go on in ten minutes."

Valerie turned toward the room Shelby indicated and was surprised to find Devon beside her as her hand went to the doorknob.

"Val, are you sure you're okay?" he said softly.

Valerie forced her eyes to meet his intense gray ones. "Yes. It's just that I've . . . never quite overcome the paralysis that strikes just about now."

Devon took her cold hands in his warm grasp and squeezed them. "When you get through, I'll buy you the biggest steak in Houston," he promised. "You have tremendous courage, Val."

Valerie blinked and lowered her eyes. Where did he get off saying that, when it ought to be obvious that she was about to perish with terror?

As she sat before the mirror inserting her contact lenses,

she tried to reflect, as she always did, on the things her father had told her just before she stood at the pulpit in front of the friendly congregation of her own church. Thoughts of Devon and Barbara kept intruding, and she wound up in a state of disorganized confusion.

Shelby rushed in with a long blue gown matching the one she was wearing and helped Valerie put it on, then she skillfully combed out Valerie's silver-blond hair. Valerie stared at the neat piles of children's Sunday school chairs in the corner and breathed deeply.

"Your young man is worried about you," Shelby said. She was a radiant woman with fluffy brown curls and large blue eyes. "I could hardly get him to sit down. He kept wanting to come back here and see about you."

Valerie's mind pushed that statement around in circles a few moments while Shelby braided her hair and pinned it up. At last she said questioningly, "Dev?"

"You're the one who should know his name," Shelby said reprovingly. "Now, Rebecca, you're going to do fine. Just get out there and support me. I need you! Think about helping me. I'll never forget how you dropped everything to come rushing over here like this."

Shelby, who genuinely loved her friends and went out of her way to encourage their spirits, chattered on in this vein while she applied more blusher to Valerie's pale cheeks and lipstick to her white lips.

"Your sister is very pretty," Shelby observed. "But she doesn't look happy."

"She isn't," Valerie said, still numb. "What are we singing? Do I need to rehearse? Where's the list?"

"Just follow my lead," Shelby said. "Maybe your sister will hear something in the music that will help her."

Valerie rose, conscious of a terrible dropping feeling in her abdomen that made her wonder if she'd left her entire middle on the bench in front of the mirror.

Shelby Winthrop was a natural performer who liked nothing better than getting out in front of an audience and ad-libbing. She could hardly wait to get onstage, and she seized Valerie's hand and pulled her along.

Valerie had learned to cope with Shelby by smiling constantly and looking as though she knew what was going on. The shell-shocked smile was on her face when Shelby pulled open the door to the small room.

Devon stood there, scanning Valerie's tense, smiling face. "Val?" he said. "Are you all right?"

Shelby smiled reassuringly. "She's fine, Devon. As soon as we get onstage, she'll be perfect. Just wait. You'll see."

Devon moved to clasp Valerie's shoulders. "You look lovely, Valerie."

He spoke gently but concentrated so much feeling into those simple words that Valerie blinked and looked at him.

"Thank you," she managed, dredging up the words from someplace deep inside her brain.

"I've been wanting to hear you sing," he said. "Do you think you could sing especially to me tonight?"

He had lowered his voice, and Shelby had discreetly dropped Valerie's hand and moved aside to give them privacy.

Valerie drew in a deep, quivering breath. More words popped into her mind, and she said, "Sure, Dev."

Devon smiled. "That sounds more like my Val. Pretend I'm the only one listening and we're on the pier fishing for crabs."

She felt his warm hands on her cold, bare arms and felt grateful for the caring she felt almost as radiant energy from him. A true smile quivered on her lips for the first time that evening.

"Sure, Dev," she said, lifting her face as naturally as she would to the sun.

Devon bent to kiss her, pressing his warm, generous mouth against her trembling lips, and came away with her lipstick gracing his face.

She looked at the red outline of lips slanting across his mouth and chuckled. Suddenly she felt that life might be worth living after all.

He grinned back at her and said, "Remember. I'm the only important person in the audience tonight."

Valerie had always considered audiences to be a single, living entity, an enemy that waited to devour her. No amount of coaching from Shelby, or self-help tapes or books had succeeded in banishing that concept.

When she walked onstage beside Shelby and the one other member of the Shelby Winthrop Quartet able to appear that night, she thought of Devon and drew courage from his image. It was almost like the Sunday she'd drawn courage from the image of Charles Dallas as he hovered in the wings near the pulpit the first time she'd sung before an audience.

The image helped banish the sick, quivering feeling that always attacked her before the group swung into its first song. She was able to concentrate on Shelby and follow her lead as she and the lone male singer backed Shelby in singing all Shelby's hits.

Shelby was a generous star, however, and always insisted that her back-up singers have their moment in the spotlight; several if they wanted. Soon she was passing the mike to Valerie, and the elaborate sound system rolled the background music for "Emanuel."

Valerie looked to the side and caught a glimpse of Barbara, who looked enthralled. Beside her, Devon stood with his eyes fixed on Valerie. Even though he hadn't showered after mowing five yards, he looked almost elegant in his jeans and plaid shirt.

Valerie stared at him, absorbing his erect carriage and the set of his broad shoulders that gave him a look of capability. She'd always found everything about him attractive, from his sun-bleached brown hair to his long, muscular legs, but this was the first time she'd paid special attention to the way he stood.

She almost missed her cue.

Shelby hissed, and Valerie jumped at once into her song, directing her words at Devon even as she faced the audience the way Shelby had taught her. Her voice gained power, and she actually began to enjoy sending the words out into the auditorium.

For the first time in the two years she'd been singing

professionally, she felt the audience's love. It was so unprecedented, she almost stumbled on her words.

She went smoothly into the third verse, and the words of the song seemed to speak to her, adding to her courage:

"The God who made all things to be,
   Who breathed this life in me."

She dwelled on those words even as she finished the verse and started the chorus:

"Emanuel, Emanuel,
   In Spirit and in truth.
Emanuel, Emanuel,
   In my life,
   In me."

It was such a successful rendition of the song, some of the audience joined her on the final chorus. By the time she reached the final words, everyone in the giant auditorium was singing with her.

Valerie left the stage, glowing with triumph.

Shelby embraced her the moment they stepped off the platform, saying, "Rebecca, I'm so proud of you! I told you audiences would love you if you let them."

Shelby's eyes had been following Devon, who was making his way through the stagehands and performers waiting in the wings.

She added, whispering, "He's very handsome. If you don't let me be in the wedding, I'll never forgive you."

Valerie opened her mouth to refute the idea that she was getting married anytime soon, then closed it as Devon reached them.

He smiled at Shelby then pulled Valerie into his arms and hugged her. "Val, you were wonderful. I was proud of the way you handled yourself tonight."

Valerie sighed with happiness and let her head rest on his chest. Then she caught sight of Barbara, who had been invisible behind Devon.

"You were beautiful," Barbara told her, with a sincerity that brought tears to Valerie's eyes. "Daddy would have been so proud."

Valerie fought back the tears and strove to remember that Barbara and Devon were probably going to get back together, even though Devon's arms were around her and not Barbara.

She managed to say, "Thank you," and hug her sister, astonished at the rush of love she felt toward Barbara.

Valerie changed clothes in the Sunday school room once more, conscious of a shift in her own inner feelings. She'd swung from devastation to numbness to intense emotion, which had yet to be identified. It felt like love, but it was mixed with triumph and a sense of controlling her own destiny at last.

She strove once more to convince herself that Devon was still in love with Barbara, but the more she thought about it, the more she realized she couldn't allow him to go back to Barbara.

Barbara had a husband already, even if he was unfaithful. She needed to work things out with him, or at least divorce him before she started running around.

And, no matter how Barbara tried to behave as though Devon was a potential business tycoon, her real feelings toward his choice of career came through.

No, Devon couldn't marry Barbara. It would be the biggest mistake of his life, and Valerie couldn't let him make it. She had to do something about it.

Hardening her resolve, Valerie removed her contacts and glared at her own blurred image in the mirror. If she had to, she'd work even harder at seducing Devon so she could force him to marry her.

Once she had him safely married to her, she'd not rest until he realized he was far happier married to Barbara's little sister rather than to Barbara.

Valerie stuck her glasses on her nose and eyed her image once more. She looked entirely different from the white-faced woman who had sat here earlier.

Devon and Barbara were waiting for her in the hall, and Barbara began chattering at once.

"Val, did you know you could become a star in the contemporary Christian music field? I was talking to Shelby Winthrop, and she says you're ready to go on your own now, and . . ."

There was much more, but Valerie tuned her out. Her soft green eyes sought Devon's gray ones, and they exchanged a long look as Barbara talked on.

"Let's go feed the star," Devon said.

"Yes, let's," Barbara agreed enthusiastically.

Before they could get away, a group of fans caught them and Valerie had to sign albums, Bibles, and programs. Devon and Barbara waited patiently for almost half an hour.

"Is it like this all the time?" Barbara asked.

"Gospel fans are very loyal and supportive," Valerie said. "They have a right to get to talk to you and have you sign their albums."

"I'm glad I got to see this," Barbara said. "Wait till I tell Mama."

In a quiet restaurant Valerie ate the steak Devon had promised her and listened absently to Barbara's chatter. Barbara was still inclined to discuss Devon's future incorporation despite a notable lack of encouragement from him.

Several times he smiled across the table at Valerie, but he didn't try to talk to her. How could he, she reasoned, with Barbara chatting determinedly about nothing?

By the time they were back on the highway heading for Winnie, racing clouds had obscured the moon and the formerly starry sky.

Devon said, "Uh-oh," and flicked on the radio.

Valerie listened with interest. "Looks like Mary was right again," she said.

"I can't believe this," Barbara said, disgusted. "This is June. Hurricanes don't strike in June."

"It *is* a hurricane," Valerie said, scrambling in her

purse for a pen. She recorded the new coordinates. "Eighty miles per hour already."

"Damn it all," Devon said. "That thing wasn't supposed to make landfall until tomorrow."

The report stated that Hurricane Allie was a minimal hurricane likely to strengthen a little more before making landfall during the early hours of the morning. Its current bearing would bring it ashore between Galveston and Port Arthur.

"That's us." Devon turned the radio down. "Looks like I'll have to secure the equipment barn tonight. Thank God we stored most of the equipment today."

"Need some help?" Valerie asked.

"You aren't coming out at this hour after everything you've done today." His voice was warm. "It won't take long. All I have to do is tape the windows at the barn and at the office."

"I can help . . ." Valerie began.

"I want you going to bed, Val. Don't argue. You were dead tired before you got Shelby's call."

Valerie said nothing about the real nature of her pretended exhaustion. She stared out the window as the first squall passed over and raindrops slashed sideways into the windshield.

"I'll drop you and Barb off first."

Valerie glanced at him and knew he intended to come back after he'd completed his preparations for the storm.

"You'd better tape that picture window in the living room, and move Meg's computer away from it," he added. "Better safe than sorry."

"A June hurricane," Barbara mused. "I wonder how it's going to affect the rice and soybean crops."

"I don't like this," Devon said, frowning out the window.

The rain was gusting in blasts that obscured his vision one moment and left it almost clear the next. A few minutes later the squall moved inland and the rain stopped.

Valerie eyed the trees lining the freeway as they

approached Winnie. The tree tops were waving wildly in the gusty wind one moment, and standing erect the next.

When they arrived home, Valerie said, "I'll make some coffee when you get through. You're liable to need it."

"I'm afraid I will," Devon said grimly. "Better get that window taped, Val. I'll be back as soon as I can."

He saw them inside and checked the house, then left quickly. Valerie watched him go, then stared at the sky. Bands of clouds were moving inland, signaling the approach of the storm.

She and Barbara worked quickly to tape the picture window, and Valerie moved Meg's computer to a safer place should the window shatter.

"I'll get some coffee going," Valerie said, heading for the kitchen.

Before she washed out the coffeepot, she carefully plotted the storm's most recent coordinates. As Mary had predicted, Hurricane Allie was heading directly their way.

The telephone rang, and Valerie leaped for it, expecting it to be Devon. It wasn't, and her blood congealed as she listened to a reiteration of her evil ways and what would be done about them very soon.

She slammed the phone down, not bothering to record the call. If the phone rang agin, Barbara could answer it.

It did ring again, just as she was washing out the coffeepot.

"Could you get that?" she called.

Barbara, lovely in red silk pajamas, picked up the telephone. To Valerie's surprise, she began carrying on a low-voiced conversation, walking to the kitchen door and standing with her back toward her sister as if to mute her words.

Valerie banged the coffeepot and ran water deliberately to show she wasn't interested.

Barbara's behavior after she hung up the phone was even more astonishing. She went to her bedroom, and the next thing Valerie knew, she reappeared wearing her khaki trousers once more and carrying her suitcase.

"Where on earth do you think you're going?" Valerie

demanded. "The weather's horrible and getting worse, it's past midnight, and a hurricane's coming."

"I have to go," Barbara said. "I don't care about the weather. Move, Val. I'm in a hurry."

"You can't go right now," Valerie insisted. "At least wait until morning, when the storm is past."

"I've got to go now," Barbara said. "Move."

"It's too dangerous . . ." Valerie began.

"Look, Val, everyone has to do something dangerous every now and then. I'm not brave like you are, but this is something I have to do, and I'm going to—"

"I'm not brave!" Valerie exploded. "Come back here."

But Barbara walked past Valerie and pulled open the door to the garage.

"Barb, it's storming out there," Valerie pointed out.

Another squall was passing over, and rain beat against the windows.

"I don't care. Look, I'll call you later, okay? I have to go."

The door to the garage slammed behind her. Valerie stared at it, still unable to believe Barbara intended to drive somewhere in the terrible weather.

She spooned coffee into the coffee maker. A strange sound, like a muffled scream, caused her to drop the coffee spoon and race to the door, spilling coffee all over the kitchen counter.

She flung open the door to the garage and stared around frantically.

The garage door had been raised, and rain and wind blasted inside. Valerie caught a glimpse of Barbara, struggling in a man's grasp as he dragged her out into the beating rain.

───────── TWELVE ─────────

Valerie stared a moment, unable to comprehend the sight. As Barbara disappeared into the slashing rain, which Valerie noted automatically was coming in almost sideways, her brain slipped back into gear.

Whoever had just called her on the phone had meant what he said when he claimed Valerie would soon get what was coming to her.

He probably didn't realize he had grabbed the wrong sister. He probably didn't care.

Valerie raced frantically to the telephone and dialed with fingers that fumbled the number twice. Then she realized the phone was dead, and stood holding the receiver a moment, wondering what to do next.

She had no choice, she realized. If Barbara was going to be saved, there was no one but Valerie to save her.

Feeling pitifully inadequate, Valerie stared blindly around the kitchen for a weapon. Butcher knives were reputed to be effective weapons, so she jerked open the utensil drawer and grabbed up the big knife, wishing she'd had the foresight to have sharpened it. She stuck it into the waist band of her jeans and hoped it would stay there.

Meg had always kept Valerie's old baseball bat in a corner in her bedroom as a weapon against burglars. Valerie raced to the bedroom and kicked over two stacks of romance novels to disclose the bat. Seizing it gratefully, she raced back to the kitchen.

The notepad on the counter beside the phone caught her eye. Devon would be back, perhaps in time to help. She scribbled a hasty note and left the pad where Devon would be sure to see it, then raced out the door and into the garage.

The moment she reached the garage, rain blasted in through the raised garage door and splattered on her glasses. Worse, the butcher knife slipped down into her jeans and began to slide down her abdomen. She had to press it with her hand to stop its progress and push it back up so she could grab it.

That cost her time. When she arrived at the garage door and peered out into the gusting rain, she couldn't see anything moving.

There were no cars visible. She hadn't heard a door slam or a motor engage. Of course the rain would have muted it, but she'd been listening and she'd have heard something.

Next door was the Broussaards' old place. Valerie stared toward it. The house, according to Meg, had been vacant for a year. If anyone had been looking at it, everyone in Winnie would have been speculating on the potential purchasers.

That had to be where he'd taken Barbara, Valerie decided, with a calmness even she recognized as due to her desperation. She forced herself to think on it even as she went toward the house.

It would explain how he knew she was home. He'd watched from the vacant house until Devon left, then he'd moved in on her.

The realization both terrified and thrilled her.

She approached cautiously, remaining behind as much shrubbery as possible, clutching the bat in one hand and the butcher knife in the other.

The wind and rain, although gusty and unpleasant, wasn't hampering her as much as she'd feared. The wind had lifted her hair off her shoulders like a cape, and the rain had thoroughly drenched it so that now it lay on her neck like a wet towel. Her blouse had plastered to her body, and despite the rain and wind, rice-field mosquitoes were attacking ferociously.

She had reached the short hedge separating Meg's property from the Broussard lot, and she skirted it swiftly, bending over in an attempt to remain invisible.

As she rounded the hedge, another squall moved over. Lightning flashed, illuminating both her and the empty house perfectly.

Valerie jumped, staring toward the house, but no one rushed out to attack her and no bullets whizzed past her ears.

Perhaps she was mistaken. Perhaps he'd dragged Barbara into a car and was hauling her to the beach.

No, she hadn't heard a car. Barbara was someplace close by, perhaps unconscious inside the house.

Valerie refused to entertain the idea that Barbara was already dead. She couldn't be. Not when Valerie was on the way to rescue her.

Sneaking across the yard during the downsplash of rain that followed the lightning, Valerie crouched at the corner of the Broussard house and waited for some sign that she'd been seen. Nothing happened, so she began a cautious circling of the house.

The rain stopped coming straight down and drove at her seemingly from every direction. Recalling a statement from a Hurricane Carla survivor about how it had rained sideways, Valerie wondered just how strong Hurricane Allie had become. So far, she was able to navigate well, except during the stronger gusts of wind.

The sideways rain did have one effect, and that was to render her glasses almost useless. Both the outer and the inside of her lenses were covered with water, and she could barely see through them, but if she took them off, she definitely wouldn't be able to see.

Valerie clutched her weapons and fought off a new terror. Suppose she did find Jonathan Wade, assuming he was the culprit. Would she be able to see well enough to smack him with the baseball bat?

She had to.

Getting a fresh grip on the bat, Valerie tucked the butcher knife in her pocket, wedging the handle in the corner of the pocket and forcing the tip to pierce the pocket lining. Her first line of defense was the bat. Failing that, she'd pull out the knife.

Valerie circled the house carefully, pausing at each window to peer inside. The house was empty, and all she saw was a uniform blackness. It was hard to see even that through the rain beating against the windows and her glasses.

Suppose she was missing Barbara because she couldn't see? Valerie resolutely squashed down the horrifying thought and kept circling. When she found Barbara, she'd see something.

She prayed, asking simply that she know when she found Barbara. Once she found her sister, she'd take it from there. According to the theology she'd gleaned from Shelby Winthrop, God gave you what you needed, and you were expected to put it to use.

It was harder to walk against the wind now, for she was heading directly into it as she came around a corner of the house. The wind was howling so loudly and the rain was driving so hard, she couldn't hear anything, including her own stumbling progress.

That meant the kidnapper couldn't hear her, either, despite the noise she'd made when she tripped over a brick and fell against the house. Valerie stuck her head up warily and peeked in the window she'd almost broken with the flailing baseball bat. She saw nothing but blackness.

She must be mistaken, she thought, despairing. He must have taken Barbara elsewhere.

In desperation, Valerie struggled against the wind and circled the entire house, even removing her glasses to peer in the black windows, but no movements or points of light were apparent to her straining eyes.

She was at the front of the house once more, and no

closer to finding Barbara than when she'd first begun. Time had dilated in the manner of Einstein's physics for Valerie, and she figured she'd spent nearly an hour circling the house. Every wasted minute brought Barbara closer to death.

Sobbing, Valerie stared wildly around her, not bothering to keep behind anything. She couldn't see, and she couldn't hear.

"Barbara!" she screamed.

Nothing answered except the wind, with another blast of sideways rain that obscured her vision even more.

She thought of the one source of human help available to her and yelled, "Devon!"

That brought no answer, either, and Valerie stumbled toward the back of the house once more. She'd have to break in at the back door and search the house before she knew for sure Barbara hadn't been taken there.

The squall was winding down as suddenly as it had begun. The lightning and thunder had moved farther north, and the rain slowed abruptly.

Valerie strained her ears, thinking she'd heard something.

The sound came once more. It was a muffled woman's scream, and it came from the garage, which was set back from the house.

Valerie sobbed a prayer of thanksgiving and shook her head violently as she ran toward the garage, trying to clear her vision enough to get in just one good shot with the baseball bat.

Shaking her head nearly resulted in the loss of her glasses. Valerie had to stop and settle them more firmly on her nose. Even with the lenses covered with rain drops, she could still see better with them than without them.

The doors to the Broussard garage were the old-fashioned double doors that opened outward. Both doors had been pulled shut, but almost an inch of space remained, and Valerie put one eye to the crack.

Inside, a kerosene lamp cast a flickering yellow light

over the scene. The first thing that met her gaze was a radio-telephone, which sat beside the kerosene lamp.

Then movement drew her eye to the struggle taking place in the center of the garage.

Valerie dug out her butcher knife and used it to pry at the crude piece of wood the kidnapper had used to bar the door. It appeared to have be a simple slab of wood with a single nail in the center, nailed so the wood could turn to either hold the doors shut or allow them to be opened. The butcher knife fitted easily through the crack, and Valerie thanked God that she'd thought to bring it.

She lifted the piece of wood easily, without anyone being aware of her.

Inside, Barbara screamed and delivered a well-aimed slap at her kidnapper.

The kidnapper cursed and struck at Barbara, who staggered, but recovered enough to deliver a kick to his groin. The man uttered more obscenities and struck at Barbara with his fists. Barbara went down and rolled over twice as Valerie pulled open the garage doors and rushed inside.

Valerie gripped the bat as if she was going to take a crack at a baseball, and swung. The man dodged, but she connected with the side of his neck and sent him reeling. Her glasses went flying with the force of her swing, but before they did, she recognized Jonathan Wade.

He'd grown his hair, and he looked infinitely harder and more dangerous. There was something inhuman about his eyes, and Valerie readied the bat for another swing.

Jonathan was a blurry figure a little more than six feet from her, and the shadowed yellow light didn't help her vision any. He was cursing her in a dogged, monotone voice, and he pulled something from the back of his trousers that she recognized even in blurry outline.

"He's got a gun!" Barbara screamed.

Valerie made up her mind to die and took desperate aim at the blurred figure. She sent up a last prayer as she brought the bat around, aided by the twisting force of her waist and hips.

To her side, she was aware of Barbara's rushing figure,

which leaped forward, almost blocking Valerie's aim as she swung the bat.

The gun fired with a roar that deafened Valerie to the cracking sound the bat made as it connected with Jonathan Wade's head. Barbara's body appeared to leap upward a foot, then crashed backward to the dirt floor of the garage.

Valerie screamed and dropped the bat. Despite her poor vision, she knew what had happened.

Barbara was lying crumpled and stunned on the ground, and blood was seeping from a wound high on her shoulder. As Valerie reached her side, she groaned and opened her eyes.

"Val? Thank God. I was afraid I'd be too slow," Barbara said. Her voice was high and light.

Valerie sobbed and managed, "Barb, why'd you do that? Look at you!"

Barbara laughed weakly. "Look at *you*. You look like a pea-eyed witch."

Valerie laughed, a hysterical, sobbing sound, but her wits returned. That had been Barbara's favorite taunt during their teen years. For once, Valerie enjoyed hearing it.

"I'm not going to die, idiot," Barbara said.

Valerie leaned down to hug her sister, feeling once more that rush of love that had so surprised her earlier.

"Val? Good God!" Devon shoved the garage door open further and rain blasted in. He shoved them closed and crossed the floor. "What . . . Good Lord!"

Valerie opened her mouth to tell him about Jonathan Wade, but it appeared Devon had seen that for himself.

Wade was trying to stagger to his feet, still stunned from Valerie's final blow, but Devon drove a fist into his chin that sent him to the floor once more. As Valerie watched, Devon bent to pick up the gun and tucked it into the waistband of his jeans. He picked up something else and brought it to Valerie.

"Your glasses," he said, placing them in her palm.

Valerie had gotten Barbara's head into her lap and was trying to staunch the flow of blood with the tails of Barbara's blouse.

"I'm glad you're here, Dev," she said calmly. "I hit him, but he shot Barbara. We have to get her to the hospital."

Devon knelt beside her and touched Barbara's shoulder gingerly. "I don't think it's too serious," he said in comforting tones. "Don't worry, Barb. We'll get you to the hospital in no time."

Valerie's senses were returning, and she raised her head as the entire garage shook beneath the roar of thunder as a new squall came in.

"Here, Val. Let me clean your glasses."

Devon took the glasses off her nose and worked them over with his handkerchief, then replaced them.

Valerie blinked as he came into clear focus. His hair was plastered to his head, and his clothes were soaked. Still, he looked better to her than any other man in the world, and it was in her eyes as she looked at him.

Devon smiled and hugged her. "Hold on, Barb," he said. "I'd better tie this creep so he can't follow us."

He took off his belt and used it to tie Wade's hands behind him. Then he tore strips from the bedroll Wade had placed on the floor and used them to secure his feet.

"There's a telephone," Valerie suddenly recalled. "Our phone is out."

"I know," Devon said grimly. "He cut the wires."

"I thought it was the storm," Valerie said, nodding toward the radio-telephone.

Devon telephoned both the Chambers County sheriff and the Houston Police Department, then came back to Valerie's side.

"Let them come get him," he said, and knelt to lift Barbara.

Barbara gasped as he lifted her. "Forget everything I said about mowing yards, Dev," she said. "If you can succeed in carrying me in this weather, yard-mowing ought to become the latest rage in strength-building exercise."

"Shut up and ride, Barb. Val, can you open the doors for me?"

Valerie stumbled to her feet and pulled, then almost got knocked over when a blast of wind caught it and added to her pulling force.

Devon struggled through the wind and rain, going slowly so he wouldn't stumble and fall. Valerie walked beside him, longing to help but unable to think of anything she could do except offer moral support.

Devon grinned at her once and shouted, "If you can't see, just grab my jeans."

Valerie's vision wasn't the best, thanks to the rain still splattering against her lenses, but she could see well enough to notice the tenderness with which Devon was handling Barbara. She could also see the way Barbara rejoiced in his strength, clinging to him with her good arm and burying her face against his chest.

Their trip was slow, but the distance was short, and they soon made it to Devon's Cherokee. He placed Barbara on the backseat, instructing her not to move, and Valerie climbed in to cradle Barbara's head in her lap.

"Lord, I hope I can see to drive," Devon said, backing out carefully.

Valerie roused herself. "Where is the storm, Dev?"

"Where *is* it?" Barbara asked. "It's here, silly."

"No, it isn't, believe it or not," Devon said. "This is the outer fringes. The eye is approaching Galveston right now."

"You're kidding," Barbara said, closing her eyes. "Wake me up when we get there."

"Don't go to sleep," Valerie said frantically. She recalled tales of people who fell asleep and died.

Barbara chuckled faintly. "I'm not going to die, pea-eyes. I sure thought *you* were going to, when you kept coming at him with that bat."

"I'd made up my mind to die," Valerie agreed, remembering. "My self-defense instructor said you were the most powerful when you decided to sacrifice your life to accomplish something. He was right."

"What are you talking about, Val?" Devon sounded almost desperate.

"Nothing," she said.

"She was going to let Jonathan Wade shoot her in order to get in one last whack with that baseball bat," Barbara said.

"Damnit, Valerie . . ." Devon began.

"Don't look at me," Valerie said. "She jumped in front of me at the last minute, which is why she has this hole in her shoulder."

"Damn!" Devon said, and swerved hard as a tree uprooted and fell in slow motion across the street.

Valerie held her breath as he drove slowly around the tree. They had to navigate a ditch, which would have been impossible if Devon hadn't been driving a four-wheel-drive vehicle. At any moment, she feared Devon would have to stop the car and carry Barbara the rest of the way.

They said nothing more during the short but difficult drive to Winnie's community hospital. The rain came down so hard, and from all angles, that they could barely see out of any of the windows. They relied on headlights to see where other cars were, and on familiar landmarks to tell them they were on the road.

Valerie held open the hospital door and Devon carried Barbara in at last, and relinquished her to a lone, emergency-room worker who said, "I just hope we can get a doctor."

"Oh, Lord," Devon said, wrapping an arm around Valerie. He smiled down at her. "Well, you've accomplished everything else tonight. Want to try your hand at removing a bullet?"

Valerie aimed an elbow at his ribs.

Devon waited at Valerie's side for nearly half an hour. Through a process of bullying and sweet talk, he procured towels and attempted to dry Valerie off as well as he could.

Valerie sat quietly and let him do it, feeling too numbed to move much, and too tired to care that in the hospital's air-conditioning, she was beginning to shiver.

"Do you think we ought to telephone her husband?" Devon asked softly.

Valerie started and looked at him blankly.

"Her husband has a right to know she's been injured," Devon said.

"I suppose so. I don't know how to get in touch with him." She rose and stared toward the room Barbara had been taken to when a well-soaked doctor had finally arrived.

"Call information," Devon suggested.

Valerie did so, and due to the nature of the emergency, was able to obtain Barbara's unlisted number with no trouble.

Harry Kilgore came on the line at once, and exclaimed in disbelief over the news Valerie told him.

She replaced the receiver and said, "I think he's totally shocked that such a thing can happen to a respected bank officer. He's on his way."

She watched Devon closely as she spoke, but he betrayed nothing but satisfaction.

"Good. Barb will have a chance to get her life back together."

Valerie lowered her eyes. He didn't sound sorry, but one never knew with a man like Devon. She resumed her seat in silence, huddling beneath the towel Devon had draped over her shoulders.

A movement near the door caught her eye, and she glanced up to see a very wet sheriff's deputy entering. She touched Devon's shoulder and pointed.

Devon crossed the shining, rain-splattered floor and conducted a low-voiced conversation with the deputy, then nodded, frowning. Valerie stared at him, loving the way his wet clothes clung to his body.

He looked up and smiled at her, then came to kneel on the floor before her. "Val, I'm going to have to leave for a while. The police will need statements from all of us eventually, but I think they'll be satisfied with mine for now."

Valerie looked at him wistfully and nodded. "I'll be

fine," she said. "I'm just going to sit here until they're through with Barb . . . I wonder what Harry's like."

Devon laughed. "I don't know, honey. Lord, I wish I had something dry to put on you. You're freezing."

"So are you," she pointed out.

"I'm about to get wet again," Devon pointed out.

He was right. Even inside the hospital, she could hear the gusting rain. Several more squalls had moved through with lightning and thunder.

Devon straightened and spoke to a nurse who had entered the waiting room. The nurse looked at Valerie, nodded, and reversed her direction.

Devon stooped and kissed her cold lips. He cupped her face in his warm hands and said, "Val, you're the bravest woman I've ever met, but if you ever put me through a night like this again, I won't answer for the consequences."

"I'm the world's worst coward and you know it, Dev Rayburn," Valerie protested. "After this, I'm probably going to be scared of storms."

"Not you," Devon said, and kissed her again.

She watched him leave, then huddled miserably on the plastic chair, but not for long. The nurse Devon had spoken to appeared with a long bathrobe and shooed Valerie into a restroom to put it on.

Valerie pulled off her soggy jeans gratefully, dried her legs with her towel, and removed her bra and blouse. It was a relief to get into something dry, even if she did look like a patient when she reentered the hall.

The nurse carried her clothes away, presumably to dry them, and Valerie wrapped the towel around her head turban-style.

When Harry Kilgore arrived, immaculate, if wet, in his khaki trousers and madras shirt, Valerie knew him immediately. Even though he was dressed casually, one could detect the ghost of a three-piece business suit hovering over his body.

She approached, putting out a friendly hand. "Harry? I'm Valerie, Barb's sister."

Harry stared at her, looking rather wild-eyed. Valerie couldn't blame him. It was going on three in the morning, and she looked like a woman caught in the middle of washing her hair.

Harry was a slim, dark-haired man with attractive blue eyes and a pale, handsome face. He was nice-looking, but Valerie would never understand why Barbara had preferred him over Devon.

He rallied and took her hand, then dropped it to give her a brotherly hug. "You're going to have to explain what happened," he said, indicating the plastic chairs. "I'm afraid I was so shocked, I didn't quite follow your explanation. Where is Barb?"

"She's in surgery to remove the bullet. They say she's going to be fine."

"Thank God." He sat down beside her, hiking his trousers carefully. "Tell me what happened. Barb was supposed to be on her way to Houston to meet me. When she didn't show, I began to get worried that she'd had an accident."

"That was *you* on the phone?" Valerie had almost forgotten the second phone call, and Barbara's subsequent desire to brave the weather. She grinned and said without thinking, "Then it's all your fault."

Poor Harry whitened, staring at her, and Valerie had to explain swiftly. Clearly, Harry didn't consider her remark a joke, and Valerie swiftly told him she didn't mean it.

She explained what had happened as clearly as she could, and bit her lip when Harry shook his head and delivered himself of his opinion.

"Barb always thinks she knows what's best for everyone," he said.

Valerie nodded, straight-faced. "You don't know how many times I've complained of that over the years."

Harry rose, paced the floor, and stood staring at Valerie with his hands in his pockets. "I don't know if she told you why she left," he said slowly.

Valerie looked noncommittal and managed to evade answering.

Harry stared at her a moment longer, then decided to speak. "Well, I've had it with banking, so I thought I'd talk it over with Barb and, you know, tell her what I'm going to do."

"Uh-oh," Valerie said.

"You can imagine how I felt when she hit the ceiling."

Valerie was curious. "What are you going to do?" she asked.

"I'm going back to school and get my Ph.D. I want to teach business. That's beside the point. The point is, Barb thinks teaching is nowhere, and kept going on about my next promotion at the bank." Harry took an angry turn about the waiting room. "It became clear she didn't care a damn about me or how I felt. All she cared about was my damn job."

Valerie made a sympathetic murmur and found she couldn't really blame this frustrated man for turning to another woman. Not when she recalled the way Barbara had pressured Devon.

"So, I thought I'd find out how she really felt about me," Harry went on. "There was a woman I'd dated before I met Barb. We'd really been just good friends, and I figured she wouldn't mind doing me a favor."

Valerie stared and said, "Oh, my God. You didn't."

"When it got back to Barb, I thought there might be hope," Harry said. "She was really upset."

"I'll bet she was," Valerie said. "You're lucky she didn't kill you."

Harry shrugged angrily. "I told her I was leaving her for a woman who loved *me* instead of my job. Do you know what she did?"

Valerie shook her head, fascinated.

"She let me leave!"

"She let you leave," Valerie repeated, and bit her lip.

"She let me leave. She didn't say a word to try and stop me. Not one word."

"Look, Harry, I think Barbara may have been too shocked at the idea that you were having an affair to react properly," Valerie said tactfully. "Maybe if you told her how she was making you feel. . . ."

Her voice trailed off, and she stared once more at Harry. Clearly, Harry had unexpected depths.

"I made up my mind to talk to her late tonight, but she'd left. So I thought I'd see if Meg knew where she was, and Barb answered."

"Barb was eager to meet you," Valerie said. "Nothing I said kept her from going out into the weather."

Harry was regretful. "I had no idea the weather was so bad in Winnie. I didn't even know there was a storm until I heard it on the radio when my car nearly got blown off the freeway."

Valerie eyed him with even greater fascination. "I can tell you'll be a fantastic professor," she said.

"Because I'm so absentminded?" Harry said, with the first gleam of humor Valerie had seen in him. "I've had a lot on my mind lately."

"I can see you have," Valerie said. "Make yourself comfortable. I'm sure she cares, or she'd never have been willing to drive all the way back to Houston at midnight with a hurricane coming in."

"I hope you're right," Harry said, and settled into the chair beside her to wait.

When Barbara was removed from surgery and taken to a private room, both Harry and Valerie were at her side when she opened groggy, emerald eyes.

Valerie leaned over her and said, "Barb? How do you feel?"

Barbara's eyes focused on Valerie. "Like hammered peas," she said.

"That's right. Insult my eyes after all I've been through tonight on your behalf."

Barbara grinned sleepily. "Actually, Dev was right. They are like peridots." Her eyes focused on Harry. "Harry? When did you get here?"

"About an hour ago, after driving through the worst weather I've ever been in," he said. "Barb, I have to talk to you. As soon as you're better—"

Barbara sought for his hand with hers. "Harry, I don't blame you for turning to Taryn. I didn't even try to understand."

Valerie began backing discretely away from the bed.

"It was all my fault, darling," Harry said. "I should have tried harder to talk to you."

Valerie shut the door behind her and walked toward the nurses' station, suddenly feeling both light at heart and dead tired. What she wanted now was her own bed, but first she had to get her own clothes.

Her clothes were dry, and she put them on thankfully, wondering if she dared bother Harry for the keys to his car.

"Need a ride?" the nurse asked. "I'm getting off duty, and I'll be happy to drop you off. You're Meg's daughter, aren't you? I know where you live."

Valerie accepted thankfully. It had been an emotionally and physically exhausting day and night, and she couldn't be on her feet much longer.

The storm had lessened to a steady, gusty rain, with occasional outbursts of thunder and lightning as squalls moved through the area. Valerie gathered the eye of the storm had moved inland, but was too tired to ask.

She walked thankfully into the house she'd left several hours earlier and stared around. Everything was unchanged. Meg's computer was behind the sofa where she'd moved it, and the masking tape she and Barbara had used to tape the windows lay on the coffee table.

She turned out the lights and went to bed, falling deeply asleep soon after crawling between the sheets.

When she awakened late the following morning, the first thing she was aware of was the sunlight coming in her window.

The second thing was the weight beside her that made her body roll toward it.

She turned and discovered Devon lying beside her, watching her with lazy gray eyes.

"You've slept with me," he said. "Now you have to marry me."

THIRTEEN

Valerie stared, certain she was neither seeing nor hearing properly. Devon was stretched out beside her, fully dressed except for his shoes.

"Well?" Devon said. "Are you going to give in peacefully, or do I have to bring on the big guns?"

"Dev?" Valerie said.

"She knows my name."

"What are you doing here? I thought I was in my own bed."

She stared around. The blurred outlines of the room were familiar.

"I came in through the garage door. Which you left unlocked, by the way. Didn't Meg teach you anything about locking doors?"

Valerie rubbed her eyes and sought to gather her wits. "I forgot about it. I was so tired last night, I just fell into bed. Sorry I left without telling you, but I'd had it."

"I know you had, darling. I went by the hospital. Barb's husband didn't know what had happened to you."

Valerie remembered Harry and gave a spurt of laughter. "Do you know he faked an affair to get Barb's attention?"

"He did? Cheez." Devon laughed and rolled closer so that his face was six inches from hers. "I'd say he got it. He was looking very happy and protective last night. He didn't even want to let me see Barb, despite my part in rescuing her.''

"That's because you're the old boyfriend. He's scared to death Barb will go back to you. I think he knows that's why she came here.''

"Well, it isn't what she told me. Do you know what she wanted to do? She wanted to fake an affair with me.''

"She *what*?'' Valerie began to laugh. "Harry got an old girlfriend to go along with him.''

"All I can say is that Barb and Harry deserve each other,'' Devon said firmly. "I told her nothing doing.''

"I'm glad.'' Valerie yawned. "All that deception is bound to cause trouble sooner or later.''

She relaxed and tried to orient herself. It was best to ignore Devon's first statement, at least until she was fully awake.

"Val, have you thought any more about your career?''

Valerie regarded him cautiously. He looked relaxed, his gray eyes bright and rested in his tanned face. His gaze was intent.

"No, I haven't. But, oddly enough, I know what I want to do,'' she added.

"Yes?''

"It all depends.''

"Yes?''

Valerie hesitated.

"Go on, please,'' Devon said.

"I can't.''

"Why not?''

Valerie shut up. How could she say it all depended on his next action?

"And just what is going on in here?'' a new voice asked sternly.

"Mama!'' Valerie gasped.

"Hello, Meg,'' Devon said, "I'm sleeping with your daughter.''

"I can see that,'' Meg said.

"He is not!'' Valerie said hotly.

"Appearances say otherwise, dear. I'm ashamed of you."

"Mama, he is not sleeping with me." Valerie pushed herself up on her elbows and reached for her glasses, which were lying on her bedside table. "Look at him. He's still dressed."

The moment she put the glasses on, Devon took them off, folded them, and placed them out of her reach. Valerie whipped her head around to glare at him.

"Val, dear, I think I'd better tell you exactly how I feel about this," Meg said firmly.

Valerie turned back to protest.

"Meg, I think I should tell you that I'm willing to do the right thing," Devon said.

Valerie whipped around to glare at him once more. "Devon Rayburn, if you don't shut up, I'm going to make sure you're incapable of doing the right thing, or anything else, for the next year or so!"

"Val, dear, the man is willing to marry you. As your mother, I insist that you accept. You know how small towns are. Believe me, everybody and his brother now knows Dev's Cherokee was parked in front of this house all night."

"Mama, I am not sleeping with him! Believe me, when we were on board that yacht, I did everything I could to entice him, but he held out. Why would he suddenly cave in now?"

"What's all this about a yacht?" Meg asked.

"She spent a week alone with me on a yacht on the Gulf of Mexico," Devon supplied.

"Val, I hate to ask you this, dear, but do you think you're pregnant? If you are, we're going to have to hurry the wedding up a bit, you know."

"Mama, I have not slept with Devon!" Valerie exploded.

"Yes, you have, dear. I got in three hours ago, and you've both been sleeping soundly until a few minutes ago."

"Well, I won't marry him. He's still not over Barbara, and I'll be darned if I—"

"Val Dallas, I am not in love with Barbara." Devon flung an arm across her shoulders and forced her back down to her pillow. He leaned over her and continued. "That ought to have been obvious to you from the first day I saw you again."

Valerie glared up at him. "Well, it wasn't. Oh, I had hopes, but what else was I supposed to think when you kept dodging every time I got you alone?"

"Well, for Pete's sake," Devon said, looking astonished.

Meg spoke from the doorway. "I'll go away long enough for you to set the wedding date." She turned back to add, "It had better be soon."

"I'm not marrying him," Valerie said.

"Yes, you are," Devon said. "You heard Meg. Everyone will be talking about me. My reputation is shot."

"Tough . . ." Valerie began, until Devon kissed her.

The kiss took all the remaining starch out of her, and she rapidly collapsed into an incoherent speech that Devon stopped with another lingering kiss.

He lifted his head at last and stared into pale-green eyes that looked dazed. "Val, I want to know one thing."

Valerie blinked at him, hardly able to comprehend that Devon was actually in bed with her, kissing her, and Meg was in the next room planning the wedding.

"How could you possibly think I'm still in love with Barbara? Even Barbara knew I was interested in you before you left."

Valerie, bemused, said, "I couldn't think of any other reason why you wouldn't . . . take me up on all the invitations I kept issuing."

"Val, you were killing me. It was everything I could do not to make love to you. It soon became clear to me that you were on the verge of being a star in your own right. I was afraid you'd get over your teenage infatuation for me and go back to your career. I wanted to be more to you than a vacation fling. Last night I began to realize why you'd gone into singing, and to hope you might mean it when you said you wanted to be a small-town music teacher."

Valerie wondered if she could be hearing correctly. Of all the reasons why Devon had kept his distance, that was one she hadn't thought of.

"Dev, how could you possibly think such a thing?" She sat up, annoyed. "Are you telling me the reason you nearly drove me crazy on that yacht was because you thought I'd ditch you for a lousy singing career?"

Devon watched her. Valerie could see the hope in his eyes, and the sight of it caused a great joy to bloom in her heart.

"Did I drive you crazy?" he asked. "You were certainly driving *me* crazy. I could hardly sleep at night for thinking of you. Several times I got up and swam laps around the boat."

Valerie glared at him. "Why do you think I couldn't sleep? Devon Rayburn, I ought to—"

Devon trapped the fist she aimed at his stomach. "Are you saying you'd rather marry me than become a gospel star?"

"That depends," Valerie said, struggling.

"On what?" He trapped both her hands.

"On whether you're marrying me because you love me or because Mama's threatening you."

He wrestled her back down to her pillow and hovered over her. "Meg isn't threatening me. She's threatening *you*." He laughed breathlessly and kept her hands trapped above her head. "I'm marrying you because I can't live without you. If you don't marry me, preferably in the next few days, I'll probably go crazy and run my tractor over every ceramic chicken between here and Beaumont."

"Dev?"

"Yes, Val?"

"Does this mean you love me?"

"You mean I haven't told you?"

"You have not."

"I love you, Val. How do I prove it?"

Valerie freed her hands and put them around his neck. "Do you really want to know?"

Devon's hands framed her face. "It's your turn."

"It is?" she asked hopefully.

"Yes. You're supposed to say you love me."

"I love you, Dev. I love you. I love you. I love you. Now, will you make love to me?"

"Valerie . . . !" he began, keeping her from pulling him down on her.

He gave in suddenly and stretched out beside her. His warm mouth settled over hers, and she parted her lips readily for him. Devon took full advantage of their positions, stroking his hands gently up and down her body.

"Breakfast's ready," Meg said, from the door.

Both Valerie and Devon jumped, then moved apart reluctantly.

"I love this scene," Meg said. "I think I'll use it when Blake and Pamela finally get together."

She stepped inside and propped an old, rusty shotgun carefully against the doorframe. Then she exited and returned a moment later with a tray.

Valerie sat up and searched for her glasses. Devon put them in her hand and they both propped pillows against the headboard and sat back to receive the tray.

Meg placed it across their laps, then she pulled Valerie's vanity bench to the side of the bed and sat on it, placing the shotgun across her knees.

Valerie eyed the contents of the tray. "What's in these cups?" She lifted one and sniffed. "Crème de cacao?"

"It's the only equivalent of champagne in the house, dear. At the moment, my duties as a mother outweigh my career."

"Is that so?" Valerie sampled the contents of the cup. "Are you going to chase Dev all the way to the church with Daddy's old shotgun?"

"Not him, dear. You. You're being very difficult. I thought I'd better show you I mean business."

Devon had broken into unrestrained laughter. "This has to be a first. A shotgun wedding with the gun poking the backside of the bride."

Valerie bit back laughter and said, "Mama, I don't know if you've thought about it, but Dev's Cherokee is parked right behind Barb's BMW. If people are talking. . . ."

"I have to admit, that had me worried at first," Meg said placidly. "Then I found Devon in bed with you, so I knew everything was fine."

Devon showed signs of choking to death with suppressed laughter.

Meg lifted her cup. "To my daughter's happiness."

The three of them tapped their cups of crème de cacao together and drank.

"Where is Barb, by the way?" Meg asked, glancing around as if expecting Barbara to appear from the closet.

Devon and Valerie looked at each other.

"Brace yourself, Meg," Devon said.

Meg's blue eyes widened and blinked.

"She's at the hospital," Valerie said baldly. "Let me begin at the beginning, or you'll never follow this."

She told Meg the entire story, and Meg listened with fascinated interest.

"Val, dear, I believe all's well that ends well," Meg said. "Poor Harry. I didn't know he had it in him to fake an affair. Well, this changes my opinion of him considerably. That I will confess. And it's a relief to me to know Barbara has something on her mind besides investment banking."

"I have to admit I never expected Barb to jump in front of the gun that way," Valerie said. "I was terrified she'd been killed."

"Your sister loves you," Meg said. "I was afraid she'd never get over being jealous of you and your courage—"

"Mama, why does everyone keep on saying I have courage?" Valerie interrupted. "I still go blank with fear every time I go onstage."

"Did I ever tell you your father was afraid of heights?" Meg said.

'Daddy?" Valerie was incredulous.

"He was like you, dear. That's where you get your determination. He decided he wasn't going to be afraid, so he started taking flying lessons and making himself go up on rooftops. Like you, when you go onstage."

Valerie subsided, embarrassed. She'd hoped her mother hadn't realized the depth of her fear, or her determination to overcome it.

"Barbara isn't like that. She never had that determination to overcome things, or to be any different from anybody else. That's why she was so jealous of you for a while there. She knew Devon was attracted to you, and that you had the personality to keep him."

There was a moment of stunned silence.

Meg glanced at them and added, "Barb has a bad habit of trying to force a man into a mold. Poor Harry was just lucky to be in a field Barb considered worthwhile."

"Meg," Devon said, "do you have eyes in the back of your head? I didn't know you paid attention to anything except your computer."

"Of course I do, dear. My children's happiness is the most important thing in the world to me. That's why I'm determined to see that Val gets to the church on time." She patted the rusty shotgun. "When is the wedding, by the way?"

"I'll let you know," Devon said, grinning. He put an arm around Valerie as well as he could while balancing the tray on his knees. "I'll have to see about a license, and line up a preacher, and a few other minor details."

"Dev, you're just the son-in-law I'd have picked for my Val. Which reminds me, did you know your little pager-thing is beeping away on the kitchen cabinet?"

"No, and I hope you don't mean to tell me, Meg."

"Sorry, dear."

"Dev, there was a storm last night," Valerie recalled. "Don't you have fifty thousand clients demanding your services, not to mention equipment to check? I told you what would happen when I planted that garden." She added gloomily, "I suppose it's been drowned."

"The clients can wait," Devon said. "I have something more important happening just now. As for your garden, you can plant another one."

"That's the kind of attitude I like to see in a man," Meg said. "I've always said Dev has his priorities straight."

"Mama, he has responsibilities. Dev, you——"

Valerie was forced to hush when Devon hooked a hand around the back of her neck and kissed her ruthlessly.

"It'll be nice to have both my daughters living near me," Meg said happily. She rose, tucking the shotgun beneath her arm. "I'd better go to the hospital and see Barb. She'll be happy to hear the good news."

Meg went out, and Valerie surfaced from Devon's kiss.

"Now you turn macho on me," she said, grinning. "Still, Mama's right. I do like your attitude."

"I've been waiting two years for this moment," Devon said. "Now that it's here, I'm not about to muff it."

Valerie got her hands beneath the tray and gently moved it off their laps and set it on the floor beside the bed. Then she removed her glasses and set them on the bedside table. She climbed back into bed and turned into Devon's arms.

She let her fingers worship every detail of his tanned face, from the straight, dark brows to the wide, mobile mouth. He was doing the same to her, stroking her brows with fingers that trembled.

"Val, I love you," he said. "If you want to keep singing, I won't stop you. You're so good, the public deserves some of you—as long as you don't forget to come home to me."

Valerie smiled, loving him even more, if possible. "Mama was right. The only reason I kept singing onstage was to try to get myself over that absolute terror of facing the audience. When you were with me last night, the terror left. Now I can quit with a clear conscience."

Devon gave a choked laugh. "I'd hate to think I was the reason you quit a promising career."

"Don't be ridiculous, Dev. I'm going to start another one. We'll buy a couple of pianos, and——"

"Pianos?"

"I'm going to teach music, remember? You said yourself I have a rare talent for teaching." She buried her fingers in his thick, sun-bleached hair. "The truth is, I don't like being on the road. I want a house, with a yard that has to be mowed and a garden that has to be tilled."

"An apartment won't do?" He grinned at her.

She frowned with mock-severity. "Not unless it has a little plot of ground I'm allowed to dig up."

"A house, then. What about the one next door?"

"The old Broussard place?" Valerie thought about it.

"You could keep an eye on Meg," he suggested.

"Let's look into it," Valerie said. She used her hold in his hair to roll him to his back. "In the meantime, I've been wanting to show you how the nineties woman deals with her mate."

"Val, cut that out. I want to make love to you so badly, it's about to kill me. I'm not touching you until we're married. Do you hear that, Valerie? Valerie!"

Three weeks later, Valerie walked down the aisle of the church to where Devon waited, impossibly handsome in his dark suit.

He smiled as he watched her walk toward him, no doubt recalling her remarks about upside-down ice cream cones, and the grooves on the sides of his mouth were pronounced.

Beside him stood his friend Flynn Sutherland, owner of the yacht they'd enjoyed. Flynn had sun-bleached blond hair and a tan as deep as Devon's, and could have passed for Devon's brother.

Valerie tried to keep her thoughts focused on the upcoming ceremony, but it was more fun to speculate on the thoughts of the people who had gathered to celebrate their wedding. She could almost hear the thoughts concerning the way the younger sister had wound up marrying Devon Rayburn while the older sister, his former girl-friend, acted as maid of honor.

The story of Jonathan Wade's capture had made national news, and both Valerie and Barbara found themselves heroines. Devon downplayed his role in Wade's capture, much to Valerie's dismay.

Wade was now connected to rape-murders in several

other states besides Texas, and would probably never get out of prison. Valerie put on a nonchalant act, but she was actually more than relieved to know it. A week after the incident, sheriff's deputies had found the stolen car Wade had been driving in a stand of tallow trees in a rice field barely two miles from the Dallas home. It was terrifying to realize how assiduously Wade had tracked her.

Not that Valerie had much time to brood. Meg Dallas, aided and abetted by Barbara, had been determined her daughter should have a big church wedding.

Barbara looked stunning as usual, and happy for once. Earlier she had been chattering in their bedroom about the way Harry was helping her plot her career path. It looked as though Barbara had decided to allow her husband to choose his own work, and was reaping the benefits of a happy man.

Valerie smiled at Devon and saw the answering warmth in his eyes. She supposed Devon was helping plot her career path. He'd bought the Broussards' old house, ordered all sorts of work done on it, and told her to pick out her pianos. Valerie had done so with joy.

She spoke her vows with even greater alacrity, and exchanged a triumphant kiss with Devon when the minister declared them husband and wife. Now all she had to do was make it through the reception and she could be alone with Devon, who had managed to evade making love to her for the past three weeks.

She gave him a portentous glance as they marched up the aisle, and he laughed.

At the reception, Flynn Sutherland said, "I've arranged transportation for you, old buddy. You're going to need it."

"I have my car . . ." Devon began.

Flynn shook his head. "Your employees have a weird sense of humor. If I were you, I'd consider ditching all those power mowers you've been so kind as to furnish them with and make them use push mowers."

"That bad?" Devon asked.

"You be the judge of that," Flynn said, grinning at

Valerie. "I've got your bags packed. Pick up your car at your equipment barn."

She smiled back, then went to change her clothes. Barbara waited to help her.

Barbara had an air of suppressed laughter, and Valerie supposed she was in on the joke.

"Val, you were beautiful," Barbara said. "If I weren't so crazy about Harry, I'd be jealous. Here. Put on this scarf."

Valerie was taking the pins from her hair and brushing it loosely around her shoulders. "Why do I need a scarf?" she protested. "It's July, and—"

"Trust me. You need it." She tied the scarf beneath Valerie's chin. "Val, I hope you're going to be happy. Heck, I know you are. Devon's a wonderful man. He just wasn't for me. Anyway, I'm glad you found each other."

Barbara's shoulder was almost healed, and she had flung herself back into investment banking with her usual zest. Valerie found herself liking her sister more than ever, even enjoying her company when she talked about the bank.

They kissed each other. Valerie stood in the center of the room, since there were no stairs, and threw her bouquet over her shoulder. Jennifer Devilier caught it.

Then beneath a shower of rice she was dashing out the door with Devon.

They stopped before a shiny green tractor that trailed three ropes of tin cans and old shoes, and had every knob decorated with white ribbons.

Devon turned to face the crowd at large. "All right, you guys," he began.

The crowd rumbled with laughter.

"I'm the one who signs your paychecks, remember?" Devon went on.

"It seemed appropriate," someone shouted from the rear.

Devon eyed the tractor. "I suppose it is. What the heck. Come on, Val. A tractor will get us there just as well as a car."

To the accompaniment of laughter and applause, Devon

climbed on the tractor and held out his arms for Valerie. Because the tractor had only one seat, she had to sit in his lap.

Devon started the motor, set the tractor in gear, and they roared out of the parking lot with the tin cans clattering.

Over the noise of the tractor and the tin cans, Devon shouted, "I can't take much more of this. Want to walk?"

"No. Flynn said rescue awaits at the equipment barn. Keep driving."

"You're enjoying this, Val Dallas."

Valerie laughed. "I've dreamed for two years of riding on a tractor with you again. It's better than I thought."

Devon grinned at her and kissed her swiftly. "Val, you're a treasure. I'm glad I finally got you."

"I think it's the other way around," she contradicted him.

He laughed and turned the tractor onto the highway.

They had to drive several miles from the reception at the church along the busy Highway 124 that ran through the center of Winnie. Three cars full of honking, cheering merrymakers followed. Anyone in town who wasn't aware that Devon Rayburn had married Valerie Dallas that day soon learned of his oversight.

Valerie removed the scarf and let the wind toss through her hair. Devon's employees were right. The tractor was appropriate.

"I first fell in love with you when you let me ride your first tractor," she shouted over the roar of the engine.

Devon smiled back. "I think I started falling in love with you then, too. You took such an interest in everything I did, how could I help but love you?"

When they arrived at the barn, the promised white Cherokee awaited.

Devon climbed off the tractor and set Valerie down, then eyed the cars that pulled in behind them.

"Hulk, you're responsible for the well-being and clean-up of this tractor. Pete, I'd better not find a single grain of rice anywhere around this property when I get back."

Loud booing greeted this pronouncement.

Devon helped Valerie into the Cherokee and grinned at his employees. "Just be glad I'm in a festive mood today. Otherwise, you'd all be fired." He paused and added, "In the meantime, my mother, in gratitude for my willingness to take this lovely creature as my wife and furnish her with grandchildren, has decreed that any of you wanting to celebrate further may join her at Val's mother's home."

Loud cheering interrupted him.

"Get going," he said. "I'll be darned if I'm having you nuts follow me all the way to Galveston."

Despite this warning, the cars followed them all the way to High Island, honking and cheering.

They reached the marina at Galveston an hour later and parked the Cherokee.

"Are you sure this is what you want?" Devon asked. "We can always check into a hotel on the Seawall, you know."

"I want to finish our vacation," Valerie said firmly. "That yacht would have been wonderful, with a little cooperation from you."

"Now, Valerie . . ." he began, looking embarrassed.

Valerie eyed him. He had escaped making love to her three weeks ago by suddenly deciding he couldn't wait to assess the storm's damage. Although the storm had merely lifted a section of tin from the roof of his equipment barn, Devon had found it necessary to see to it immediately.

He wasn't going to escape this time, she vowed.

It took them two hours to get aboard the yacht, cast off, and travel far enough out in the Gulf to obtain privacy, and Devon still didn't appear to be satisfied.

She grinned at him and asked, "Are you planning to take us to Cuba?"

Devon glanced at her and kept steering. "I just want to be sure we're alone. What's a honeymoon without total isolation?"

"I'd say we've achieved that," Valerie pointed out. "Unless you're interested in the solitary confinement cell in a Cuban prison."

"Now, Val, I'm quite a way from Cuba and you know it."

"Dev?"

He tilted his head toward her, gray eyes shielded by his lowered lids. "Yes, Val?"

"Stop this boat."

"Are you going to turn out to be one of those bossy wives who drive from the backseat?"

"I'm going to be worse than that," Valerie warned.

Devon's eyelids lifted, and his gray eyes were warm on her. "You don't appear to appreciate my noble restraint," he said.

"I'm afraid I don't. I'm beginning to worry that you don't find me physically attractive, and you know how that worries a woman."

"I don't find you physically attractive?" Devon repeated in astonishment. He cut the boat's motor and turned to stare at her in disbelief. "Let me tell you something, Val Dallas."

He left the control chair and stalked her.

Valerie, her heart beating fast with excitement, slipped out of the chair beside his and backed up. When he reached for her, she scurried down the stairs to the deck.

Devon followed her. As he came nearer, she retreated, pleasurably exhilarated by the blaze of passion in his eyes. So far, he'd been carefully banking his passion. The fact that he felt free now to let it show excited her further.

She kept walking backward, just out of his reach.

"Remember two years ago when Barb accused me of looking at you when your dress fell open?"

"Yes," she said breathlessly.

"I was."

Valerie turned and raced down the companionway.

Devon followed, catching her at the entrance to the forward cabin.

"If you liked what you saw, then I'm glad," she said as he turned her into his embrace.

"Oh, I liked it, Val. I liked it a lot."

He crushed her against his chest and kissed her until

she realized exactly how much restraint he'd been exercising over the past few weeks. Her glasses slipped from her nose, and he caught them.

Valerie trembled and locked her arms around his neck, wondering if she'd be able to stand up much longer. Her knees weren't behaving in their usual stalwart manner at all, and her heart had begun a strange, new rhythm.

He lifted his head and stared into her dazed, pale-green eyes.

"That night outside Jen Devilier's," he said, "I was so afraid Jonathan Wade had made you fear men. That's why I sat there and let you make all the moves."

Valerie smiled. "And when did you begin to realize that I was fine in that regard?"

He chuckled and slipped his hands, glasses and all, into her silver-blond hair. "About five minutes later. Lord, I don't know what would have happened if that car door hadn't slammed."

"I'd like to have found out," Valerie said, urging his face down to hers.

"Temptress."

"You bet."

Devon kissed her again, parting her lips to stroke deeply into her mouth with his tongue, savoring her sweetness in all the ways he'd been avoiding for three weeks.

Valerie trembled anew, and wondered if she'd hold out beneath this passion. It was far more powerful than she'd dreamed, and seemed likely to reduce her to a pile of ashes before it was spent.

Devon lifted her in his arms and placed her on the bed. Then he laid her glasses on the bedside table. Stretching out beside her, he continued kissing her, adding other caresses that made her arch toward him.

By the time he began removing her clothes, Valerie was only aware that the clothes were in her way. So were his, and she unbuttoned his shirt to smooth her hands over his magnificent chest.

Devon shuddered and lay back to let her explore him

as she pleased. While she did, he cupped her breasts and teased her nipples with his thumbs.

The rush of sensation was everything she remembered, and she soon forgot everything but the way he was making her feel. When his mouth replaced his thumbs, she was certain she was going out of her mind.

"Dev?" she whispered.

"Yes, darling?"

"I love you so much. You are going to finish this, aren't you?"

Her head was thrown back, and she had arched her back to give him better access. Her nails were digging into his shoulders, although he wasn't complaining.

His gray eyes were smiling as he moved over her. "Val, I love you. Of course I'm going to finish it."

And he did.

FUN & FANTASY—IN YOUR MAILBOX!!

Your friend didn't return one of your new Kismet Romances? Well, get yours back and show them how they can get one of their very own!!

No. 1 ALWAYS by Catherine Sellers
A modern day "knight in shining armor." Forever . . . for always!

No. 2 NO HIDING PLACE by Brooke Sinclair
Pretty government agent—handsome professor. Mystery and romance with no escape possible.

No. 3 SOUTHERN HOSPITALITY by Sally Falcon
North meets South. War is declared. Both sides win!!!

No. 4 WINTERFIRE by Lois Faye Dyer
Beautiful New York model and ruggedly, handsome Idaho rancher find their own winter magic.

No. 5 A LITTLE INCONVENIENCE by Judy Christenberry
Never one to give up easily, Liz overcomes every obstacle Jason throws in her path and loses her heart in the process.

No. 6 CHANGE OF PACE by Sharon Brondos
Police Chief Sam Cassidy was everyone's protector but could he protect himself from the green-eyed temptress?

No. 7 SILENT ENCHANTMENT by Lacey Dancer
She was elusive and she was beautiful. Was she real? She was Alex's true-to-life fairy-tale princess.

No. 8 STORM WARNING by Kathryn Brocato
The tempest on the outside was mild compared to the raging passion of Valerie and Devon—and there was no warning!
